Aeon Rises

Jim Cronin

ALL RIGHTS RESERVED

Publisher's Note:

This is a work of fiction. All names, characters, places, and events are the work of the author's imagination.

Any resemblance to real persons, places, or events is coincidental.

Solstice Publishing - www.solsticepublishing.com

Aeon Rises

by

Jim Cronin

I dedicate this book to my grandchildren. We have shared
so many wonderful story times together that I hope to
provide all of you with one of my stories, even when I am
not around to read it to you.

Prologue

Keldon Ankara, first citizen of the Ankara family, one of the leading and most powerful families in the Skutaran government, stood before the council in full ceremonial dress. The long gold sash across his chest, decorated with the many badges and emblems received over his long career in service to the emperor, perfectly balanced the deep maroon coat and black trousers. On his head sat the golden ceremonial cap of his office as chief of the science and development branch of the government. His dark skin glistened with perspiration under the glaring lights of the council chamber.

"It is true that our research is not yet complete, and there is still much to understand, but the possibility of reversing the effects of criminal digitization has profound possibilities for the future of Skutara and our military forces. The war has lasted far longer than any of us predicted and our personnel resources are reaching their limits. Millions of digitized minds could provide the reinforcements we so desperately need. All we need is the support of this council to proceed with our research."

Silence filled the dark chamber as the emperor and his advisors glared at Keldon. With a slight raise of one finger, the emperor signaled for the speaker of the council to give their reply.

"Keldon Ankara, we have reviewed your proposal and have concluded that this would be too dangerous a course of action to take. We therefore decline our support and forbid any further research into the matter. All of your research will be turned over to our security force immediately for deletion. You, and your colleagues, will submit yourselves for mind wiping within two days."

Keldon's mouth dropped open for a second before he regained his composure. "How can this be your decision? Our soldiers need reinforcement. We have stretched ourselves into too many star systems for us to continue on this path without the aid of my digitization reversal procedure. Without my research, we cannot hope to win the war. I only ask—"

"Enough!" Tolpan Accra, emperor of all Skutara, slammed his hand on the table in front of him. His face twisted with anger and disgust. "Keldon Ankara, who are you to presume to question this council, and me, in such matters? You are no general and have no military credentials other than your service as a minor officer on a space transport thirty years ago. What do you know of military strategy and troop dispersions?"

"You are correct, my emperor. I am no soldier. And I would never presume to second guess this esteemed council in military matters. I wish only to bring to you a way to increase our reserves that could ensure our eventual victory. I do not understand why the council would not take advantage of this opportunity."

The emperor took a deep breath and shook his head. Lowering his voice dangerously, he leaned forward to address Keldon. "Your understanding is not required, and frankly, not expected. It is only out of respect to your late father that we are even continuing this discussion. Let me explain so you might understand, Keldon Ankara. Digitization is reserved for crimes of sedition, treason, and enemies of the state. In recent decades, we have extended this policy to include captured enemy soldiers. Our resources are limited and we cannot afford to feed and house millions of our enemy's forces, so digitization became a practical solution. For most crimes, we recognize the individual is still able to contribute in some way to society, even from isolated confinement, but those guilty of sedition and our wartime enemies are far too dangerous to allow for even the slightest possibility of escape from imprisonment. They are always a threat to my rule, unless only their minds, converted to digital engrams in our computer systems, remain. There, we can harvest their intelligence and experience, without danger of an uprising. And now you want us to release these threats back into our world?"

Keldon suddenly recognized the danger he was in. "Please, esteemed council... my emperor, we have taken every precaution. There will be extreme safeguards to ensure that none of the traitors ever rise up against us. We can separate out those engrams that create the seditionist mentality, even limit the engrams we transfer to only those required by soldiers."

"And how are you to be trusted with this? I am leery of someone with your well-documented ambitions, Keldon Ankara. What safeguards can you provide to ensure you are not raising your own private army to overthrow me while my forces are spread across light years of space? I am of a mind to have you digitized and remove this possibility permanently." The emperor sat back, arms folded, still glaring at Keldon.

Shaken to his core, sweat beaded on Keldon's dark-skinned forehead. "My emperor, how can you say such things? I am no traitor! I have no desire to overthrow you. I only want to help Skutara in our hour of need."

One side of Tolpan Accra's mouth twisted up in an evil grin. He waved one hand in front of him dismissively. "Enough, Keldon Ankara. You will not be digitized today. Be satisfied with our decision to only eliminate your research and wipe any memory of the procedures from your mind. Of course your department will be disbanded and your colleagues dispersed. Of course you will be closely monitored as a precaution. One of your ambitions needs to be watched."

"But my career! Who will hire me if I am under constant surveillance?"

"You should have considered this before you started this line of research. A loyal subject would have seen the possible ramifications of your work and chosen a different path. Your time is up." As one, the emperor and the council members stood and left the room, leaving one guard to escort a stunned Keldon Ankara out, handing him a summons to report for mind wiping the next morning.

***

"All the files copied over successfully, sir. All we need to do now is get to the spaceport and hope the others were able to commandeer a long-range transport for us." Marcus Dakar shut the portable computer, securing it inside his carrier as he hurried over to Keldon's desk.

Keldon looked up at his assistant's approach and gave another searching glance around the office. "All done here as well. Let's get out of here before those hypocrites and sycophants figure out what we're doing."

"Don't worry, sir, it's only been a few hours since they disgraced you. They can't possibly suspect anything." Marcus reached out to lay one hand on his superior's back and urge him to the door.

Keldon's dark features screwed up in anger at the memory of his ruination before the council. "The short-sighted fools! Paranoid and delusional, all of them! They think I'm a threat? Well then, so be it. I've given my life in service to Skutara. How dare they mock my work and call me a traitor." He gave one last look at his former office and stormed out.

At the spaceport, Keldon and Marcus located another of their allies who waved them over. He hopped in their vehicle before it came to a full stop. "Everything is arranged. The captain is willing to join us and file a false flight plan. It took a small fortune to seal the deal, but his operations are not strictly all legal so he knows what to do. The supplies should all be loaded by the time we reach the ship. Take a left up ahead and drive to pad 27."

Keldon, still fuming, tried to control his anger with only minimal success. "Are you sure about our destination, Martin?"

"Absolutely, sir. Plenty of sentient life, low-level technology, only minor exploration forays into their immediate solar system, breathable atmosphere and suitable food availability. And, once our captain returns, leaving us stranded on the planet, far enough to not be worth anyone's trouble to come after us."

"How breathable is the atmosphere? Your figures give very low oxygen levels, and almost no methane. The planet must smell terrible."

Martin nodded, but did not face Keldon. "Agreed, sir, but levels are sufficient, if not ideal."

Keldon scratched at his ear as he considered this information. "Are the beings on this world suitable for our purposes? Will their bodies be able to manipulate our technology?"

Martin hesitated, glancing over his monitor to gather his thoughts. "We believe so, sir. They are bipedal, two arms with five digits each, and an opposable thumb. From the images we have collected from their transmissions, their tech is not all that dissimilar to ours. They should be compatible."

"Do not underestimate the emperor's anger, Martin. Be absolutely you lay down sufficient false trails to hide our true destination. Mere remoteness will not provide enough security."

"Yes, sir. The protocols have already begun. You may rest assured that, with the ongoing battles pressing the emperor's forces on so many fronts, he will not waste valuable resources looking for us for long. They will consider us banished and without the ability to return for at least another century or two, not their concern." Martin Mumbai flicked the screen on his personal tablet to search for any additional helpful information.

Keldon nodded, eyes closed. "And what is the name of this backwater world again?"

Martin swiped through his device's screen again. "Its inhabitants call it Earth."

Chapter One

"Okay Mom," he yelled, yanking the blankets over his head. "Okay, I'm up already! Gimme a break! I don't know why I have to get up before the sun. It only takes a minute to get ready." Struggling through the fog in his head, Justin rubbed his eyes and shook his head trying to clear it.

"Man, that dream was so real." The dream, so vivid only minutes ago, faded quickly as he awoke fully. Only a vague memory of his father, long dead now, spoke to him as they stood together among the stars. While most of the conversation was gone now, there was something about it being time. *Time for what? That was so fricking weird.*

As the dream faded completely, Justin gave in to the inevitable, sat up, and tossed the covers to one side.

Today began as every other day began... unfortunately for Justin. Still having homework with only a week left in the school year, his ever growing and never-ending mountain of chores, his ancient cell phone, and, most important of all, the lack of privacy in his own home were chief among his gripes.

"Don't give me that tone of yours, young man. Just get yourself up here with a smile on your face and get your breakfast before you miss your bus."

Mumbling through his hands as he scrubbed his face, Justin argued back. "Maybe if you would drive me to school I wouldn't have to get up so fricking early just to catch the bus." He made that mistake once before of saying this sort of thing loud enough for his mother to hear and did not want a repeat of that long lecture again, so he was more careful to not let her actually hear his response. The twice-daily torment on the rolling yellow prison was unbearable.

Did she really need to remind me about the bus? As he brushed his teeth, a new strategy came to him and his mood brightened. His mind searched through dozens of ways to open the conversation once again before settling on what he considered the most irrefutable, and logical argument. Putting on his best Mom-pleasing smile and one last check in the mirror, he bounded up the stairs. The meadowlarks sang sweetly in the field behind the house as he entered the kitchen.

"So Mom, I heard they're going to start charging extra to ride the bus next year…"

"Hurry and finish breakfast so you can fix your lunch, young man. The bus will be here before you know it." Justin poured a bowl of Apple Jacks and chugged his orange juice, then went to examine the fridge. PB and J on whole grain bread, an apple and an organic juice box. "Don't forget to take one of those packs of carrots too," his mom called out as he stuffed everything into a reusable bag.

"And another thing. I'm not going to be your personal chauffer, mister. We are perfectly able to afford any sort of bus fee. It won't kill you to take the bus. You could even do some homework or extra studying on the ride if you put your mind to it. Your grades aren't so perfect you couldn't put more effort into them, you know…" Her soapbox speech lasted for a good three minutes, rambling from one pointless reason to the next. Justin zoned her out — a skill perfected by most teenagers. He only caught the edges of her diatribe and forgot the details.

He sat back at the table and added some milk to his cereal, but did not lift the spoon to eat any of it. Two fingers of his left hand scratched nervously at the table. "I don't like the bus. They bully me on the bus and nobody does anything about it."

She moved to empty the dishwasher, but cocked her head, carefully measuring her son's mood. "Have you reported it to the dean at school?"

Realizing he had made the comment too loudly, Justin shrugged his shoulders, sighed, and decided his best course of action was to finish his complaint before the "I am your mother and you can tell me anything," speech started up. He gobbled up a mouthful of cereal while he organized his thoughts. "I tried once, but that only made it worse. Nobody would be a witness so all they got was a warning. Everyone except Kevin looks at me like I'm some sort of freak. I try to fit in, but I don't know anything about the benefits of Xbox versus PlayStation. I can't text them, or go on Snapchat to talk with them. They all laugh at me in the lunchroom. I don't fit in with them, so I'm a target. You don't understand. The school can't do anything about it so I just try to ignore it. Besides, they're right. I'm weird."

Justin's mom stood up with a handful of plates and turned to face him. Her eyes narrowed as she tilted her head. "What do you mean weird? What makes you say such a thing?"

Justin swallowed another spoonful of his breakfast, sat back, and leaned on one elbow as he faced his mom. "You know… just weird. I don't like the same things other kids my age like. Those video games they play all the time give me headaches. The glasses you got me help some, but they're trash. Can't I get contacts like everyone else? I don't get what they see in all those dumb YouTube videos. I mean, like really, what's so hilarious about cats playing the piano after the first eighty-three times you've seen it? And I enjoy reading real books, not Audible or Overdrive everyone has. I mean, like real paper books. Real books never give me migraines. Those books just don't feel right to me. You see? I'm just weird."

His mother sighed and placed a gentle hand on Justin's shoulder. "All that means is you have better things to occupy your brain and your time with than all the nonsense those other kids are filling their brains with. You're not weird, honey, you're more mature than they are. You'll see. In a few years they'll all catch up with you and things won't seem so bad."

Justin rolled his eyes at her well-meant remark, knowing she simply did not understand the problem. "So, in the meantime, can you like give me a ride in to school instead of making me ride the bus?" Her look instantly told him the answer had not changed. "Well then, can I get a real phone instead of this piece of crap? At least they won't be able to mess with me about having a junk phone." That last statement escaped his lips before he even realized it. He knew it was a mistake but just couldn't help himself again. *Oh crap!*

"Justin Madrid, we've been over this before." His mother's voices suddenly became a lot less motherly as she continued her efforts to clean up the kitchen. "You said it yourself: going on the internet gives you headaches, and you know how I feel about kids your age being able to text anyone at any time. You don't need that sort of distraction. You know I don't even have one of those idiotic smart phones myself. A phone should just be a phone. Now let's not have any more of this nonsense. I have work to do. Finish your breakfast. If you want, I'll go in and have a talk with the principal about the bullying."

"No!" he shouted, spewing cereal from his mouth. "Don't talk to anybody about anything, Mom." He turned to face her. His hands gripped the table so hard his knuckles turned white. "You'll only make things worse. I can deal with it on my own. School is just about over anyway. Maybe next year I won't feel like such an alien."

She turned to face him, her eyes wide as if in shock. The muscles in her forearms knotted as her grip on the dish towel tightened. The morning sun coming through the window caught Justin at the perfect angle. For a mere second, his eyes reflected golden the soft light, the way a dog or cat's eyes reflect a car's headlights at night.

His mother's face paled and she dropped the plate she was drying. It shattered loudly all over the floor. She grabbed the counter top to steady herself before kneeling down to recover the shards.

"Mom! Are you okay?" He jumped up to help her pick up the pieces off the floor.

"I'm fine. It just slipped. Must have still been wet, I guess. What was it you said?"

"Nothing."

"No, I'm serious." Her voice trembled slightly despite her effort to control the fear. "What did you say about being an alien?"

Justin sighed, rolled his eyes again, and reached for another piece of broken plate, forcing up a few tears for added effect. "I just said that sometimes I feel like I'm so different from everyone else my age I must be from another planet or something. Don't go all crazy over it, okay? You have enough to worry about taking care of us on your own and all. It's just… like a kid thing, Okay? Let's not turn it into a big deal. Don't worry about me, I'll figure it out."

His mom sat up onto her knees and took Justin's hands in hers, capturing his attention with her gentleness. "Justin, I know things have been tough for you lately. I've tried to be both parents to you, but you're getting older now and I'm not sure how to handle some of the things you're going through. I'm sorry your dad can't be here for you."

He felt her hands shaking as he saw the worry on her face. "I'm fine, Mom. You're the best mom ever and I love you. The only way I even know anything at all about him is because of all the stories you tell me. Are you sure you're okay?"

She tousled his hair and placed one hand on his cheek. "Just go get yourself changed before you miss the bus. I'll finish up here."

He looked at the clock on the microwave and knew he had to hurry. He wasn't the one who dropped the dish after all, so he didn't feel too terribly guilty about not picking up any more, especially since his attempted guilt trip didn't work and he still had to ride the bus. "Sorry I can't help more, Mom, but it's getting late and I need to change." He ran downstairs to his basement room. After a quick change of clothes and another check in the mirror, he headed back up. This time he tried to be stealthier in the hope of reaching the door before his mom could intercept him with another emotional outburst. As he reached the top of the stairs though, he overheard her on the phone. He crept as close as he dared and crouched low to avoid being seen so he could hear better.

"Yes, Jonah, I need your help. I noticed the first sign this morning over breakfast." She hesitated, listening to the voice on the other end, nodding her head in response. "Yes, no question at all. And he's starting to ask questions about it too. He is noticing the differences. Can you come over?" She ran her fingers through her hair as she listened again. "That would be great. We'll be celebrating his birthday this weekend so you can come for that. You know he would love to see you again. Maybe it would be best for you to talk to him about it." Another brief pause and she smiled. "Wonderful! We'll see you then. I have to go now, before he comes back up. See you soon."

Justin could not wrap his head around that one. He knew she was talking to his uncle Jonah, his father's older brother, but nothing made much sense. What signs was she talking about? What differences was he noticing that she felt were so important to ask Uncle Jonah to come over? He decided she obviously did not want him to know about the call, so he silently backed down a few steps before loudly running up again.

"Who were you talking to?" He watched her, praying she wouldn't lie.

"Just checking in with the office." She avoided looking at him directly, focusing instead on tidying up the countertop. "Things are kind of slow lately so I was thinking about taking the day off. Want me to drive you in this morning?"

Great! Something is wrong with me and she needs Uncle Jonah to help her talk to me about it. Why can't she tell me what's wrong? I don't feel sick or anything. If it was serious she would tell me... I think. Then another thought occurred to him. *Oh, crap. Am I going blind, or have cancer or something? Does she need his help to tell me I'm dying?* Justin fought to control the rising panic, took a deep breath and let out a long breath. *Nothing to do but wait, I guess. After all, a ride is a ride.* "Sure!" He tried not to sound too overly excited. "Can we take Kevin too?"

She rolled her eyes and sighed heavily, threw her arms in the air and brought as much overwrought mom drama as possible into her reply. "Sure. Whatever makes you happy, honey."

***

Jonah Madrid hung up the phone and sat quietly for a moment, his hand still resting on the black plastic receiver of the ancient rotary phone. His dark brow furrowed in thought. The small windowless room was spartan, typical of all military bases across the country. The green metal desk held a small lamp, blotter calendar, and rolodex file. The wire frame inbox contained far more papers than the adjoining outbox. The overhead fluorescent lights cast an unnatural starkness to everything. *So it begins. Our long wait is finally over.*

He raised himself up out of the chair and walked around his desk to the safe mounted in the wall of his office. He dialed in the combination and pulled open the door. Inside was a rectangular silver box. Jonah carefully removed the shiny container in his strong, well-tanned hands and studied its ornate carvings. *So many lives lost to obtain this. I hope the boy is everything we hope he is.*

He ran his fingers over the seemingly random patterns and pictographs engraved into the surface of the box. A knock at the door brought Jonah out of his contemplations. He returned the box to the safe, locking it securely before answering. "Come in." The wooden chair behind his desk creaked as he settled into it.

"Good morning, sir." The young lieutenant entered and handed over a thick manila folder. "I have the surveillance reports from yesterday."

"Anything new requiring my immediate attention, Lieutenant?" He took the folder and started flipping through the pages. "And you don't have to keep calling me sir. I'm not part of your military."

"No, sir. Everything is status quo. They do not seem to be making any significant progress at this time."

Jonah sighed, shaking his head. "Very well. Since everything appears to be pretty much static for now, I need you to arrange some transportation for me to Buckley Air Force Base in Aurora, Colorado. Some urgent family matters have arisen requiring my attention."

"Yes, sir." He flipped open his notebook and snapped the pen into readiness. "When will you need the transport?"

"Friday afternoon should be good. And be sure to arrange quarters for me on the base."

"Yes, sir. Anything else, sir?"

"Set up a meeting for me with the General as soon as possible. I have some news he needs to hear before I leave."

"Very well, sir," said the soldier. He turned sharply on his heels and exited the room.

Jonah glanced at the folder on his desk. "Oh, hell, not now. I need some air." He shoved away from the desk and headed toward the elevator.

Outside, Jonah squinted and held up his hand to shield his eyes from the glare of the rising sun over the Pintwater Range beyond Groom Lake.

After a few minutes walking around the base, he wiped the sweat from his forehead. *Don't think I'll ever get used to the heat out here in this desert. So much hotter than home.* He headed toward the shade of one of the dozens of hangars nearby and sat cross-legged on the ground. His black hair ruffled slightly in the quiet breeze. *Alright, my brother. A life for a life. I promised you long ago to protect them both and now that time has come. I will not fail this time. You will be proud of us.* After an hour of silent meditation, the heat grew too great, even in the dwindling shade. Jonah stood up to his full six-foot four-inch height, stretched his long, powerful legs and arms, and rubbed his brown face with both hands. He returned to the bleak, but much cooler, confines of his air-conditioned office to prepare for his meeting with the General.

Chapter Two

"Tenth frame, Justin. Just one more strike and you can break one-twenty," said Kevin. "An all-time record."

Jason hoisted his ball from the rack. "I know, quit trying to jinx me."

"Hey, there's no crying in baseball, or bowling." Kevin put on his most innocent, wide-eyed expression and smiled a great toothy grin.

"Yeah, right. Shut up and let me do this." He held the ball in front of his chin and placed his feet on the little dot marking the spot he used when he got a strike two frames ago. His eyes riveted to the small arrow just right of the center mark a few feet down the lane. Taking a deep breath and exhaling slowly, Justin stepped forward, swung the ball, and released it. At first, the trajectory of the ball looked flawless, but the ball began to veer left during the last five feet and hit the head pin dead on. Justin closed his eyes, listening to the clash of pins. Peering out between his fingers, he saw his fate written as two pins remained upright.

"Wow, a seven-ten split. At least you go down in style, dude. Looks like I win again."

"Hey, I still have one more throw here. Don't start celebrating yet. I could still get a spare, ya know!" Justin looked up at the overhead screen, calculated the maximum score still possible, dried his hand in the air vent, and grabbed for the ball as it arrived back on the rail. Stepping to the far left side of the lane, he held it up in front of him, laughed, muttered, "My precious." He aimed carefully and let the ball fly. Straight down the middle.

Kevin slapped his friend on the back, smiling as the final scores appeared on the overhead projection. "Too bad. That would have been cool. So where's your mom and uncle? I'm hungry."

Justin sat staring up at the score sheet as he removed his rental shoes. "Same! They went to go get some food. They're probably waiting for us back in the snack bar. Let's turn in the shoes and go find them."

Kevin stopped in front of the video game room and grabbed Justin's arm. "Hey look, the Air Hockey is open. C'mon, let's play."

Justin pulled loose as Kevin entered the game room. "Not now, Kevin. I'm hungry. Let's go find Mom and Uncle Jonah." Justin rubbed his eyes. Even from a distance, the glare of active screens started to give him a headache. Instead of the images of action heroes fighting dragons, or cute characters racing cars through various scenarios, all Justin saw was a flickering, stop-action motion, interrupted by flashes of static, and what appeared to be computer code. It was the same thing with any electronic screen. If he looked at them for more than a few seconds, the stabbing pain in his head grew unbearable. Ever since he'd turned twelve, the devices gradually became more difficult to watch, until he could no longer tolerate being in the same room with all the games his friends loved. He turned away from the arcade to see his uncle walking toward them.

"You okay, Justin?" Jonah examined Justin's face, even using two fingers to hold open his eyelids.

Justin swatted away the fingers stretching open his eyes. "Yeah, I'm fine, just hungry. Is the pizza ready?"

Jonah scrutinized his eyes a moment longer, smiled, and placed his arm around Justin's shoulder. "That's why I came looking for you. You go ahead, I'll get Kevin."

***

An hour and two large pepperoni pizzas later, Justin, his mom, Kevin, and Uncle Jonah walked out of the bowling alley and piled into their car.

"Thanks for coming out to see us this weekend, Uncle Jonah. I'm glad you could make it." *Maybe what they need to tell me isn't too bad after all. I mean, they wouldn't take us bowling and out to eat if anything was seriously wrong? Would they?*

"Wouldn't miss it for the world. Things were getting slow down there in the desert and I needed to get away. Your mom reminded me about your birthday so I hopped on a plane." He tipped his hat to Justin and his hazel eyes sparkled. "After all, it's not every day you turn fifteen."

"Mom says she'll take me to get my learner's permit over summer break."

"Oh great," said Kevin. "Better alert the cops. The streets really won't be safe anymore." He punched Justin in the arm and the two exchanged harder and harder jabs until…

"Alright you two, enough of that. No more distractions unless you want me to plow us into a light pole and spend the rest of your birthday in the hospital."

"Sorry, Mom." Justin took one last quick poke at his friend before settling back.

They arrived home and piled out of the car. Jonah glanced up and down the block before heading into the house with the others. His expression was suddenly grim, but only for a moment. Regaining his composure, he smiled and closed the door behind him. "Justin, why don't you and Kevin go outside for a bit? There's still a couple of hours before sunset so why don't you let me and your mom catch up some before we go out for ice cream."

"Cool! We'll be down by the creek." He and Kevin wasted no time running out the back door.

Once the boys were safely out of earshot, Emily came into the family room with two cups of coffee. She handed one to Jonah and curled her feet under her as she sat in the large recliner. Jonah took a seat on the sofa across from her.

"You're right, Emily," His dark complexion seemed to grow even darker as he stared at the cup in his hands. "I saw the signs too. He's the one we need for this operation. If I read the signs correctly, he may be even better than his father."

"He's only a boy, Jonah. He doesn't know anything about his true origins, or any of this business. Certainly nothing about the war. I just couldn't bring myself to tell him after Karl died. I know it was selfish, but I wanted him to have a normal happy life. We were never fully convinced he would inherit Karl's talent. Is that so terrible of me?" Her eyes showed anxious excitement she felt growing inside and she took a sip of her tea to help calm her nerves.

"No, Emily, it wasn't selfish of you at all," He set his cup on the nearby tray and sat leaning forward on the edge of the sofa. "You've done a fine job raising him. My brother would be proud of everything you've accomplished. We only suspected who he might be. There was never any proof. But now there is no doubt and we must move quickly, before the enemy finds out and starts looking for him… if they haven't already."

Emily spilled some of her coffee as she jerked upright in her chair. "Do you think they know? How could they? It's only been a few days since I first noticed the signs."

"Their headquarters is hidden around here somewhere. They have their spies out searching for the one the prophecies allude to. Who knows where they've infiltrated. The school is the only place we've been able to survey completely so we know he's safe there, but …"

Jonah held up his hands shaking his head. "We need him and his ability to locate the Suldat's main base and destroy them once and for all."

"But he doesn't know about his ability. All he knows is that too much TV or video games give him headaches. He complains about static on the computer sometimes, but he doesn't really know what it means, or what he can do."

Jonah stood and paced the room. "I can teach him. I'll go back to the base and make all the arrangements. Next weekend, after school is over, I'll come back and invite him to spend the summer with me down in New Mexico. It'll be good for him to get away... and you too. You could use a break from being a single mom."

Emily stood and took Jonah's hands in hers, searching his face for answers. "Are you sure about this, Jonah? Isn't there another way to win this war?" Tears began to well up in her eyes as she thought about the dangers facing her son.

"There's no other way. If there were, we would have found it by now. No, Justin is the only one who can do this. Both our worlds are depending on him."

The door burst open as the boys slammed back into the house in a tumble of arms and legs. "I win!" Justin's chest heaved with every breath as he untangled himself and got to his feet.

"Boys! Not in the house! How many times do I have to tell you?"

"Sorry, Mom."

"Sorry, Mrs. Madrid."

Jonah laughed but controlled himself at a stern look from his sister-in-law, trying to disguise it as a throat clearing. "Come in here Justin. I have something for you." He pulled up his briefcase from the side of the sofa and opened it. Inside sat a long rectangular silver box. Jonah picked up the box and held it out to Justin.

"For me?"

Jonah laughed. "You know anyone else around here with a birthday? Of course, it's for you. Something very special. Your father wanted you to have this when you were old enough."

Justin stopped in mid-reach, his mouth hung open as he stared at the box. "My father?"

"Yes, Justin, Karl found it on our last mission and wanted to give it to you when you were old enough. Be very careful with it. This box is very valuable." He pressed the container into Justin's hands, watching him closely.

Kevin peered over Justin's shoulder, pointing at the engraving as they examined the container. "What are these markings? They look kind of like hieroglyphics or something,"

Jonah shook his head and lounged back in his chair. "Not hieroglyphics. They're more ancient than that."

There was a faint noise of something inside the box shifting and sliding as Justin took the back the box, tilting it in the process. "How do I open it?"

"Read the instructions," said Jonah with a smile.

"What instructions?"

Jonah pointed to the figures on the surface of the case. "That's what the markings are,"

Justin frowned and held the gift closer to his eyes, searching for some clue. "I can't read this. What's the secret?"

Jonah waggled his finger in the air. "Oh, no, I'm not going to ruin the fun for you by just giving you the answer. Tell you what, why don't you try to figure it out on your own for a week or so. I'll come back next weekend and we can talk about it then. If you still haven't figured it out I can take you back to Nevada with me for the summer and we can work on it together. How about that?"

Justin froze for a second, and then looked up at his uncle in shock. "You want me to spend the summer with you? Wow! Mom, is that okay? Can I go?"

Emily laughed, reached out and gave Justin's shoulder a squeeze. "Of course, you can. Your uncle and I talked it over and we think you'll have a great time."

Kevin gave Justin a shove, nearly knocking him over. "That's lit! Lucky!"

"Sorry you can't come on this trip with us, Kevin," said Jonah. "Maybe next time."

"That's fine, Mr. Madrid, I understand. Maybe you can teach him how to play basketball without tripping over his feet."

***

The week dragged on, as all last weeks of school do. The teachers valiantly pretended to make everything seem important while the students pretended to care, or at least tolerate their teachers' efforts. Every afternoon Justin and Kevin charged home from the bus stop to work on the puzzle of the silver box. Even the taunts, shoulder bumps, and crude remarks of the upperclassmen were ignored in his efforts to penetrate the mystery of the box.

Kevin tried pushing on a few of the markings without success, then picked up a pencil from Justin's desk and waved it over the box. "I solemnly swear I am up to no good." He slumped down to the floor and stretched out his legs. "Oh well, it was worth a try."

Justin reclaimed the box and frowned in frustration as he turned it over in his hands. "I can't explain it, but there's something almost familiar about these markings. Like I should know what they are. I don't get it."

"They're all Greek to me. Any luck over at the library last night?"

"Nothing. I went over to the Mission Viejo branch, but the librarians just looked at me like I did something all jacked-up when I told them it was a school project I was working on."

"They were probably upset you made them do some work this week. Who in their right mind goes to the library during the last week of school? You can ask Siri, ya know."

Justin glared at his friend and exhaled in disgust. "It wasn't only that. When I showed them the rubbing we took of the markings, they seemed to get really upset... almost angry. The head guy finally came out and calmed them all down, but he asked a lot of questions. Wanted to know where I found the symbols and all."

Kevin rolled onto his back and looked up at Justin. "Did you tell him about the box and your uncle?"

"Not on your life. I just said one of my teachers gave me the paper and wanted me to find out what language it was. He kept asking about what teacher and why he wanted to know. It was creepy the way they all got after me about it so I left."

Kevin grabbed for the box again, turning it over in his hands, listening to the sounds from inside. "They're a bunch of weirdoes over there if you ask me. Maybe they've been sniffing too much of that old book dust."

"What about you? Find anything on your computer that might help us?"

Kevin shook his head and scowled. "Bupkus. I even sent a scan of the rubbings to a few sites and they were just as stumped. You sure this isn't just some prank your uncle is playing?"

"Bupkus?" Justin shrugged his shoulders as he gave his friend a quizzical look.

"Yeah, cool word huh? It means like zero, nada, zilch. Think it will catch on?"

***

Each day the two boys explored new avenues of solving the box's riddle. Each day proved just as fruitless as the last. Then Friday arrived. School finally ended for the summer. Justin ran home, dumped his backpack on his bed, saw the neat piles of clothes his mother had apparently laid out for him to pack, and had just finished stuffing clothes into it when the doorbell rang.

Justin raced upstairs, tripping over the top step. Recovering his balance, he tossed the pack onto the sofa, ran to the door and yanked on the knob. "Uncle Jonah! You made it!"

Jonah walked in and placed a large brown hand on Justin's shoulder. "Hello to you too, Justin. Is your mom around?"

"In the kitchen!"

She came around the corner wiping her hands with a towel and gave her brother-in-law a hug. Eyeing the clothes hanging out of Justin's backpack, she turned to give him the Mom stare. "Those clothes were neatly folded for you. Try putting them in the bag so they won't get permanently wrinkled. So good to see you, Jonah. Do you have time for dinner?"

"Thanks, Emily, but no. The plane is getting refueled and the pilot wants to get going." He turned to Justin and smiled. "We might just have time to grab your friend Kevin and go get some pie down at the pancake house on the corner if you want to say goodbye before we leave."

"Can we? That would be great!" Justin ran to the phone and called his friend.

Emily's brow furrowed as she placed her hands on her hips. "You have time for pie with Kevin, but not dinner?"

Jonah took her by the shoulders and smiled. "Come on, Emily. You know how boys are. Kevin may be Justin's only confidant and I am separating them for the summer. They need a proper goodbye. He doesn't need his mother right now, Emily. He needs this."

"I know, but I'm his mother. I was hoping for one last moment before he left." She settled into Jonah's arms for a long hug.

***

Justin tossed his backpack into the trunk and before long, the three were sitting in a corner booth digging into huge slices of apple, strawberry rhubarb, and peach pie ala mode.

"So where in Nevada do you live, Mr. Madrid? Justin said it was at a military base or something. You gonna go fishing or camping? I hear there's some insane ATV trails in the hills down there. That would be cool."

Jonah laughed, trying to swallow the mouthful of pie. "Whoa, slow down Kevin. Try chewing your food once in a while. We don't want you choking to death on us here." He took another bite of his pie and wiped his chin with a napkin. "We're going to a place called Groom Lake. It's a small military base, usually pretty quiet, but yes, there are some hills nearby. I can get us an ATV, or maybe some dirt bikes if that's something you would like, Justin."

Justin's eyes lit up and bits of pie sputtered out of his mouth as he replied. "An ATV? Can I drive it? Dirt bikes would be cool too. Maybe you could talk one of the pilots into giving me a ride in one of the jets, maybe an F-16 like the ones flying over our house every day."

Jonah smiled as he swallowed the last of his pie. "Yes, the off-road rules allow a fifteen-year old to drive, and the F-16 joy ride is doubtful, but I'll look into it."

"Oh, man, you have to send me pics of that!" Kevin punched Justin's arm to punctuate the command.

Half an hour later. Uncle Jonah looked at his watch and pushed his plate aside. "Time to go, boys. We can drop you off Kevin, and then head on to the base." He left a tip on the table, paid the bill and they drove off, heading north to take Kevin home. That's when the trouble began.

The whoop of a siren and the flashing lights made them all jump. Jonah saw the police cruiser in his rearview mirror. "Great. What now?" He pulled over, rolled down the window, and waited as the officer slowly approached the car.

Jonah adjusted his glasses as he observed the patrolman. His face suddenly grew grim, his grip on the steering wheel firm. "Can I help you, officer?"

"Caught you doing 45 back there, sir," said the police officer as he leaned down to see inside the car. "I need to see your license and registration."

As the patrolman turned toward him, Justin felt a strong sense of wrongness. He couldn't quite place the feeling… but something wasn't right.

"Of course, constable. Let me just get them out of the glove compartment over here." Jonah reached over to open the glove compartment, then turned and punched the patrolman in the face with a powerful blow, knocking him off his feet into the street. A car horn blared and missed the cop by inches as it swerved clear. Jonah stomped on the gas pedal and the tires squealed as they raced away.

"Hold on tight, boys. We have a slight change in plans."

The policeman rose to his knee and pulled his revolver, aiming it at the speeding vehicle. He fired three shots. One glanced off the rear window, cracking it, causing Justin and Kevin to duck low. A second round broke the driver side mirror, scattering bits of glass into the car. The third missed. In a matter of seconds, the man was back in the patrol car, lights and siren blasting and in full pursuit.

Justin crouched in the back seat brushing broken glass from his hair. "Uncle Jonah, what's going on? You hit a cop!"

Jonah made a high-speed turn squealing onto a side street. "He's not a cop, Justin, he's one of the enemy. I wasn't expecting them to find us so soon."

"What enemy? What are you talking about?"

"I can't explain right now, boys. I need to get you out of here first. I'll explain it all later. For now, just hang on and stay down. If we can make to Buckley, we'll be fine."

He swerved around another corner just as he caught sight of his pursuer. Despite his evasive maneuvers, the patrol car gained on them. Two more shots hit the rear window. Cracks spread from the points of impact like spider webs.

Jonah glanced around at the neighborhood as he slammed the brakes before careening right at the next intersection. "This is too dangerous. Too many people could get hurt if that idiot keeps shooting at us. I have to get back on the main road. We should be close enough to keep ahead of him until we get to the base." He took another corner, nearly tipping the car onto its side, leaving a long trail of rubber behind. Two more turns and he was back on the road headed north toward the Air Force base. "Only a couple more miles, boys," he told them.

The phony cop gained slightly, but Jonah managed to weave in and out of traffic enough to evade him until they reached their destination. He made a quick right turn, and then left, into the entrance to Buckley Air Force base. He hit the brakes to slow their momentum. Kevin and Justin peeked up to see the guards with weapons at the ready and Jonah holding up his ID. He was shouting at the guards. "Jonah Madrid, special federal liaison. We're being chased by an individual posing as an Aurora police officer."

The guard, noting the badge and official sticker on the windshield, signaled his companion to open the gate and waved the car through.

The fake policeman careened around the corner to see his target escaping through the guard station, noticing the armed soldiers who suddenly appeared to take an unhealthy interest in him. He hit the gas and sped off down the road, away from the gate.

Once inside, Jonah drove to the hanger containing his jet, a shiny white Learjet70. He stepped out of the car, flashed his ID badge to the soldier on duty, and waved for the boys to join him. "Alright, you two. We need to talk."

He led the boys to a small glass walled office inside the hangar. He poured them both a glass of water and sat behind the desk.

"First things first though. We need to take care of Kevin here. How would you like to go with us to New Mexico?"

"Who, me? No. I want to go home. What's going on?" Kevin's hands were shaking.

Jonah leaned forward, resting his chin in folded hands, his elbows on the desk. "We can't let you go home. They will have your description by now, so it won't be safe for you there."

Kevin jumped to his feet, eyes wide, choking on his water a bit before replying. "What do you mean it won't be safe? What about my mom? Who are you talking about?"

"I'm sorry, Kevin. We never meant to involve you in any of this. Nevertheless, right now you need to come with us to New Mexico. I can arrange it with your mom so she thinks we invited you at the last minute to spend the summer with Justin and me. She will be safe. We can arrange things so she is invited to work on a short-term project for one of her company's branches in another state." He pressed a few buttons on the phone by his chair, gave some instructions and hung up. "She should get a call in a couple of hours from her boss, so she will be delighted you will be taken care of while she is gone."

Justin finally found his voice again. "Safe from *who*? What are you talking about, Uncle Jonah? Tell us what's going on!"

He stood up and walked around the desk, kneeling down to face his nephew. "Trust me, Justin. There is something incredibly important you need to do, but I can't tell you anything more until we are gone from here. Your mom called me last week when she recognized it was time for you to learn the truth about yourself. It is my responsibility to teach you the things you need to learn. It will all make sense in time. Can you do that? Can you trust me for just a little while longer?"

Justin fought to calm himself and thought carefully before responding. After a moment, he nodded and looked his uncle in the eye. "Yeah, I can do that."

Jonah turned to Kevin with a stern, but sympathetic look in his eyes. "And you, my young friend, it may help Justin on his journey to have a friend like you at his side. Are you that sort of friend?"

Kevin's shaking subsided as he listened to Jonah. He took another sip from his glass, gave Justin a long look before allowing a slight smile to grow. "If you're sure my mom will be safe, count me in too." Kevin looked toward Justin, a gleam growing in his eyes. "Strange things are afoot at the Circle K."

Justin returned the smile. "You said it, Socrates," pronouncing it like in the movie.

Jonah clapped Justin and Kevin on the back. "Good boys. Now let's convince Kevin's mom that he is with us on a nice, wonderful vacation."

After enlisting Emily's aid in the conspiracy, Jonah helped Kevin make a three-way phone call to his mother. Kevin's mom couldn't believe her luck. She quickly explained about the amazing opportunity she had just been offered and was more than happy to give her permission for Kevin to join Justin and his uncle on vacation.

After Kevin's mother hung up, Jonah covered the mouthpiece of his phone with a cupped hand as he whispered into the receiver. "One more thing, Emily. Get to the safe house as quickly as you can. It's only a matter of time before they try getting to him through you."

"Okay, Jonah. I understand. Take care of him."

Jonah hung up and led the boys back to the car to retrieve Justin's belongings. Two soldiers were quickly dispatched to Kevin's house, with Kevin's key, to gather up the clothes and other items he would need for the trip. An hour later, the Learjet70 was speeding down the runway, tilting up toward the sky.

Jonah unbuckled himself and turned in the swivel chair to face the wide-eyed boys. "I suppose you two are wondering what just happened." He examined their faces, took a deep breath, staring at the ceiling as he gathered his thoughts. "Guess I probably should start at the beginning. Justin, you're not from Earth."

***

Keldon Ankara, head librarian, shoved his phone back in his pocket and slammed his fist into the wall. "That idiot! He endangered our entire operation with his reckless stunt."

Marcus Dakar, dressed in his usual tailored gray suit, remained seated behind his desk in the dimly lit underground bunker. "How could they have known who he was? Humans don't have the technology to penetrate our disguise."

Keldon suppressed the rage rising in his mind. He wanted to kill something, but he needed Marcus. At least for now. "Obviously he was not a human. A Zarminan agent got to the boy before we did. Are we tracking the plane?"

Marcus checked his computer. "No, sir. They must have stealth capability. We've lost them."

Keldon stormed out of the bunker, punching the elevator button with his fist. "Find them! We need to get that boy and learn how he came into possession of that box. Our entire operation depends on it. Contact that Bork idiot and have him set some of his Earthling lackeys on their trail. Let's see if our puppet can be useful for something besides his money. And have Martin Mumbai report to me immediately. His failure needs to serve as a warning to everyone." He rearranged his face to show a calm, pleasant, and concerned appearance as the doors opened to the main floor of the library, a small branch in the Aurora city system. He approached an anxious-appearing patron. "Hello, Mrs. Graham. I'm sorry your book wasn't here, but I have placed it on hold for you. As soon as it comes back in, we'll be sure to notify you."

Chapter Three

The hum of the jet engines filled the cabin as Justin and Kevin absorbed this statement. Justin's eyes jumped between his uncle and Kevin, not sure he wanted to hear the answer. "What do you mean I'm not from Earth?"

"This is going to be a bit much to take in all at once," said Jonah, taking a deep breath. "I'll try to spill it out in small doses so you can get a grip on it all and ask any questions you may have." He paused for a moment to gather and organize his thoughts, deciding the best way to proceed. Jonah held up one hand, stopping Justin as he started to ask a question. "Be patient for a minute. We have lots of time. As I said, you are not from Earth. Your home world is a planet astronomers here call Trappist-1d. We call it Zarmina."

Kevin swallowed hard as he stared at his friend and Jonah, scrunching back as far as he could manage into his seat. "Are you talking aliens? Like from another planet out in space aliens? His face suddenly took on a look of terror. "You're not trying to take over the Earth, are you? Or space pirates or something?"

Justin stared in horror at his friend, realizing he might be part of an extraterrestrial plot to overthrow the Earth and enslave its people. What would his mother think?

Jonah laughed. "Calm down, Kevin. In fact, we're here with the blessings of your government attempting to prevent an invasion. We're the good guys."

Kevin smiled and leaned forward resting his elbows on his knees. "Oh wow, that's insane! you mean you and Justin are fighting a space war? Like Halo? Super cool!"

He turned to face Justin, his expression displaying a slight hurt. "How come you never told me?"

Justin woke from his confused stupor at the question. "What are you talking about? I didn't know about any of this." He turned toward Jonah, his voice trembling with fear. "Does Mom know?"

Jonah reached out, placing a hand on Justin's knee. "Yes, Justin. She knows. Your mom is an incredibly brave woman. She is Zarminan as well, but after your father died, she chose to raise you alone, as a normal Earther. She convinced us it was the best way to protect you until we learned if you were indeed the one. I've been her only contact with our people since you were an infant."

"Are you really my uncle?"

"Yes, I am. Karl was my youngest brother, just as we told you. He and your mother were pair-bonded when they entered the academy. How she has managed to do everything on her own after the bond was broken is beyond me."

Justin opened his mouth to speak, closed it, his brow corrugated as he tried again. "What happened…? I mean how…?"

"How did he die?"

Justin nodded his head.

Jonah took a deep breath and let it out slowly through pursed lips. "I knew this time would come. I hoped it would be easier after all these years." He rubbed the back of his neck, then slid to the edge of his chair. "Your father was the smartest, most courageous Zarminan I ever knew. He and your mother were agents placed here on Earth to track down and interfere with our enemy's plot to invade. His ability to see their codes in Earthly technology made him invaluable. From the time you were conceived he was convinced you would develop the same abilities he had to see those Skutaran codes. When you were born there were some indications he was right, but nothing substantial… until now."

Kevin sat up straighter, his eyes even wider. "Skutaran? What the frak is a Skutaran?"

Jonah turned to look at Kevin, his face grave. "Skutarans are a race of warriors intent on conquering as many systems as they can. Fortunately, Zarmina is too strong for them, but some of us have joined forces with other threatened worlds to try to stop them. Your father noticed some strange transmissions between Earth and Skutara. Very unexpected since Earth is so distant and has such low technologically that they were of no strategic value to anyone. After a little investigation, your father learned this was a rogue group of Skutarans with their own plans for earth. We sent him and your mother there, with a number of others for support, to find out exactly what they were up to."

"Can you see these codes?"

"No. None of us can. In fact, on Zarmina, most of us thought Karl's ability was a learning disability. He couldn't read, or text, or use any of the normal technology we take for granted on our world. The schools had to furnish him with specially made printed copies of all the required materials in the form of what you know as books. His classmates were quite cruel to him because of this."

Justin slumped back in his chair. "Yeah, I know all about that. I guess kids are jerks everywhere."

"Yes. One more thing our two species have in common. Hopefully it's something we will both out grow of in time. It was only when he joined the military and accidentally noticed the hidden codes in some intelligence reports we realized what he had. This ability to see beyond the screens gave us our first hints as to what the Skutarans were up to. Your father was the first to make contact with the governments here and to set up bases around the world. It was Karl who tracked their main base of operations to somewhere around Denver. That's why he and your mother set up their home there. They both worked undercover trying to narrow down the exact location. And then you were born."

Justin absorbed the words as he sat staring into the floor of the jet. "You haven't said how he died… I need to know how he died."

Jonah sighed heavily, reached out, and laid a gentle hand on Justin's shoulder. "Karl was leading a small group of us on a mission to destroy a Skutaran outpost. More of a research facility actually, so not heavily guarded. We eliminated a couple of sentries at a side entrance to the facility and began our reconnaissance of the interior, looking for anything to tell us what they were up to. I took one group to the upper floors while your father took the rest to the lower floors. After a while, we heard the firefight and raced to rejoin with his group. We met up near the entrance and held off a superior force long enough to begin a withdrawal. We took several casualties, but nothing serious, until we headed into the hills where we hid the lander. Another patrol of Skutarans cut us off, nearly surrounding us. Karl took two men to lead a breakout. By the time my group caught up with him, they had taken heavy casualties, your father among them. I got there too late and found him only minutes before he died. Your mother was home with you so she could not heal him through the pair-bond. Before he died, he gave me that silver box and told me to get it to you."

Justin felt his throat tighten as if a pair of invisible hands had him in a strangle hold. He looked up at his uncle, vision blurred with tears. "So, he died a hero? He saved Mom and me?"

"He did indeed, Justin." Jonah gathered up Justin in a strong, protective embrace. "His last words were to ask me to watch over you and your mother, and to keep you both safe until you could take his place."

Sniffling back the mucus running from his nose, and pulling back to wipe it on his sleeve, Justin again looked up into his uncle's hazel eyes. "Why didn't anyone tell me about this? All this time I thought he died is a car accident. Why didn't anyone tell me the truth?"

"Your mother and I thought the best way to protect you was to keep your true identity a secret, even from you. If you grew up believing you were a normal human, you couldn't accidentally give yourself away to the enemy."

"Normal? I've never been normal. All this time I just thought I was some sort of freak… and so did everyone else."

Kevin punched Justin on the arm. "Yeah, but we always thought you were a normal human freak, not some space alien."

Justin laughed, despite himself. "Oh, that makes me feel a whole lot better."

Kevin smiled as his eyes twinkled mischievously. "E.T. need to phone home?"

Realization intruded on Justin's thoughts. "So how did they find us again? What went wrong?"

Jonah stood up and walked back to the galley, picking up some sandwiches and sodas for each of them. "I'm not sure, Justin. We still don't know exactly where the Skutaran base is, so maybe you stumbled onto them somehow." He passed out the food, opened his turkey on rye and took a bite. "Can you remember anything unusual happening while I was gone?"

Justin unwrapped his sandwich, popped the top on his Coke and ate while he thought. "Not really. We spent most of our time after school trying to decipher that box you gave me. We never did figure it out." He took another swallow of the soda. "There's something familiar about it though. Like I should know what it is, but I can't quite get it."

Kevin barely managed to speak through a huge mouthful of peanut butter and jelly. "Yeah, even that wacko librarian didn't know anything about it."

Jonah's head jerked up, his eyes narrowing as he glanced quickly from Justin to Kevin and back again. "What librarian? The one at your school?"

Justin shook his head as he held his sandwich halfway between the table and his mouth. "No. She's okay with our school research and stuff, but how would she know anything about those markings? I went to the Mission Viejo library. I figured they might know more."

"You took the box to a public library?"

"No, not the box. I made a rubbing of the engravings and showed that to the head guy there. He sort of freaked out about it so I made up something about it being a school project and left."

Jonah folded his hands and tented his fingers under his chin as he glared at the boys. "You are lucky to be alive, Justin. I think you accidentally exposed yourself to the Skutarans, and may have discovered where they are hiding." He leaned back in his seat, folding his arms across his chest. "It's my fault for not warning you to keep the box secret. Not sure what I was thinking. I should have guessed you two would try searching outside resources to learn more."

Justin rubbed the back of his neck as he tried to absorb everything. "Let me get this straight. You and my parents are aliens fighting a war to save Earth. I'm an alien with some strange ability to see secret messages in cyberspace, and not just a kid with some genetic disorder. The enemy killed my father and is now trying to kill me. You need my ability to end this war we are waging against a bunch of… space librarians?"

Kevin laughed, slapping Justin on the back. "Not a bad way to start summer vacation."

Jonah shook his head, trying unsuccessfully to suppress a smile. "That's about the gist of it. They're only posing as librarians, at least it appears that way, and we'll know more once we get to our base. How are you holding up? I know this is a lot to take in all at once."

"My head feels like it's about to explode, but in a weird sort of way it feels right, like it makes sense of everything. I'll be okay—I just need time to rethink pretty much everything I thought was my life." He turned to stare out the window at the solid layer of clouds below them.

Kevin raised his hand. "So where, exactly, are we going?"

"We have a base at Groom Lake. We should be there in another hour or so."

Kevin checked outside his window. "Never heard of it. I don't see any landmarks below, too many clouds. But according to the sun we're flying southwest."

"Exactly right. You may know it by another name. Area 51."

Chapter Four

The "fasten seat belts" sign flashed overhead in the cabin as they began their descent. The jet bounced a bit as it passed through the clouds, but settled comfortably once below them. Looking out the window, Justin and Kevin saw only the greyish-brown dirt of the Nevada desert, sparsely vegetated with sage and cactus. Tire tracks traced randomly intersecting lines, evidence of the popularity of four-wheeling in the area.

"Is that where we're headed?" Kevin pointed ahead of them toward a complex of concrete buildings and parallel runways nestled against some hills.

Jonah nodded with a grin. "Groom Lake, and the Nevada Test and Training Range. Home of several detachments from Edwards Air Force Base—"

"And alien central. There really are aliens here, just like everyone thinks." Kevin plopped back in his seat, eyes wide and smiling from ear to ear.

"No better cover than the truth shouted by a bunch of fanatics nobody will take seriously. We couldn't have planned it any better."

Justin stared out the window at the approaching runways. "So it really is true? I'm from another planet?"

Jonah reached out and placed a strong hand on Justin's shoulder. "Yes, Justin. And you have a tremendous responsibility before you now. I wish we could have prepared you more for all of this, but we can't change the past. I'm here for you whenever you need to talk. You're not alone."

Kevin sat looking out the window. "If everything is ready here on the dark side of the moon, play the five tones."

Justin whistled the five notes from the movie in reply.

Jonah stared at both boys, shook his head and laughed.

The plane lurched as it touched down. The whine of the engines grew as they reversed power to brake down to taxiing speed. A few minutes later, the door swung open and a staircase rolled up to the opening.

"Holy crap on a cracker!" Kevin held his hands up to shade his eyes as he stepped out of the plane. The thin cloud cover did little to reduce the sun's glare. "It's hotter than an oven out here."

"We're in the middle of a desert, dummy. What did you expect… polar bears and reindeer?" Justin punched his friend in the arm, feeling the sweat dripping from his own brow.

A few minutes later, inside the air-conditioned bunker, Jonah filled out the required paperwork as the boys drank sodas provided by one of the sentries. The room could have been a recruiting poster for military décor magazine. Tan metal filing cabinets along one wall, a 1950's wire-framed fan sat slowly turning left to right as it clanked and circulated the air, a green metal desk with matching roller chair against one wall and a mix of aircraft photos on the walls, some dating back to the 1950's. A large map of the base hung behind the desk. A door opened to their left. Justin's heart skipped a beat as he saw a girl about their age approach.

"Good afternoon Major Madrid. I hope your flight was pleasant." She extended a hand to Jonah in greeting instead of saluting.

"Good afternoon, Myah. You're right on time. May I introduce my nephew, Justin Madrid, and his friend Kevin

Samson. Justin, Kevin, this is Myah Helsinki. She is assigned to be your liaison for the duration of your stay here on the base."

Her smile lit up the room. Her long golden hair seemed to shimmer a light of its own. She wore a black short sleeved shirt and torn, faded jeans with black Converse cross trainers. She carried a worn and faded jean jacket in the crook of her left arm. Justin felt his face flush and his palms grow sweaty as she looked him over.

"So this is our newfound hero. I hope you're worth all the trouble you've caused around here."

Kevin stepped forward, reaching out to shake Myah's hand, his most winning smile beaming. "Oh, don't mind him. He excels at causing trouble wherever he goes. Nice to meet you Myah. So what's a girl like you doing in a place like this?"

Jonah fought back a laugh as Myah sent him a withering glance. "You've got to be kidding me. Are all Earth boys so hopeless?"

"You'll have to forgive Myah, boys. She is one of our brightest computer specialists, but we have stolen her away from her studies on Zarmina to assist with your acclimation to all of this."

Justin's mind went blank, with the exception of one thought. *Help me, Obi-Wan Kenobi. You're my only hope.* The image of the beautiful Zarminan girl dressed in a white robe, pleading for his help, flashed before him. A jab in his ribs from Kevin, and a whispered "Use the force, Luke." startled him out of his paralysis.

Justin stuttered a barely audible "Hi, I'm Luke… uh, Justin."

"It's okay, Major. I can spare some time away, for now, to help out. I know how rough it can be to find yourself in unfamiliar surroundings." She turned to Justin, giving Kevin nothing more than a nose-wrinkled shake of her head. "I can imagine how unsettling all of this must be for you. I remember when I first arrived from Zarmina. Everything on Earth was terribly strange. It took a while to get accustomed to, but I managed to find my way eventually, and so will you." She held out her hand for Justin.

Justin realized she had been speaking to him and startled out of his trance, wondering what she had said, but her hand was out to him so he shook it, hoping she didn't mind the clamminess too much.

***

The screams faded, eventually ending as Martin Mumbai lost consciousness. Two large Skutaran guards carried the body off to the incinerator. Keldon Ankara faced the score of personnel assembled to witness the educational execution. The circular room, dug several stories below the library, contained twelve steep rows of seats, similar to images of old operating theatres. A bank of powerful overhead lights illuminated the central stage, leaving the audience in deep shadows. Three cameras transmitted the lesson to other Skutaran bases scattered across the face of the planet. In the center of the floor sat a heavy chair. Its arm, leg and head straps, now bloodied, hung loose.

"I trust there will be no more independent foolishness to be dealt with in the future. That one's carelessness might have exposed our entire operation. Is the lesson learned?"

The witnesses jumped to attention, their left fist raised in salute. "All hail the revolution!" He stood rigidly examining their faces for any signs of weakness or sympathy for the traitor. Finding none, he continued. "Our priority is now two-fold. We must first double our efforts to complete the mind wiping of the earthlings as soon as possible. If the Zarminans have discovered the location of this base, they will attack us very soon. We must complete our mission before then. The emperor will not forgive failure. In addition, we must locate the boy. If the traitor's information is correct, and the son of the Zarminan spy can read our signals in the Earthers' technology, then he must be eliminated, like his father before him. Without him, they cannot prevent us from conquering this planet and using its pathetic inhabitants to build our army and overthrow the emperor. You have your assignments. You know the consequences of failure. Go."

***

Back in his office, two floors above the main auditorium, and three floors below the library, Keldon Ankara gathered a crate of supplies. "Are they gathered yet?"

"Yes, sir. They are awaiting your arrival. There are still a few minutes before the appointed time."

"Good. I hate these programs, but we must keep up appearances. Especially now that we are so close to completion."

"And what is the topic of this program, if I may ask, sir?"

"An Alice in Wonderland Tea Party. The children will make construction paper hats and we have games and snacks for them." Keldon composed himself into the perfect imitation of happy excitement. "Am I presentable?"

"Perfect, sir. They'll never suspect a thing."

***

Phillip Bork, entrepreneur, self-made baron of stocks and bonds, multi-millionaire, was a true believer. Aliens from distant worlds were here on Earth, studying us, preparing for who-knows-what. Somebody had to do something, and he was just the man for the job.

Most of the actual work running his empire was done by the various managers and boards of directors. He played the role of benevolent father figure, whose only real job was to give the annual state-of-the-company speech at the stockholder's meeting. The bulk of his time was spent researching the thousands of alien conspiracy theories and sightings, collecting rare alien artifacts, and providing support to various conspiracy organizations, his favorite being the Red Angus Party. They were one of the few getting real results.

Now that his new investors, represented by a Mr. Keldon Ankara, assumed even greater control over most of the operations, he was free to pursue this more vital quest. Curious that he had never heard of Ankara before; he usually made it his business to know everyone who could be a potential competitor, or partner, but the organization's background check was spotless. New pop-up companies burst onto the tech radar from time to time, so it really was not that unusual.

For now, he had to decide how to proceed with the information request he received from Mr. Ankara. Given the nature of the security restrictions required for this job, The Red Angus were the perfect choice. He opened the desk drawer with the key kept in his pocket, took up the phone and punched the contact button for Zach Litson.

Chapter Five

"Ooph. Where's the Tylenol?" Justin's eyes tried to focus in the dim morning light filtering through the window of his shared room, but the pain in his head was too great.

"In the bathroom, dude, right where you left it last night... R2D2, you know better than to trust a strange computer." Kevin leaned up in his bed, rubbed his head and plopped back onto the pillow. The small bed creaked as he resettled his body into the thin mattress. He yanked the grey blanket over his head as Justin turned on the light.

"It's my destiny." He shuffled like an old man with arthritis toward the bathroom, ignoring the light switch. The cold dingy white tiles froze his toes, but he was too sore to move any faster. He leaned on the sink counter, pulling open the mirrored medicine cabinet, straining to read the labels as he searched for the bottle of painkiller. "If I have to look at another computer screen I think my brain will explode. Are they trying to kill me?"

"And what's up with all the physical training? I've never done so many burpees in my life. Even coach Hargrave wasn't as sadistic as drill sergeant Myah. Who does she think she is?"

A far too animated female voice crackled through the loudspeaker in the ceiling. "Rise and shine, campers. Daylight is wasting away. Chow is at oh six-thirty. Be on time today, boys."

A pillow flew through the air, hit the speaker, knocking over the table lamp as it fell.

***

"Come on Justin. You can do this. Focus your mind on the message hidden in the static." Myah, dressed in her typical faded jeans, black t-shirt and jean jacket, long blond hair tied back, leaned over him at the terminal. "You almost had it yesterday. Block out all the distractions and let your mind do what it knows how to do. You simply need to get out of its way."

"I'm trying!"

Kevin replied automatically to the obvious opening. "Do or do not. There is no try."

"Ugh. Why didn't I take the blue pill?"

"Hey, no mixing franchises."

Myah gave Kevin another withering glare. She simply could not understand the need these two had for communicating in movie quotes. "Maybe you should leave if you can't be more help."

The three sat together in small four-wheeled metal chairs in front of a grey-green metal desk in front of the computer. Fluorescent lights glared and flickered in a string of banks hanging from the ceiling. A dozen soldiers in tan uniforms sat at other desks around the underground bunker talking on phones, filling out forms, or typing on their own computers.

The static on the screen drilled into his mind like thousands of hot needles stabbing at his brain. Despite the new glasses, his eyes felt as if they would explode any second. He winced and inhaled sharply. The scent of Myah's shampoo filled his nostrils. He suddenly became aware of her hand resting on his shoulder. In spite of himself, and despite his irritation at her no-nonsense dedication to an all-out assault on overcoming Justin's inability to read the alien code, he felt a stirring in the pit of his stomach. He lost himself in the sweet smell of green apples. Justin found his imagination taking him to a grassy hillside, where he stretched out under an apple tree. Above him, nothing but blue sky, dotted with puffy white cumulus clouds drifting on the gentle winds.

"That one looks like a dragon." Myah's voice, next to his ear, and soft, like a song, made his heart skip a beat. He smiled. Gazing into her brown eyes gave him goosebumps. Her soft golden hair flowed across her neck and shoulder. She was the most beautiful girl he had ever seen. He reached out to take her hand.

"Open your eyes, Justin. You'll never get it sitting there with your eyes shut." Reality landed on him with a thud.

Opening his eyes, Justin let out a startled gasp. "I see it!" He looked up at Myah, eyes wide, and pain free for the first time in a week. "It's all there as clear as day! The static is gone!"

Myah gripped his shoulder hard and spun him around to face her. "You can read the alien code? For real?" Her face grew stern, eyes squinting as she studied his face. "You're not just saying that to get an early rest period are you?"

"No, for real. Give me a pencil and paper and I'll write it down for you." Excited as he was at finally breaking through the barriers, he felt a twinge of disappointment that Myah doubted him. She was very pretty when she smiled at him.

Five minutes later, Myah grabbed the paper and ran it over to one of the soldiers. "Deliver this to Major Madrid. Tell him Justin has learned to read the code."

The soldier saluted, and marched out of the room. Justin watched as Myah walked back to him. He had never noticed before how the light shimmered in her hair, or the way she seemed to float when she was happy. He sighed, then startled back to his senses. *What are you thinking? She'd kill me if she knew I was daydreaming like that. Besides, she probably has a hundred other guys to pick from. Get a grip.*

"So what happened? How did you finally crack it?" She sat in the chair next to him, tossing her ponytail off her shoulder, that beautiful ponytail.

Justin felt all the blood in his body fill his face. "Well, uhmmm, you know, I did what you said. I let my mind wander and it just happened. All the static vanished, along with the headache. And the words were there."

Myah smiled again. "Did you think about anything in particular? It might help to know exactly what you did, in case you need to do it again."

Justin's voice cracked a full octave and a half. "Nothing." He cleared his throat. "Nothing special. I, uhmmm, don't even remember...I just let go and relaxed, then it happened." He pointed at the screen. "I can still read it, plain as day. I don't think we need to worry. It feels like something switched on in me."

"What about your migraines? Does it still hurt when you try to read the codes?" Myah's face reflected her concern over Justin's struggles to overcome the pain of his efforts.

He thought for a moment, eyes turning upward as he made an internal search for the pain, then grinned. "No! The pain is gone! Once the static vanished and the messages became clear, the headaches disappeared."

Myah smiled in return. "Good. We were getting worried about you. But let's go slow for a while, just to make sure they don't come back."

Before Justin could respond, Jonah Madrid burst through the doorway, practically running toward his nephew. He held the paper Myah had sent in a tight grip. "You did it? You can read the enemy's code? Show me."

Justin took another sheet of paper and began copying the information as he read it off the monitor. Jonah and Myah watched silently, staring alternately at the paper, Justin, and the monitor, which to them appeared to be a static filled screen. After filling half the page with the new intelligence, Justin held out the paper for his uncle. He felt his heart leap as he glanced at Myah's beaming face.

"Marvelous. Absolutely marvelous. I'll tell the general we're ready to begin Phase Two." He slapped Justin on the back, nearly knocking him out of the chair. "Well done, Justin. I'm proud of you. You too, Myah. I'll make sure the general knows the part you played in helping Justin."

"Thank you, sir." She smiled her beautiful smile again, and patted Justin's knee. He nearly fainted. "I'm glad to have helped. All he needed was a little encouragement."

Jonah stood up, studying both papers. "In any case, you two have earned a break. Take the rest of the day off and go have some fun." He strode out of the room, followed by two soldiers.

Myah leaned back, stretching her arms and back, undoing her ponytail, tousling her hair loose. "Wonderful. Let's get in a good workout before lunch." She stood up and leaned in to give him a hug. "Congratulations, Justin. You may have just learned how to help us save the people of Earth." Then she was off. Justin felt his heart leap in joy… and his armpits gush.

He turned to Kevin and raised his hand for a high-five. Together they shouted, "Mischief managed!"

As he stood to head toward the gym and another torture session, the ache in his legs returned and he groaned at the thought of trying to lift another kettle bell.

***

"Yes, Lord Keldon. Our section is working day and night to complete our portion of the programming for the engram revitalization process. Our coders are most encouraged by their progress. We will be ready to begin operations within three Earth months, possibly sooner. All glory to the revolution!"

Keldon Ankara switched off the communicator and breathed a sigh of relief as the face of the section leader faded from the monitor. He pushed back from the heavy wooden desk, cracked his interlaced fingers as he walked across the room, reaching out to touch the marble busts sitting on stands underneath the works of art hanging on the walls, and stopped in front of a huge map on an easel. From above, two spotlights illuminated the map. Colored pins marked several dozen strategic locations of additional Skutaran bases and warehouses across the globe, as well as key Earth military and corporate facilities. He fingered the intercom device on his wrist.

"Marcus Dakar, you can make your report now."

The door opened and Keldon's second in command strode in, his digital tablet in his left hand. He stood silently, standing on the thick rug covering the floor of Keldon's plush office. His forehead wrinkled, scowling as he waited.

Keldon glanced over his shoulder. "You still disapprove of my choice of furnishings?"

"It is not my place to approve or disapprove, Lord Ankara."

Keldon sniffed. "And yet you do." He turned to face his underling. "If we are required to take refuge here on this pitiful planet, the least we can do is afford ourselves of its few luxuries. You do not need to live in squalor, Dakar. We will fulfill our destiny and return to Skutara with a force of millions soon, so you might as well enjoy what it has to offer."

"Yes, my lord. Are you ready for my report?" Marcus stiffened, his face turned blank. He held up his tablet, ready to proceed.

Keldon wandered across the room, gazing up at one of the paintings. "I hope your news is as good as those of the others. I would not want to hear you have disappointed me once again."

Marcus cleared his throat and scrolled through several pages on the tablet. "No, my lord. We will be ready."

Chapter Six

"Lord Ankara, the test subjects are assembled and ready for the engram compatibility protocols. We only await your passcodes to proceed." Marcus Dakar stood at attention in the sub-level bunker beneath the library. He tried to ignore the disgraceful display of opulent decadence on display in his commander's office, but his absolute hatred of all things to do with the Earth beings was difficult to keep from his face. His own spartan quarters were the ideal image of a Skutaran officer and citizen of the realm. None of the comforts that soften the body and mind soiled his life.

Keldon Ankara sat in his heavy well-padded chair as if on a throne, carefully ignoring his second in command, as he appeared to study a recent report on the visipanel on his desk. Calculating the precise time required to make sub-commander Dakar uncomfortable waiting for his reply, he slowly added his biodata signature to the bottom of the report and sent it on its way down the chain of command before turning off the visipanel. "All of the test subjects have been properly conditioned with the primary and secondary level protocols?'

Marcus stiffened at the intentional questioning of his attention to important details but held himself firmly in control. "Yes, my Lord. The subjects have all been regular participants in the previous after school programs we have held for their age group and all have been eager to attempt the next level of the video games they believe we have been providing them. They suspect nothing and already show signs of brainwave conditioning."

"Very well, then. Let us proceed with the compatibility protocols." Keldon rose from his chair and led the way to his private elevator. Rising up the five sub-levels to the main floor of the library, he carried out his ritual of altering his character to that of the head librarian. The smile he fixed on his face barely reached his eyes, and was almost painful to maintain. He hated these Earth beings, almost as much as he hated the fools of the emperor's council, but in particular, the younglings he was forced to deal with on a daily basis. His self-imposed exile to this remote world only served to increase his anger at the emperor and the humiliation he received before the council. He would show them all, though. With careful strategic planning, and the recruitment of the finest scientific minds of Skutara, Keldon Ankara managed to turn their fears of an uprising of re-implanted digitized minds into reality. He would show them how wrong they were to spurn him. He would overthrow them all.

The elevator doors opened to a small antechamber hidden behind a bookshelf in Keldon's office. He went to his small, crowded desk and opened up a password-protected program entitled "Space Warriors – Engram Protocols". He entered the requested passcode to initialize the program and watched the screen load an impressive looking video game. Along the left side of the screen, a banner of scrolling commands, the mind-altering code of this crucial phase in their plans for conquest, worked flawlessly. "All is ready," said Keldon. "All hail the revolution and our imperial destiny."

"All hail the revolution," replied Marcus. And the two left the head librarian's office, making sure to lock the door behind them.

The commotion of a dozen teenagers grew in volume as Keldon approached the community room. "Gather around everyone," he called to the assembled computer club members. "Today, as promised, you will be the first to beta test a new chapter in the Space Warrior video game franchise."

A wild cheer erupted from the teens. "Space Warriors! Space Warriors! Space Warriors!"

Keldon raised his hands, palms down to regain their attention. "But before we can start, remember the rules. You can tell no one about anything dealing with this game, even its existence. There are strict copyright and test participation requirements we must follow, or we will be denied any further testing privileges, and you yourselves could be liable in the case of any breech of secrecy. Does everyone understand?"

"Of course."

"We know the rules."

"No problem here."

One by one, each member of the club reaffirmed their agreement of absolute secrecy.

"Very well then. Each of you has a computer assigned to you, so log in and begin. Be sure to answer all the questions as they appear on the screen during the game. This data will be invaluable to the designers." He waved them off and each teen raced to their computers lining the walls, placed the headphones on their ears, and set to tapping madly on their keyboards. As the screens loaded up, they picked up the game controller, double-checked the function of each button and stick, and then settled in to become Space Warriors.

As the game began, Keldon motioned for Marcus and two additional library staffers to enter the room, shut doors behind them, and monitor the test subjects. Within minutes, and at regular intervals, a series of questions flashed on the screens.

"How do you feel about those in authority over you? Press A for good or B for bad."

"A good citizen conforms to everything without question. Press A for true or B for False."

"I am a good citizen. Press A for true or B for False."

"Skutaran citizenship is better for everyone. Press A for True or B for False."

"Compliance to Skutaran authority is what makes me happy. Press A for True or B for False."

Each of the dozen or so questions had been carefully selected to reveal the effectiveness of the conditioning process to make the earthlings wholly compliant to any form of authority, even an alien force intent on conquering their world.

During each series of questions, the subjects' fingers continued to work the game's controls, but their shoulders slumped, and their mouths hung slightly open. Their eyes lost focus and stared without blinking at the monitors before them. Once the questions were completed, the game resumed and the subjects' focus and activity levels returned to normal. To any accidental observer, it would appear the children were completely immersed in their activity. No indication of anything but a high tech video game appeared on the monitors. But to the Skutarans, the brain wave altering code flashed regular instructions as it worked on the minds of the players.

The librarians wandered back and forth behind their assigned test subjects recording the answers each one provided to the questions, carefully documenting how those responses changed as the game progressed, and how the changes indicated greater compliance to authority. After two hours, Keldon gave a signal and Marcus ushered the library assistants out of the room. The game ended to the groans and disappointment of the players.

"Hey, we didn't get to finish! What's the deal?"

"Now you all know this was simply a beta test of the game. The full version is not complete yet. The designers only want to know if what they are creating will be as popular as they hope. What do you think?"

"It was amazing! Super cool."

"Everyone sit down for a minute." Keldon's grin became more natural as the teens complied without argument.

"I am so glad you enjoyed the game. I will tell my friends at Design Tech how much fun you had. Now I want you to write down the usernames and passwords to each of your home and school devices for me. Here is some paper and pencils for each of you."

Without question, each of the kids complied, giving the sensitive information as requested. Keldon collected the papers and placed them in his jacket pocket. "Now I want each of you to stand up and go home. Tonight, you will refuse to eat anything but your vegetables at dinner, no matter how strenuously your parents argue with you. This is the Skutaran way."

"The Skutaran way is what makes me happy," they all replied in unison as they stood up and quietly left the library.

The next day, during the parents' council meeting, Keldon overheard many of the parents complaining to each other how difficult dinner last night had been.

"It's hard to complain about John eating his vegetables, but he absolutely refused to eat anything else. Now if that isn't strange, I don't know what is."

"The same thing happened with Mary, and Anne told me her two boys did the same thing. I bet you dimes to dollars it's something they cooked up together as a prank to pull on us."

"That must be it. Just some crazy teen prank. So what do you think about the new curriculum the school is proposing for next year?"

That evening, alone at his underground luxury office, Keldon reported the success of the program to his colleagues across the globe. "Now we know the brains of these pathetic earthlings are suitable for engram implantation. It is only a matter of time before we make the final calculations to complete the procedure. How long do you estimate before we can begin?"

The others conferred quickly, sharing data on their tablets before agreeing on a timeframe. "Another three months should suffice, maybe more, but we think that should be adequate time given how susceptible the humans were to the procedure."

Keldon tented his fingers under his chin as he leaned back in his chair and considered the schedule. *Three months. That should be sufficient. Approximately a week to remotely implant the engrams into the millions of unsuspecting earthlings, then another two years of concentrated work to build the transports required to return them all to Skutara.*

Marcus Dakaar interrupted Keldon's thoughts. "There are still a few improvements we would like to make in the programming, based on the subject responses we received."

"Excellent, but keep to the schedule. Do not fail me, gentlemen. The emperor and his toadies have had their way long enough. It is time for somebody with true vision to take control. With our army of dissidents implanted into their new bodies, nothing will stop us. Nobody on Skutara will expect an attack coming from Earth. Has our old transport ship been refitted for battle?'

Marcus swiped through his tablet for a second before responding. "Yes, sir. Final alterations were completed last week. The ship is now in orbit, utilizing stealth mode to hide from Earth's radar. If any of the Zarminans try anything, we will be ready."

***

The roar of the four-cylinder engine filled Justin's ears as he fought the ATV for control over the uneven hard packed sands of the desert he raced across. Kevin's whoops of joy blared through the earpiece in his helmet. Windblown sand stung Justin as beads of sweat carved channels through the grit caked on his face.

He startled from his revelry at the sound of a shout. "I am the Knightrider!!"

"Hey! Pay attention, Kevin! You almost ran right into me on that last turn."

"Sounds like a loser complaining to me! Watch this!"

"Loser, huh? Go ahead and do your worst! I'll show you who's a loser. I feel the need...the need for speed!"

The boys weaved across each other's tracks, narrowly missing colliding on several passes. Rooster tails of sand flew behind them as they careened across the flats of the military base on one of their few extended recreation breaks.

"I've got you now," shouted Justin over the cacophony of engines.

"Holy crap on a cracker! What was that?" Kevin's shouts almost hurt Justin's ears.

In an instant, a thick cloud of sand obscured his view of the desert and filled his open mouth with grit. Spewing desert crud in thick globs, Justin wiped his goggles enough to see a third ATV race ahead of him. A blond ponytail whipped in the breeze from under the driver's helmet. About a hundred yards ahead, the contestant performed a perfect donut, coming to a halt facing Justin and Kevin. As they approached, the driver stood up in the vehicle and pulled off her helmet. Long golden hair flew out behind her in the desert breeze, practically glowing in the bright sun.

"Myah? Where did she come from?" Kevin sputtered in disbelief. "Don't tell anyone I said this, but she just made us look like a couple of rookies."

"We are a couple of rookies, you idiot." Justin slowed his approach so as to keep the dust to a minimum. His heart skipped a beat, or two, as it always did when he saw Myah Helsinki. He lifted his hand to wave, but the left front tire caught a rock, sending his ATV swerving suddenly. He fought to regain control and came to a skidding halt. The resulting dust from his mishandled arrival covered Myah. She emerged from the cloud spitting sand and using her fingers to comb the grit from her hair. Lifting her goggles, she shook her head at Justin as she hopped down and walked toward him.

Myah leaned in close, hands clutching the roll bar. "Nice. Maybe next time we should put some training wheels on your ride." She ran her fingers once more through her hair and flicked the sand at Justin before turning back to her car.

Justin watched mutely as she marched away. A swat on the back of his helmet brought him back to reality.

"Way to impress the lady, man. Did she come over to ask you to the prom?" Kevin plopped himself down on heavily treaded tire laughing at his friend.

"Just shut up, Kevin. I don't see you doing any better. At least I don't make a complete pest of myself around her." He lifted his goggled, revealing raccoon eyes as he sat them on his helmet.

The roar of Myah's engine cut off any further exchange between them.

"Come on, you two. We're needed back on the base. Turn your vehicles into maintenance and get cleaned up before reporting to your station." Without another glance, she took off in a cloud of sand. Her rooster tail covered the two boys as a final statement of superiority.

As she sped off, Myah grinned and even laughed at her little show. *That ought to show them who's boss on these wheels.* Her brows furrowed and her mouth twisted as her thoughts continued. *Maybe I should lighten up on Justin a bit. He has made some incredible strides and never gives up, no matter how hard I push him. If only he would loosen up and talk more. I guess this is all a bit much for anyone to take in. and he is sort of cute. Maybe I should give him a break... or not.*

She parked her ATV into its assigned slot in the maintenance shed and marched off to her quarters. The sound of Justin and Kevin approaching caused her to look back over her shoulder and smile.

Chapter Seven

"Rise and shine, Chosen One. You have a busy day ahead."

Myah's voice, as usual, insanely cheerful for such an early hour, blared over the loudspeaker in Justin and Kevin's shared room.

"Ugh, what time is it?" asked Kevin as he burrowed deeper under his blanket.

Justin rubbed the sleep from his eyes and tried to focus on the red numbers illuminated on his desk clock. "Holy crap on a cracker, it's only four-thirty in the freaking morning."

"I don't care if you worship the ground she walks on, dude. That girl needs some serious mental readjustment." Kevin pulled his pillow over his head and curled up into a ball.

Justin threw his pillow at Kevin's back and sat up, recoiling as his bare feet hit the cold tile floor. "I do NOT worship the … oh for Pete's sake, just get a life and get dressed. Something must be up to wake us up so early."

Before they could finish their morning routine, and only half dressed, a loud bang on their door caused both boys to jump. "Are you two up yet?" The door flew open and crashed into the wall as Myah strode into the room. Her long flaxen hair hung loose around her shoulders, backlit by the hallway fluorescents. "Jonah has a special treat in store for the both of you today and you don't want to be late. Get a move on."

Justin and Kevin dove for their blankets to cover themselves, even though they both had their jeans fully on. "What the hell! You can't just barge in here like that!

We're not dressed yet," Kevin's voice declared, about half an octave too high. Justin, mute as usual, simply blushed nine shades of red.

Myah laughed with hands on her hips. "If you don't want me to see you like this, then get up and dressed a bit faster next time. Besides, we've gone swimming before so this is nothing I haven't seen already." Even with her face backlit and in shadows, Justin could see her wink at him. "Get moving. Breakfast is in five minutes and lift-off in forty-five." She turned and marched out of the doorway, leaving it wide open.

Both boys stood speechless, still clinging to their blankets and staring at the empty doorway in disbelief. Justin finally shook himself out of his stupor and looked around for his shirt and socks. "Alright, let's get a move on and get to breakfast before they shut it down. She and my uncle must have something… wait, what did she say? Lift off in forty-five minutes? What is she talking about?"

"As I said before, strange things are afoot at the Circle K." Kevin dropped his covering and started his search for clothes, shaking his head in reply. "I have no freaking idea, man, but whatever it is, I'm sure she found a new way to torture us. I don't get it. One minute she is talking to us like old friends, then she suddenly starts acting like Attila the she-hulk drill sergeant. If all girls are as crazy as she is, I may never want a girlfriend. Too much weirdness."

Justin finished tying his shoes and headed toward the hallway. "Give her a break, dude. It's her job to teach us, and get us in shape to fight the bad guys. It could be worse."

"How do you know?"

Justin turned his back on Kevin and walked several paces ahead of him on their way to the mess hall. "Just can it."

They found Myah, in her typical black shirt, sleeveless today, and torn jeans, hair pulled back into a complicated braid, already half-way through her powdered eggs and grapefruit. They picked up a plastic tray and found their way to the steam bins keeping the food warm. Eggs, sausage, bacon, hash browns, toast with a small packet of strawberry jelly, pineapple juice and a carton of chocolate milk. The breakfast of champions, fueling alien invasion force battling teens.

After gathering their breakfast, the boys stood looking around the room, debating whether to take a chance on joining their mentor at her table, or not. Loud whispers and elbow jostling got them at least slowly headed in her direction.

"Come on, boys. I won't bite. At least not too hard. Pull up a chair and chow down." Her tan shoulders bounced as she laughed at her own joke and waved them over.

Kevin swung one leg over his chair and slid his tray onto the table. "So what's up with the extra early wake-up call today?" He shoveled a forkful of eggs into his mouth.

"Not a chance, guys. Your uncle Jonah wants to tell you this little nugget himself." She motioned toward the entry to the mess hall with her fork.

Justin turned to face the tall figure approaching them at a brisk pace, swallowing hard a mouthful of sausage. "Uncle Jonah, where have you been? I haven't seen you in two days and nobody would tell me anything. And what's going on today? Myah says you have something special, but…"

"Whoa, Justin. Slow down. Chew your food before you choke on it." Jonah sat in the fourth chair at their table and stole a piece of jellied toast from Justin's tray. "I've been away on business, arranging a few things. Our leaders have decided it is time to meet you in person."

Justin's eyes narrowed in suspicion as he took another bite of eggs. "I've already met the General. Who are you talking about? Is this something I have to get dressed up for?"

Jonah chuckled as he licked the jelly drippings from his fingers. "Not the leaders of this world, Justin. I'm taking you on a little trip home. To Zarmina. And yeah, you should probably spruce up a bit. You are quite a celebrity on our world and you probably would like to make a good first impression."

Justin froze with his fork suspended halfway between tray and mouth, staring slack-jawed at his uncle. Wha...what do you mean you're taking me to Zarmina? You mean in space? Another planet? I thought you said Zarmina was forty light years away. How can we possibly go there?"

"We can, and have been, traveling between our worlds for about seventy years. Earth technology is about four hundred years behind us, so they haven't solved FTL quantum paradoxes yet. The trip only takes about two hours in our ships."

Justin lowered his fork to his plate and sat back, staring at his uncle, attempting to articulate questions, but without success. He pressed both palms into his eyes hard enough to see flashes of light, then ran his fingers through his hair. "You want me to go with you into outer space to a planet, my home world, forty light years away, in just a couple of hours?"

"We lift off to dock with our ship in fifteen minutes, but the journey itself will only take two hours. One hour to leave this solar system, Almost no time in hyperspace, then another hour to reach Zarmina."

Kevin choked on his juice, using his napkin to catch the spray. "Hold on, hyperspace? Like in that scifi book, what was it...oh yeah, *Foundation*? The one that Asimov guy wrote? That's just a story. You're making all this up. Some sort of joke."

Jonah tilted his head and winked at Kevin with a smile. "Where do you think old Isaac got the idea in the first place?"

Kevin sat back and laughed. "No way, man! Holy crap on a cracker. That stuff is real?"

"Some of it. But most is just a good imaginative story."

"So if you guys are so smart, and all, how come you need Justin the wonder boy here to fight these Skutarans?"

"The enemy is just as advanced as we are, Kevin. Their home planet is in your constellation of Libra, orbiting around a star your astronomers call Gliese 581g. They have been able to mask our attempts to trace or decode their signals. Justin is a biological mutation, like his father. He can attune his senses to locate and unravel specific electromagnetic wavelengths. All he had to do was learn how to isolate the Skutaran signal from all the others on Earth. Once he learned control, the rest was easy. Notice how his migraines have vanished."

Jonah held up a hand to stop Kevin as he started to ask further questions. "Sorry, that's all I can tell you for now. State secrets and all. You understand."

Kevin deflated a bit, but leaned back and gave Justin a friendly shove. "Guess we better get packing if we leave in fifteen minutes."

"Sorry, Kevin. You need to sit this one out. Native Earthers, at least those without the highest clearances, are not permitted to make this interstellar journey. We'll be back tomorrow morning so there won't be much time for sightseeing."

"Bummer. Maybe next time?" He turned to his friend and raised his hand in a Vulcan salute. "The needs of the many outweigh the needs of the few… or the one."

Justin returned the salute. "Live long and prosper."

Jonah and Myah looked at each other, shrugging. "Let's go, Justin. We have just enough time to make the next shuttle."

***

As they arrived at the launch pad, disguised as a landing pad for F35 Lightning II aircraft, Justin's jaw dropped when he saw the spaceship rolling out from its hangar. Not quite the circular flying saucer shape of science fiction movies, it was more oblong, nearly fifty yards long and at least as tall as a three-story building. His first thought was of the saucer section of the U.S.S. Enterprise of *Star Trek* fame.

"She's a beauty, don't you think, Justin? The payments set me back quite a bit, but I always loved the looks and power of the Quark model. I named her Sunna." Jonah brought Justin to the ship and examined it carefully before approaching the entry.

"Wait… this is yours?" Justin froze, gaping at his uncle.

Jonah proudly brushed his hand along the underside of the blue-grey vessel. "All mine. One of the perks of my status as envoy to Earth. They let me use my own ship, but specially modified with weaponry and sensors provided by our military due to the nature of our mission."

"Very cool," replied Justin as he followed Jonah into the ship. The hallway they walked along hugged the interior contours of the ship and was intersected by several spokes of corridors leading to the central bridge. There were status panels at regular intervals, each displaying a variety of information about the ship as it was prepared for take-off. A voice over the intercom gave additional updates and information, only some of which Justin understood. There were two more interior circular halls containing living quarters, storage, engineering, medical facilities, and other areas which purposes Justin could not guess.

They came to one of the living quarters located on the inner ring, close to the bridge. Jonah stopped in front of the door and waved his hand in front of a panel next to the entry. "This will be your room during the voyage. Mine is next door. I have to go to the bridge now, so strap yourself down in the chair and get ready. I'll be back in a few minutes."

Justin saw a large padded reclining chair on a pedestal in front of a computer panel. "You're leaving me here? But I want to watch the take-off."

Jonah led the way into the room and approached the panel by the chair. He pressed a control button and the large screen lit up with a view of the ship's exterior. "There you go. You can see just as well from here. We're leaving in less than five minutes, so don't waste any time getting into the chair. See you soon."

He left, the door closing behind him. Justin was left with the intercom voice announcing departure in only two minutes. He hopped into the chair, tightened the heavy straps and tensed himself for the g-forces of the acceleration to come.

Moments later, the ship shuddered and Justin felt a slight pressure on his chest. He looked out the window and saw the ground rapidly vanish below, clouds streaming by his viewport. In less than a minute, Justin could see the curvature of the limb of the earth in the distance.

The door to his room slid open with a slight swish and Jonah entered. "So what do you think of your first launch?"

Justin stared for a second before replying. "That was it? No noise? No shaking around? What happened to the g-forces the astronauts talk about?"

Jonah laughed. "Sunna is not just some clunky Earth ship. She's state of the art Zarminan tech. Come on, let me show you the bridge now. We're about to leave orbit. You'll want to see this from the best seat in the house."

Once they arrived at the bridge, alarms flashed through the ship. Crew members ran to their posts and Uncle Jonah took Justin by the arm, pulling him to the side. "This is the most protected section on the ship. Take the seat over by that panel and strap in. Things will get a bit rough for a while."

Justin struggled with the chair's straps as his fingers shook and fumbled with the locking mechanism. A young man seated next to him reached over and helped secure him. "There, you're strapped in now. Just sit tight. Jonah will get us through this."

Justin faced his rescuer with wide eyes, his knuckles white as he gripped the straps holding him in place. "What's happening?"

"A Skutaran vessel came out from behind Mars and is on an intercept course. They don't manage to shoot any of us down very often, but they are a threat."

The young officer turned to work the various controls on his panel so Justin swiveled to face his uncle, now seated in the command chair. A large visiscreen filled the forward bulkhead of the bridge, showing empty space.

"Visiscreen to isolate on the approaching enemy vessel. Maximum magnification."

The screen shifted and a large, randomly shaped spaceship appeared. Having been constructed in space, solely for travel in space, no aerodynamics were required, but it did give the appearance of something a five-year-old would construct from his mega Lego blocks.

"Range to target?"

"Forty-seven million miles and closing fast. Weapons range in five minutes, sir."

"No response to our hails?"

"No, sir. No response."

Jonah examined the tactical information displayed to the left and right of the main image and made his decision. "Evasive maneuver muta eln, all weapons engaged and lock on target at earliest opportunity."

The officers responded wordlessly as their fingers flew over their controls. Justin watched as the seemingly incoherent lights and data displayed on the main screen changed. The lights suddenly changed from normal daylight to a deep violet.

"Enemy in range and locked onto, sir."

"Steady now... wait for my command."

As Justin watched the visiscreen, the Skutaran ship produced an array of eight energy beams from various spots on their ship's surface."

"Evasive maneuver decca quor, now!"

Justin felt the ship lurch to one side just as an impact struck. Lights flashed, a loud bang, as if someone struck a large metal beam with a sledgehammer resounded through the vessel.

"No damage, sir. The energy shielding is holding firm."

"Return fire!"

Justin watched as a single much brighter and larger energy beam struck the Skutaran craft. A large hole burned through the point of impact. In moments, debris flew from the hull breech and the Skutarans veered off, accelerating on a vector out of the solar system, away from the Zarminans.

Jonah watched them grow smaller in the visiscreen for a minute longer, then released his restraints and swiveled the command chair to face the others. "Well done, everyone. Prepare for solar system departure. Keep all sensors on maximum range, just in case."

Justin stared at his uncle, mouth hanging open, brows arched high on his forehead, still white-knuckling his straps.

"You can let go now," said the young officer next to him, reaching over to help undo the restraints. "You must be very proud. Jonah is one of the greats. Almost as great as his brother, but you already know all that, don't you."

Without facing the Zarminan officer, Justin shook his head. "No, I had no idea."

***

The rest of the trip proved uneventful, and disappointingly unexciting. It turned out the quickest way to leave the solar system, apparently necessary for the hyperdrive engines to work with any reliability, was to head straight up, above the plane of the ecliptic and not pass near any of the other planets. Only a momentary dizzy spell and a sudden shift is the stars gave any indication the trip through hyperspace occurred at all. As the ship approached Zarmina, from above, just as before, Justin had difficulty seeing anything other than the red dwarf star known as Trappist-1. Zarmina, the fourth planet, about the size of earth, hid in its glare.

Nearing the planet, Justin saw white clouds floating above a vast blueness, broken by two large land masses and spotted with several dozen smaller islands. "It looks a lot like Earth. Not like a strange alien thing at all."

Jonah chuckled and rested his hand on Justin's shoulder as they stood together at the portal. "Does that surprise you so much? Wouldn't conditions have to be similar to Earth's for us to look so much alike?"

"But wait, the information my computer gave about Zarmina made it sound a lot different from this. Smaller and only questionable signs of water or an atmosphere."

"Remember, Earth's tech is not as advanced as ours. They cannot see so far away with any degree of accuracy. Your computer only accesses their databases."

"But why didn't you tell me?"

"You didn't ask. I had hoped we would have more time, but our responsibilities kept us apart much of the time. Myah tells me you never talk to her about Zarmina, so I figured you weren't ready yet. Guess you'll learn on the fly. It is time to warn you though." Jonah turned Justin and locked eyes with him. "There is a very serious purpose for this trip. The Imperator, and several important members of his staff want to personally verify that you can correctly interpret the Skutaran code. They are planning a test for you to prove your ability."

Justin furrowed his brow and glanced out the window at the approaching planet. "What sort of test?"

"I'm not sure, but they do want to make sure you are the real thing before they invest so heavily in this war for the sake of Earth. After all, other than yourself, only your father had this ability. His accidental discovery of the Skutaran signals led us to Earth and their plan to invade. There has always been tension between our worlds, but never outright war. They need to be certain you are as reliable as your father."

Justin slumped into the bench in front of the window. "I'm terrible at tests."

"Jonah took a seat next to him and held his gaze again. "Don't worry. From what I've seen, you will do fine. There's nothing to worry about, and nothing to study for. Just do what you've been doing and everything will be fine. Now go get buckled in. We're about to land."

***

Justin stayed glued to the transport window on the trip to the Imperator's offices. The scene was something like a view inside the mind of his favorite science fiction writers' brains. The car he and uncle Jonah traveled in fit snugly into a transparent pneumatic tube, flying them along at incredible speed. Massive structures made of spiraling glass and metal towers were widely dispersed. The expanses between were filled with forests, some open grass, and ponds, others of varying mixes of greenery. Outside the public transportation system of pneumatic tubes, Justin saw a wide range of personal transport vehicles of all sizes, shapes and colors traveling in well-marked paths like areal roadways, one stacked above the other, six levels deep. Rising above the horizon was a very large moon, four times the size of earth's moon, glowing a deep orange-red, reflecting the red dwarf's less intense energy.

Justin leaned back just enough to turn to his uncle without quite taking his eyes off the view. "It's not as crowded as I thought it would be. You said this was the capital. Where is everyone?"

"This is the height of what on Earth you call rush hour. Everyone is heading in to work or going home at the end of their shift. There aren't as many of us on Zarmina as you humans on Earth. A few hundred years ago our population was severely decimated by a manufactured virus. It spread so rapidly in the crowded conditions of those days, the ones who survived enacted strict population control measures and required safe zones between living centers to restrict the spread of any future plagues. It is also what instigated our reaching out to spread ourselves among the stars."

Justin tilted his head, his mouth screwed in consternation. "The sun looks awfully close to the horizon, but it doesn't seem to be getting any closer to setting. What gives?"

"Zarmina has some very different orbital dynamics than you have on Earth. One orbit of our red sun takes about one and a half of your months, but the planet's rotation is very slow. One day on Zarmina is about four of your months. The atmosphere here is a bit thicker than on earth, so the climate is warm enough, even during the long nights. Give it a few days and you'll see the changes as the sun rises ever so slowly. You haven't been with us long enough to notice, but we live mostly underground so we can control the hours of light and dark. Your quarters are set to simulate earth day and night, but for the rest of us, it's been light for the entire time you've been with us, and will be so for some time yet. Our biological rhythms are set to other cues than light and dark, so we sleep regardless of light conditions. We can talk about all this more later, but now there are other more important matters to focus on. Get ready. Here come the Imperator's officers."

Chapter Eight

"So glad to meet you, young man. We hear marvelous things about your progress here in the capitol. Can you truly decipher the enemy's codes? Of course you can, we've seen the reports. How silly of me to even ask." The Imperator strode up to Justin, nodding acknowledgement toward Jonah, and held him by both shoulders, patting him roughly. Dressed in what appeared to be a tailored business suit, Justin was not sure of this man's identity, until he noticed everyone's deference toward him. The Imperator's personal office certainly gave no outward appearance of his status as the head of the planet's government. It could have passed for any well-off executive's place of business back on Earth.

"Come, join me for some refreshments in the conference room. Much more comfortable in there. So glad to meet you at last. The loss of your father was a terrible blow to us all. How is your mother?" He wrapped an arm around Justin's shoulder and led the small entourage into an adjoining chamber. Two walls were uninterrupted glass, or at least glass-like material—who knew on an alien world? The reddish glow of the sun was added to by several glowing panels in the ceiling. Colorful foods of all descriptions filled the center of an oblong table in the center of the well-lit room. Justin recognized only a few of the offerings as some of his mother's favorites. He had always assumed she shopped for them at some specialty store, but now...

He leaned over to his uncle as they sat next to each other. "This is really the Imperator? The ruler of all Zarmina? He certainly doesn't seem like a king."

Jonah chuckled and plucked a greenish-yellow berry from a nearby plate. "I guess he would seem strange to you. Zarminans are not as impressed with status as people of Earth. We honor accomplishment and ability, but also honesty and consider true service to others as the highest calling. Would you be surprised to learn that here, teachers are among the highest paid and most respected people on the planet?"

"No way!"

The remainder of the gathering consisted of various questions directed at Justin about his ability to see the codes and what it was like. Did he think he could teach others how to see the code too? What did he think about earth? What did he think about Zarmina? Condolences regarding his father, and regards to pass along to his mother. Justin answered as politely and honestly as he could but made certain everyone remembered he only discovered his ability, and heritage, a few weeks ago. This was all terribly strange to him.

Later that night, Justin found himself drifting off staring up through the transparent ceiling of his assigned room at the star-filled sky. The patterns were strange. No Big Dipper or Orion anywhere in the cosmos above. As he fell into sleep, dreams of standing in front of a panel of inquisitors wearing nothing but his Star Wars briefs (he hadn't worn those for nine years) filled his mind and made for a restless night.

After breakfast—a delicious assortment of foods Justin did not recognize—Justin and Jonah headed off to the testing chamber on another floor of the Imperator's office complex.

Inside the chamber, Justin saw a single table in the center of the room with what appeared to be a computer monitor. At the far end was a long curved and elevated bench. Behind the bench sat the Imperator at the center, flanked by six others. Justin watched as Jonah took the seventh seat. The Imperator nodded his head and the woman to his right, dressed in an elegant, but no-frills deep red business suit, stood to begin the proceedings.

"Justin Madrid, you are here to verify for all concerned you possess the ability to detect and successfully decode the embedded communication signals of the Skutarans." She raised one hand and pointed at the table in the center of the room. "You will take your place and tell us what the messages appearing before you say. Do you have any questions?"

Justin swallowed a massive lump in his throat and stammered his reply. "No, Your Majesty, um, Your Honor." He closed his mouth and looked no further than his shoes as he made his way to the assigned chair.

Several seconds passed before the monitor began to glow. In a bright flash, Patterns now familiar to Justin scrolled across the screen. Justin translated the message and new information replaced it as soon as he was done. The test continued in this manner for several more minutes without interruption, though he did hear whispered voices making comments from the bench.

As quickly as it began, the screen went dark and Justin swiveled to face the Imperator.

The leader of the Zarminans turned to face Jonah. "Are you certain this young man has not been prepared in any way to assist him with this test?"

Jonah faced his superior without hesitation. "No, sir. Only the translations he has provided at our base on Earth. Nothing more. He was not even aware there would be a test until we were about to land yesterday."

"Astonishing! Even better than your brother. We are impressed." He nodded to Jonah, rose as one with the rest of the panel, and exited the room out the door behind them. Jonah stood and clapped his hands as he walked toward Justin.

"Well done, nephew. I knew you were good, but that was incredible. Your father took hours to decode what you just did in minutes."

Justin stood as Jonah approached. "That was it? All I did was read what they put in front of me."

Laughing out loud, Jonah swatted Justin on the back, nearly knocking him over. "My boy, all anyone else saw on the monitors was static. What you do is remarkable. Even your father was not as fast at the decoding as you are."

A look of confusion crossed Justin's face. "But if nobody else can see what I see, how do they know I was right?"

"Simple," replied Jonah. "They fed you transmissions your father decoded for us several years ago. We authenticated those messages through many months of intensive undercover operations against the Skutarans. You even improved a bit on the decoding to fill in a few gaps your father was not certain about. Your mother would be very proud of you, as am I."

"So now the Imperator will support the war against Skutara invading Earth?"

"It won't be a war, exactly, but yes, all thanks to you. Officially, we have a neutrality agreement with the Skutarans. They leave us alone and we do the same. Of course, each side provides some low levels of support to each other's adversaries, but we all ignore those. Diplomatic channels have confirmed our suspicions about the enemy on Earth, though. They are an outcast group of criminals, deserters, stranded on Earth and not worth the effort for the Skutaran government to do anything about. Our attempts to provide any warnings about what they may be up to is not their concern, officially. The Imperator has authorized us to do what we can, with the forces we already possess, and try to stop them. If things become too big for us, he will reconsider any increase in support. Now it is time for some lunch. There is quite the celebration honoring your success set up in the main audience chamber. After that, we need to get home."

Two hours later, after much handshaking, congratulatory and inspirational speeches, and only a few quick bites between dignitaries, Uncle Jonah stood and bowed to everyone assembled. "Honored sirs and ladies, I despair at having to break up this grand occasion, but my nephew and I need to return to Earth within the hour so we must depart. Be well and serve well."

The Imperator stood and bowed in return. "Of course, Jonah. We regret your necessary departure, but we understand and wish you well on this vital mission on Earth. Be well and serve well. It was a great honor to meet you, Justin. Your father was a great friend and served us all. We are honored to meet you and assist you on the successful completion of your mission."

Justin stood and copied the actions of the others. "Thank you, Imperator. Be well and serve well." He followed his uncle out of the building and into the waiting tube transport.

"You did that very well, Justin. Your mother and father would be very proud. As am I."

Justin lowered his head and stared at his lap as the tube car accelerated. "Thank you. I guess it just hit me how real all of this is. I really am a Zarminan, and I am really part of a fight to stop an invasion of the Earth."

Jonah moved to sit next to his nephew and placed a strong arm around him. "That's a lot to place on your shoulders so quickly, I know, but you're not alone. I know Myah would protect you with her life, if required. She wasn't so certain at first, even requested a transfer. But she came to me a while back, after getting to know you, and asked me to tear up the request. She is not easily impressed, but you have made her sit up and take notice."

Justin looked up at his uncle, and blushed.

Four hours later, Justin walked through the doors to the gym, after learning Kevin and Myah were there shooting hoops. He thought about what Uncle Jonah told him about Myah and the strange feelings in his gut started up again as he watched her sinking a difficult long distance lob with ease.

He waited until Kevin was about to shoot before announcing his return. "Hello, boys. I'm baaack! So you two didn't kill each other while I was gone?"

Kevin fumbled his throw at Justin's shout. "No, but I might strangle you for making me miss the winning shot."

"Welcome back Chosen One. What did you think of you home world?" Myah dribbled the ball and tossed it to Justin. "And by the way, in case you hadn't noticed, I'm not a boy."

Justin blushed furiously and fumbled a bit trying to catch the ball. "Oh, no… I know you're not a… I mean it was a movie quote and…" He stuttered a while longer trying to extricate himself. He gave up when he saw his friends watching and laughing. "Zarmina was nice. It will take some getting used to, though." He dribbled closer, then sank a three-pointer.

Myah stopped in her tracks, glaring at Justin. "Nice? Is that all you have to say? Nice? Prepare yourself for a major beat-down mister." She snatched up the ball as it rolled near her foot and spun it on her finger, challenging him with her stare to a game of one-on-one.

Chapter Nine

The sun beat down, scorching the ground so nothing stirred, even in these early hours of the summer morning, except for Justin and his companions carving up the desert in their ATVs. Now that Justin and Kevin had some experience in their vehicles, and were handling them well, Myah decided it was time to allow them more freedom in their escapades.

"Alright, watch this one," called Kevin through his helmet communication system. He proceeded to spin his car into a half-donut, switched into reverse, and drove tail first without losing momentum.

"Easy! Here goes," replied Justin as he duplicated the maneuver. "Woohoo! Bet you can't do this one!" Justin completed a series of half-donut spins, in and out of reverse, finishing off with a full circle spin continuing forward at full speed.

Kevin followed his friend's stunt, adding an additional half spin to exit in reverse, still at full throttle. "I thought you were going to give me a challenge today. Got anything really good?"

"Don't get careless out here, guys. We don't want any stupid accidents." Myah's voice cut in over their chatter.

"Yes, mother," they replied in unison without slowing down.

Kevin waved his arm to his left, gesturing the direction he wanted to go. "Let's see what we can do over in the dry wash over to the east. Maybe get some air under these things."

"Last one there is a boring Earthling," shouted Justin as he sped into the lead.

In less than five minutes, all three reached the steep banks of the dried up river bed and, one after another, jumped into the sandy bottom sending large sprays of sand up behind them. Several gravel beds provided excellent jumping ramps and the dry desert air was filled with a mix of engines and whoops of excitement.

After a brief water and energy bar break, Kevin spotted a particularly enticing spot on the bank to attempt some big air. "Alright you aliens, try not to chicken out of this one." He hopped into his ATV and sped off. Hitting the slope of the bank at a full forty-five mph, he flew high above the ground beyond, and out of sight of the others. When he did not reappear, Myah and Justin jumped into their vehicles and raced to the edge, climbing a more sedate slope to reach the top.

"You idiot," shouted Myah. "We thought you killed yourself. Don't ever do that again."

Kevin stood up, leaning on his roll bar, laughing. "That was incredible! You've got to try it!" He returned to his seat and drove back to his friends. Jumping out, he pointed at a spot about thirty yards away from the edge where the ground was torn up by his landing. "What a rush! Go ahead, it was amazing! I bet neither of you can do better."

Without a word, Justin revved his engine and sped back down the slope.

Myah swung around to watch him leave. "Justin, I don't think this is such a good idea. You guys are still novices on these things. Kevin was lucky he didn't flip and break his neck."

"No way, Myah. I'm not letting him show me up on this one. Stand back and watch. Wax on… Wax off!" Justin gunned his engine and accelerated across the dry sandy riverbed. About thirty yards before the steep bank, Justin felt a sharp jolt and heard a loud, metallic bang. The world suddenly disjointed itself as ground and sky spun in haphazard mixes before going black.

***

A look of terror froze on Kevin and Myah's faces as they watched their friend's car tumble at high speed and crash into the steep bank below them. Leaving their cars behind, the two scrambled down the crumbling slope. They stared in disbelief as the saw Justin hanging limp and bleeding, upside down in his broken and smoking ATV.

"You undo his restraints and I'll pull him free," ordered Myah. "We need to get him out of there before it catches fire."

Kevin ran to the other side and squeezed down between the wall of gravel and twisted metal wreckage. Leaning in, he pulled at the release catch and caught Justin as he fell loose, passing him to Myah.

Myah grabbed Justin under his arms and used her legs to drag him out of the vehicle. When safely away, she began a quick assessment of his injuries. "He's still breathing, but unconscious. Looks like his left leg, and both arms are broken. We need to put a bandage on those bleeders." She pointed to several spreading red areas seeping through Justin's shirt and pants. She turned to Kevin as he scrambled to her side. "Get up there and grab the first aid kit, and call for a chopper rescue crew. We need to get him to the hospital ASAP."

As the two worked furiously to bandage Justin's wounds as best they could, his breathing became irregular and his face turned ashen.

"No, no, no!" yelled Myah as she leaned over Justin, trying to think what to do. "Where are those medics?"

Kevin pressed in close and applied pressure to some of Justin's still unbandaged injuries. Without warning,

Kevin and Myah felt a surge of energy flow through them and into Justin. Their nerves tingled as the energy flowed, and Justin's breathing calmed to near normal levels. His bleeding also slowed considerably.

Kevin sat up with a jerk as the sensation ended. "What just happened?"

Myah's eyes shot wide with surprise. "You felt that? That's impossible. At least I've never heard of a non-Zarminan joining in a bonding. And certainly never anything like this. It's always a pair. A pair-bonding. It was the only way I could think of to save him. You should not have been affected."

"Earth to Myah, you're not making any sense."

"The pair bond. It's how two Zarminans commit to each other. Our soldiers are always pair-bonded to another so deaths on the battlefield are very low. If one is injured, the other can provide some of his or her life energy to provide some initial healing until more sophisticated medical help arrives. The pair bond is also how two Zarminans are joined in civil life. It provides a level of connection like no other."

"You mean like getting married?" Kevin thought for a moment when his face registered the reality of the situation. "Wait… you're not saying the, the three of us just got married, are you?"

Myah blew out an exasperated breath. "No, you idiot. Well, not exactly… maybe. I don't know. Like I said, I've never heard of anything like this. I don't know if a triad-bond is even possible. We have to report this." She joined Kevin in confusion over the situation as the sounds of a chopper closed in on them.

***

The darkness faded into a pale greyish-tan light and an incessant beeping assaulted his ears as Justin slowly dragged himself back to consciousness. His first attempt to open his eyes and see his surroundings resulted in a stabbing pain to his frontal lobe. *Well, that was brilliant. My migraines are back.* He tried to rub his eyes, but found himself unable to move either arm more than a few inches. The attempts shot waves of pain through both arms. *What the frak? What's going on with me? Where am I?* He let out a groan, and that too was painful, as if the desert sands now coated his throat.

"Justin, thank goodness. I'll call the doctor."

His head spun with confusion. *Doctor? What doctor? Was that Uncle Jonah?* He tried opening his eyes again, only a slit this time. The light was not so painfully bright this time, so he blinked and slowly brought everything into focus. The first thing he noticed was the white tiles on the ceiling. Then he realized he was surrounded by a sort of cage with cables crisscrossing through a series of pulleys mounted on the framework, eventually leading to both his arms and his right leg. The cables elevated his arms and leg, all in thick casts, above the sheets of a hospital bed. *Holy crap on a cracker… What did I do now?*

"It's alive! It's alive! How you doing there, Dr. Frankenstein?" Kevin's voice came from somewhere behind him.

Justin started to chuckle, but the pain proved too much. He winced and groaned out the expected response. "That's Frahnkesteen. Hi, Kevin."

Kevin stepped into his field of view. "That's Eyegore." He was about to say more when the door opened again.

"Hey kiddo, glad to see you're awake. You had us all worried." Uncle Jonah strode back into the room, followed by two doctors and a bevy of nurses, all intent on probing every inch of him.

"Uncle Jonah, what happened? Where am I? No, wait, I know I'm in a hospital, but where? I can't move anything. What happened?"

Jonah sat carefully on the edge of the bed and laid a gentle hand on Justin's uncasted leg. "Do you remember racing around the desert in your ATV with Kevin and Myah?"

Justin rolled his eyes to the ceiling trying to remember. He winced as a nurse adjusted the IV in his right hand. "Umm, yeah. We stopped for lunch, but that's the last thing I remember."

Jonah gave a heavy sigh. "Apparently, you tried to play Evil Knievel and wiped out. That was yesterday, early afternoon. We got the call you were hurt and the chopper lifted you back to the hospital here on the base. Fortunately, one of *our* best doctors was on call and reset everything without difficulty. With some help from Zarminan medicine, you should be back in full operation by next week. The doc says the bones are already starting to knit, and your internal injuries have almost healed already."

Justin blinked, trying to focus his thoughts and attention on his uncle. "Did you say next week? How is that possible?"

"Zarminan medical science is several centuries ahead of Earth's, just like our technology. Disease, genetic disorders, and aging maladies, all are things of the past with us. Unfortunately, we've been unable to adapt our medicines to Earth physiology as of yet, but our best genetic specialists are working on the problem."

"You mean we might be able to make a pill people can take to never get sick? That would be so cool. No more colds or flu." Kevin ran his fingers through his hair as he considered the implications. "Could we reverse the effects of Alzheimer's for my grandfather?"

"Not yet, Kevin, but maybe soon. We are very encouraged for your generation being the first to benefit from our assistance." Jonah squeezed Kevin's shoulder in sympathy. "How would you like to live twice as long as the average person on Earth today?"

Kevin shot a startled glance up at Jonah. "What, you mean like we could live for a couple of hundred years?"

"At least, if our projections are true. Without disease, we Zarminans live far longer than you here on earth. I myself am one-hundred seventy-five years old, according to your calendar."

"Holy crap on a cracker," muttered Kevin under his breath.

Returning his attention to Justin, Jonah patted him on his uninjured shoulder and stood to leave. "Hang in there, kiddo. You should be out of here tomorrow or the day after. I have some work to do, but I'll be back later to check in on you." As the door behind him closed, he heard Justin and Kevin discussing the exciting possibilities of living for centuries.

Back in his office, Jonah hit the com button to call his aide. "Is the report on the ATV accident ready yet?"

The small box crackled in response. "Yes, sir. It just arrived. It's just like we suspected. I'll bring it in now."

Two minutes later a knock sounded on Jonah's door and it opened, ushering in a tall, immaculately dressed Marine lieutenant carrying a small flash drive. Jonah held out his hand and accepted the drive. "Sit down, Lieutenant. I want to discuss options with you as soon as I look this over."

Jonah plugged the device into his computer and typed a few commands to open the secure file. Instantly, text and photographic images filled his screen detailing the cause of his nephew's accident. Scrolling through the text, Jonah flipped back and forth to the corresponding images until he reached the end of the document.

"You're right, Lieutenant. Just as we thought, this was no accident. Someone deliberately damaged the axle so it would fail during high stress maneuvers. Exactly the sort of tricks those kids were doing out there. Have we found who was responsible yet?"

"Not yet, sir," replied the straight-backed Marine. "But it's only a matter of time before the forensics team gathers the evidence."

"Keep an eye on this one, Lieutenant. If we have a saboteur on the base, we need to find him fast. And my nephew was nearly killed. Is this somehow directed at him, or possibly our mission here? We need to know what's going on."

"Yes, sir. I'll make sure this one is top priority." The soldier rose, saluted, spun on his heels, and strode out of the room.

***

Lying prone on top of a sage-covered dune, Edward Davidson peered through binoculars at the trio of kids racing around the desert on their ATVs. As one of the base mechanics, Davidson had been the one who checked out the vehicles to the kids and filed the report on where they were headed. He spoke into the cell phone at his side, set to the speaker phone feature so he could talk and observe simultaneously.

"Damn reckless kids. Probably kill themselves out there like that. Maybe I need to call them back in." His deep, gravelly voice rumbled into the phone.

"Negative, Davidson. Continue as planned."

"You sure about that? Dead kids don't talk much. Maybe we should... Oh shit!"

Davidson watched as the new kid attempted a dangerous stunt, causing a catastrophic failure of the axle. What had been intended to be a mildly jolting accident during a typical afternoon excursion into the desert became a disaster.

"Davidson, report! What the hell is going on?" The voice shouted over the speakerphone.

"No time. I need to get back to my post. Abort. Repeat, abort. I think we just killed him." Davidson turned off his phone, crawled back down the slope and ran to his jeep. His huge bulk shook the entire vehicle as he jumped in. Slamming the door shut, he gunned the engine and took a trail back to the motor pool at high speed.

As he pulled the jeep into the designated space, he saw the frantic activity taking place. As one of his fellow mechanics ran up to him. "Man, did you get back from lunch just in time. There's been an accident and the chief has been yelling for you. Better get over there on the double." He waved toward the main hangar where the chief's office was located and headed off at a run.

"There you are," growled the chief as Davidson hurried into the hangar. "My office, now!"

Davidson followed the chief mechanic into his office and shut the door behind him. Standing loosely at attention, his broad shoulders completely blocking the closed door behind him, he waited for the chief to compose himself.

"I've been a jarhead longer than you've been alive, son, and this is one of the biggest cluster fu ... oh hell, no time for that now. You checked out those vehicles to the kids this morning, right?"

"Yes, sir."

"I shouldn't have to ask this of my best mechanic, but the book requires me to ask if you followed the safety checklist before giving them the keys."

Davidson hesitated briefly, squeezing his massive fists tighter to control his reactions. Every muscle in his body tensed, but he respected the chief and measured his response. "Yes, sir. Everything checked out fine. May I ask why, sir?"

The chief leaned forward in his chair, arms folded on his desk as he glared. "We don't know what happened, yet. Some sort of accident, nearly killed one of those kids. The Colonel's nephew, for cryin' out loud. They're bringing in the ATV's now and I want you on it as soon as they arrive."

Davidson began to sweat. "Nearly killed, sir. He okay?" His rumbling voice held a bit of a deep trembling in it.

"They say he'll live, but it's a damn miracle from what I hear."

"How long before the vehicles get here, sir?" Davidson gave an internal sigh of relief that he was not a murderer after all. He would have had no choice but to turn himself in if that was the case. Even now, he struggled with the thought of causing such an accident. He only wanted to strand the kids, not hurt them, even if they were one of the damn aliens.

"About an hour," replied the chief. "They want to make sure to document the site thoroughly and do a double sweep for any debris they might have missed. You have some time, son." He noticed the sand and scuffs on Davidson's uniform. "Go get yourself cleaned up and get something to drink. Once they get back, it may be a while before you get another break."

Davidson looked down at his shoes for a moment, then stood straight, all six foot-five inches of him, and looked at the chief directly. "Thank you, sir."

The chief watched Davidson for a moment before relaxing. "I know this post has been tough on you, son, and I know you have some pretty damn peculiar ideas about some of the civilians here on the base, but that never bothered me. You are one hell of a mechanic. Maybe the best I've ever seen." He hesitated a second or two before continuing. "Let me give you a bit of advice. I'm due to be retired out of the service in a few months. I won't be here to smooth things over for you after that. Your enlistment is about over, so you might want to think about not reenlisting and look for something in the civilian world. I can write you a hell of a resume. The next guy in this chair might not be as forgiving as me with some of your ideas about how things ought to be."

Davidson's eyes lost their focus for a minute as he considered the chief's advice. "Thank you, sir. I'll do my best."

"Go on, get out of here. And make sure you give that ATV a complete run down."

"Yes, sir." Davidson left the hangar, drove his jeep to his barracks, and went inside. He needed to pack enough supplies to last him at least a week on the road. He was done with the military—he never really fit in anyway, Now he needed to reconnect with his friends in the Red Angus Party. They were the only ones who shared his anger at the aliens he knew were here on Earth, and at the base. They were the only ones who wanted to get rid of them as badly as he did. Throwing everything he could pack into the back of his '66 Chevy Impala, Davidson pulled the pass he hadn't used last weekend out of his wallet so it was ready to show the gate guard. He gave one glance in the rearview mirror at the motor pool, and sped off to the little used east gate.

Edward Davidson pulled his ancient Chevy into the lonely gas station along Route 66 heading west. He filled his tank and went into the store to pick up some supplies. He aimed a huge thumb toward the antique pay phone outside the store. "Phone out there work?" he asked the clerk as he paid for his purchases.

"Sometimes. Not many folks use it anymore since we got the new cellphone tower down the road, so I'm not sure."

Davidson nodded his understanding and walked outside into the oppressive desert heat. He tossed the bag onto the front seat and strode to the old payphone. Picking up the receiver, he smiled as he heard the distinctive dial tone. He plunked a couple of quarters into the coin slot and dialed the number he had memorized. After a couple of rings, a voice answered on the other end.

"Yeah?"

"Davidson. Zach there?"

"Yeah, just a sec."

Davidson tried to shift his huge bulk to fit more comfortably inside the glass booth, without much luck, as he waited. A rustling on the line alerted him to Zach's arrival.

"Davidson, is that you?"

"Yeah."

"Good. We'll meet up in a few hours. You sure the kid survived the accident? Would have served him right."

Davidson only grunted in response.

"I filled in the boss. He was pissed, but he says the clients have given us a new mission. Only a few more details to work out, but yeah, we're ready. Meet us at the safe house."

"Two, maybe three days. Need to be sure no one is following me."

Davidson hung up the phone, spat into the dusty ground, and returned to his car. With a grinding start-up, the engine caught and roared as he gunned the gas pedal. Gravel flew as he shifted into drive and floored it, continuing west down the empty road.

Chapter Ten

Justin limped to his station in the tech surveillance room three floors beneath Groom Lake. He winced as he lowered himself gingerly into the swivel chair and set his cane hanging on a hook next to his small desk.

"Don't be such a baby. What are you complaining about? It was only a flesh wound. The treatments are working and you should be fully healed in another day or two," Myah called out to him without looking up from her monitor.

Justin turned on his computer and turned to face her, grunting with the sudden movement. "It still hurts, for cryin' out loud. Give me a break, I should have died in that wreck. And did you just quote *The Holy Grail*?"

"The holy what? Maybe, how would I even know that? Oh crap, the bond, it's working already." Myah let her shoulders slump ever so slightly, took a deep breath, and swiveled in her chair to face Justin. "I know. It scares me to think just how close it was. We need you, Justin. You can't be so careless again. Besides, without you around, I'd only have Kevin to hang out with. I'd never forgive you for doing that to me." She winked and returned to her work.

Justin sat watching her for a moment. "So you do care about me, at least a little. And what's the bond?"

She rolled her eyes and shook her head as she continued to read the reports on her screen. "Something for another time, just not now."

He smiled and turned back to his own computer as it came to life. "Yep, you like me."

An hour later, Justin stopped the scrolling symbols on his monitor and re-read several lines. "Hey, Myah, look at this. I think I found something."

"What is it?" Myah leaned over his shoulder, one hand on the back of his chair, careful not to put any pressure on his aching body. One lock of long blond hair fell down and brushed against Justin's ear, sending a shiver up his spine and bringing a flush to his cheeks. "You know all this looks like random garbage to the rest of us. Translation please."

"Oh, right. Sorry, I keep forgetting." He pointed to a line of symbols. "This looks like a typical order for supplies, at least at the start, but look at the amounts."

Myah flicked his ear in frustration. "Translation?"

"Oh yeah, here, let me type it out for you." His fingers flew over the keyboard as he converted the symbols into English.

New order: PO# 60793346
39 reams computer paper, 650 book stickers, 65 rolls of book tape, 44 bags of mixed rubber bands
Returns for distribution or removal from database:
104 defective paint sets, 80 unused pencil sets, 94 unusable glue sticks, 39 spine-damaged used books

Myah examined the information but shook her head. "I'm not seeing anything significant, just a weird supply order."

Justin frowned, but then a smile grew on his face. "Fair enough, but look at what happens when I print it out in the same format and layout as the original message. It was the way it presented itself on my screen that helped me see what it was." He pressed a few more keys and then hit Enter. His monitor flashed and a new display filled the screen.

39 reams computer paper
650 book stickers
65 rolls of book tape
44 bags of mixed rubber bands
-104 paint sets (damaged returned)
80 unused pencil sets
94 unusable glue sticks
39 spine-damaged used books

Myah studied the information a minute longer before scowling again and scratching at her neck. "I'm still not seeing anything. What are you getting at?"

"When I was a Boy Scout, the last badge I earned was Orienteering. We had to do a lot of work with compasses and map reading. I think these are longitude and latitude coordinates. The first set of numbers could be the latitude if we add a decimal after the first number like this, and the second numbers, longitude, has three digits before the decimal so..." He hit Enter again and a new set of numbers appeared. 39.6506544 and -104.809439.

Myah stood up, her eyes widened is realization. "So where is this location, if it is indeed a set of coordinates?"

"Let's look it up. But I think I already know." Justin copied the values and called up a mapping program. He pasted in the coordinates and watched as the map zoomed in to the specified location. "Holy crap on a cracker! I think we just found their base. It all makes sense!"

Myah grabbed the phone on her desk and hit the first speed dial number. "Jonah, you need to get down her right away. Justin may have found their base." She listened, nodding quickly. "Yes, sir." She hung up the phone and tuned off the monitor on Justin's computer.

"Wait... Ouch! What did you do that for?" Justin jerked back, called out in reaction to the pain he self-inflicted again by turning too quickly, and stared up at the girl in shock.

"Don't worry, I didn't lose anything. I just turned off the screen so nobody can see what you found. Jonah ordered us to keep it secret until he gets here. He's on his way now."

Five minutes later, Jonah's booming voice reverberated across the room. "Attention, everyone. I am enacting a Code Gamma C5 shut down of this area, effective immediately. Save your work, shut everything down, and clear the room. You have one minute."

A flurry of clicks filled the air and dozens of monitors went dark in quick succession. Lines of men and women stood, gathered their personal belongings, and silently headed toward the exits at either end of the room.

Myah grabbed Justin's wrist as he started to reach for the keyboard. "He doesn't mean us, genius."

Justin flushed as he pulled his hand back. "Oh yeah, right. My teachers all use that voice when they are super serious. Guess I've been conditioned." He sat back carefully, giving a sheepish smile in the process.

Stone-faced Air Force guards, complete with side arms unclipped on their belts, positioned themselves outside the doors as the last person filed out of the chamber. Only the sounds of a flickering fluorescent light, and Uncle Jonah's rapid footsteps echoed in the eerie silence.

"What have you got?" Jonah's voice brooked no nonsense as he approached the pair of teens.

Myah stood at attention, brushing a vagrant strand of hair from her face. "We think Justin has finally located the Skutaran base, sir."

Jonah's attention focused on his nephew with an intensity Justin had never witnessed before.

"I, umm, well, there was this message and I, umm…"

Jonah softened his stance and placed a gentle hand on Justin's shoulder. "It's okay, Justin. No need to be scared. Tell me what you found."

Justin let out a calming breath and pushed the button to turn his monitor on. "I was reading what looked like a standard supply order form, when I noticed something weird about the numbers. The way they were laid out struck me as familiar somehow. When I stopped the feed to look more closely at them, the format clicked in my mind and it all made sense. Look here." Justin pointed first to the translated columns of the form. "It hit me that they look like map coordinates, so I wrote them out as latitude and longitude values like this." He showed Jonah the rearranged values. "Then Myah and I plugged them into a map and this is what showed up." He punched another button on his keyboard and displayed the map. A purple circle appeared at the given coordinates.

Jonah stared at the map for a few seconds before his eyes lit up in recognition. "But this is…"

"Yeah, this is the library near home where I went to see if someone there could help me with the symbols on the silver box you gave me for my birthday."

"And then we got chased by that bogus police officer a couple of days later. It all ties together. Well done, you two." Jonah stood up and beamed at the youngsters. "I thought this might be where they were after your incident there, so I've had them under loose surveillance ever since with no definite results. This, however, is fairly condemning evidence. I'm going to order more invasive reconnaissance of the library at once. Let's see if we can catch them in the act."

"I'm sorry, Uncle Jonah. I never meant to put you and Kevin is danger. We could have been killed that day because of my stupidity."

Jonah pulled over the chair from Myah's desk and sat, wheeling himself in close to Justin. "You have nothing to apologize for, Justin. I should have warned you against revealing those symbols to anyone else. You had no idea about any of this. It wasn't your fault."

"He's right, you know," chimed in Myah. "You still thought you were a normal, if odd, Earther teenager at the time. And nobody got hurt. You can't change what happened, so let it go and let's get down to business and do something to end the invasion of these evil librarians."

"And let's not forget whoever tried to eliminate you by arranging that ATV to self-destruct. That was not a Skutaran. He may have been one of their brainwashed operatives, but I'm not convinced of that, since the Skutarans do not know we are operating from here. At least we are fairly certain they don't know. I believe we have another player in the game. One not related to the invasion at all."

Justin slumped back in his chair again, rubbing his eyes with one hand. "Great! Now I'm not only the target of an alien invasion force, but also some lunatic who just hates my guts for some mysterious, unknown reason. What ever happened to good old-fashioned teenage problems?"

"Well, if it helps," said Myah with a grin, "your voice does crack from time to time and you do have a pimple just left of your nose."

Jonah laughed as he stood up. "And that's my signal to get back to the paperwork on my desk and organize a new front of action. Keep up the good work, you two. By the way, Justin, it's time I told you how to open that box and showed you how to use what's inside. Bring it to my office in the morning."

Justin looked down toward the floor and ran one hand through his hair. "Umm, about the box…"

Jonah's face reddened and his voice grew angry. "What about the box?"

"Well, the thing is… we sort of left it at Kevin's house."

"What? I told you to keep it safe! I told you it was important! How could you leave it behind?"

Justin's lips trembled as he gripped his hands tighter. "I'm sorry, Uncle Jonah... really. We didn't mean to leave it behind. We were studying it at Kevin's house the night before we went for pie. I was going to pick it up when we dropped Kevin off, but then, well... you know. In all the excitement I sort of forgot about the box until a few days after we got here. I've been trying to figure out a way to tell you ever since, but..."

Jonah sighed heavily, rubbed his face with both hands, and leaned back in his chair. "Okay, I'm sorry to have gotten angry, Justin. It's not your fault. We'll just have to go back and get it. The item inside is critical to the next level of your training. It too belonged to your father, and he used it to help him with decoding the signals. We need to see what you can do with it."

***

Keldon Ankara walked in the park near his library/base of operations. The sky was a brilliant blue with a bright summer sun warming the late morning air. Birds sang in the newly leafed-out trees and children laughed as they explored the playground equipment nearby. He scowled, hating all of it. *What a miserable planet. If it wasn't for the shortsighted fools back home I could have handed them the galaxy by now. But they will pay the price for scorning me. They will see their folly when I lead millions of implanted engrams into their midst and throw them all in the chair for digitizing. Then nobody will stand in my way, especially that simpering witless Marcus Dakar. How I ever saddled myself with such a worthless imbecile is beyond me. Even this infernal atmosphere with its foul-smelling flower scents is better than another minute spent listening to his whining reports.*

Keldon recalled their earlier meeting with extreme distaste.

"We have some indications the Zarminans may have discovered this base, Lord Ankara. One of our observation posts thinks he picked up a scanning signal last night."

"Has it been confirmed?"

"No, my lord. The signal was so fleeting it was not even recorded."

"Then it is nothing more than some fool operative trying to impress you. Our systems have full shielding and cannot be penetrated by those pitiful Zarminans. Why do you waste my time when your real purpose here still goes unfulfilled? Have you and your techs finished the final codes for implanting the engrams yet?"

"Not yet, my lord. There are very intricate and delicate sequences still to be worked out, but we will have them solved in time."

Keldon leaned forward with a deadly gaze. "See that you do not fail, Marcus. Our operatives in the fleet are nearly ready to begin their coup. After all these years of carefully maneuvering our compatriots into position, we will soon have enough ships to begin transporting our revived engrams back to Skutara to start the revolution. Do not bother me with these flights of fancy from minorlings."

Marcus snapped to attention and saluted with fist to his temple. Turning with a snap, he exited his superior's office. Keldon shoved a pile of report discs to the floor and stormed out to stem his anger before he found an excuse to execute the incompetent fool.

***

Edward Davidson rose from the thin mattress of his cot, squinting into the slit of morning sun, the fourth sunrise in this miserable trailer, peeking through an open slit in the striped curtain. Groaning, he stretched his back and arms trying to loosen them after a restless night on a hopelessly inadequate bunk. His feet, and most of his heavily muscled calves, hung beyond the bottom of the cot. Stumbling his way to the bathroom, he pulled on a dirty t-shirt and pulled the chain to turn on the suddenly blinding bare bulb hanging from the ceiling. Scratching at his three-day-old beard, he finished emptying his bladder and returned to his bed, sat down and pulled on the same pants he had worn since arriving at the Red Angus safe house. He smelled the socks and reluctantly yanked them over his size fourteen, dirt-encrusted feet before sliding them into his military boots. Regaining his feet, Davidson shuffled into the tiny kitchenette where he flipped on the fluorescent overhead light and grabbed a box of stale Cheerios and the last semi-clean bowl from a shelf. Opening the fridge, he found a half-used bottle of milk, smelled it, and decided it wasn't quite rancid yet. Plopping down into the 1950's style dining set, he proceeded to eat breakfast, dribbling milk down his chin in the process. He glanced around the room at the newspaper clippings tacked to the walls. "UFO Sighting over Phoenix," "Mysterious Lights In Sky Over Las Vegas." Dozens of reports of supposed alien encounters were each connected to a large map with a string leading to each location. Above the map hung a framed, faded portrait of a heavily mustached man, William "Red" Angus. He was an Old West lawman in Wyoming from 1888-1893. As with many lawmen of that time, Red once had his picture displayed on wanted posters across the territory. He was elected as sheriff because he understood the outlaws and was handy with a gun. During his reign as sheriff, he sided with the vanishing breed of cattle barons against the rise of farmers and settlers arriving with the railroads. He lost his post when he led a raid against a group of small ranch owners, in support of the large barons. It was this brand of law, support for those who ran the industries and against the ungrateful masses who benefited from the jobs and growth provided by these leaders, that inspired those who belonged to Red Angus. They found their niche in the world raising the cry against invaders from beyond the earth. Nobody else seemed to recognize the threat these invaders created. It was up to them to keep the country, and the Earth safe.

When finished, he dumped the dirty dishes into the already filled sink, deciding again to tackle that job later. Making his way to the dark living room, he sank into the torn Lazy Boy recliner and used the remote to turn on the TV. Just as he started to doze off in front of some bunch of screaming women intent on proving some poor schmuck was the father of their baby, the door burst open, flooding the room with painful light.

"Wake up, Davidson. Time to… Shit! What is that smell? How can you stand it in here? Open a window and take a shower, dude. It's rank in here."

"What the… oh, it's you, Zach. You're late."

Zach went around the motorhome opening up the few windows and opening the curtains. "I had to be careful, man. Had to be sure nobody was tailing me. Who knows what evidence they found? You're the prime suspect now, and they might have found something that connects us. The boss warned me to take extra precautions."

Davidson jerked upright in his chair. "How is the kid? "

"Relax, our friend's still on the base reported back that not only is he not dead, but he's up and around like nothing happened. Not even a scratch. And now all sorts of shit has broken loose back there." Zach grabbed a Coke from the fridge and slammed half of it down in one shot.

Davidson sat impassively, watching his partner.

"They know it was you, or at least they sent out a massive manhunt for you. Military police, FBI, federal marshals, no stone unturned. I had to make sure they hadn't pegged me as well. They already identified a couple of our group on the base. Not everyone, but most."

Davidson scratched at his side. "Still safe here? What about Mexico?"

"No worries, man. There's no place you can go any safer than this. And they'll catch you for sure if you try to cross the border. Best to stay here for now. The boss will protect us. Besides, there's something else going on. Something big. Our sources say it looks like they're gearing up for a major offensive."

Davidson looked up with interest. If the aliens were up to something, he wanted to be in on helping to stop them. "What offensive?"

"I have no idea. Our friends aren't in a position to know any details, but they have orders to prepare all sorts of equipment for what looks to be a major surveillance detail, possibly more."

"Those effing aliens preparing to attack us?"

"I don't think so, not yet anyway. This could be something else. I think they might be trying to gather intelligence on some government officials. The operation appears to be someplace around Denver. There's a big federal center around there someplace, and don't forget DIA. We know about their facility underground there. We'll keep an eye on them for sure."

Davidson's voice rumbled like a tank. "We need to do something."

"Right now, I'm going in to town to pick up some food for you, and report in with the boss. While I'm gone, get this place cleaned up, and take a shower. My grandmother would kill us if she ever saw her home like this."

"She's in a nursing home, man."

"I know, you idiot. She's still my grandma. Have a little respect." Zach let the screen door slam as he left.

Davidson stared mutely at the mess, picked up a pile of old newspapers from the floor and headed into the kitchenette.

***

Phillip Bork switched off his phone and returned it to the drawer in his desk, then locked the drawer. This was the phone kept for secret communications with members of Red Angus, as well as his powerful investors. Highly encrypted and untraceable, not even his personal secretary knew of its existence. He went to pour himself a drink and looked out the window of his home high in the Rockies about twenty miles outside Vail, Colorado. The view on this spring morning was spectacular. Recent spring snows covered the mountains, but today, the sky was blue with a forecast high in the sixties. His investments during the last recession paid off handsomely now, and, while he had always enjoyed the privileges of wealth, he now luxuriated in the lifestyle of the top 0.5% of the wealthiest men in the world. This home, really a cabin compared to most of his properties around the world, was his favorite. All due to the insights and resources provided by his investment partner, known to him only as Mr. Ankara.

A voice from behind him startled Phillip out of his reflections.

"Good afternoon, Mr. Bork. I have some papers from Mr. Ankara requiring your signature." The large man, dressed in an expensive Armani suit, gave an imitation of a smile as he approached.

Spilling half of his gin and tonic as he spun around, Bork grabbed the silk handkerchief out of his pocket to wipe up the mess on his sleeve and scowled at the intruder. "How did you get in here? Where is my security?"

The man showed no interest in what Phillip said, set his briefcase on the desk, pulled out a tablet, and called up a set of documents. He handed the tablet to Phillip.

"I said, how did you get in here? Who are you? I warn you…"

"No need for threats, Mr. Bork. As I said, I represent Mr. Ankara. Please provide your signature on page twelve."

Bork started to read the file, eyes widening in horror before reaching the third page. "This will turn my entire business over to Ankara! Who does he think he is? Tell him I want to have a word with him about this farce." He tossed the tablet onto the desk, turning his back to the messenger.

"Mr. Ankara is not available at the moment, sir. But he left explicit instructions regarding how to proceed if you refused to cooperate." He pulled out an odd-looking weapon and pointed it at Phillip. "Your signature, please."

"I won't be intimidated like this! You can go tell…"

A red beam split the air and the large window shattered, spraying glass into the room. "Let's not be difficult, Mr. Bork. My superior has left you with a sizeable portion of your estate, more than enough to live the rest of your days in comfort. Your signature now, sir. Please." He aimed the pistol at Phillip's chest.

Shaking violently, Bork collapsed into his chair and fumbled a barely recognizable signature on the tablet.

"Thank you, sir. That concludes our business." A second beam of red energy burned a hole in Phillip Bork's chest. He fell to the floor, unbelieving eyes staring at the ceiling.

Pulling a phone out of his coat pocket, the messenger pressed the contact listed as Keldon Ankara. "Mission completed, sir. We have the signature and Mr. Bork has been retired."

He listened as a voice on the other end responded. "Yes, sir, I have enough recording of his voice for our system to replicate reliably."

Keldon Ankara interrupted with another set of instructions. "Yes, sir. His conspiracy friends never saw him in person, so we can simulate his voice when dealing with them. I will send you a copy of the transfer papers, and a second copy to the lawyers. We can take care of all future inquiries by phone, video, or text once we have his profile in our system." A quick nod at Ankara's reply, and the man returned the phone to his pocket. Exiting the room, he left instructions for the other Skutaran soldiers to clean up the bodies and dispose of them properly, saving Bork's in storage for later. He straightened his tie and headed back to his car.

Chapter Eleven

"We have the woman, Lord Keldon. She will be at the communication center within the hour."

Keldon Ankara stood in the doorway of his private elevator, a look of disgust on his face after removing himself from the library's weekly computer training workshop for seniors. "What are you talking about, Marcus? What woman?" He stepped past his subordinate into the underground passageway leading to his quarters.

"The Madrid woman, the mother of that boy who possessed the Zarminan silver puzzle box a few weeks back. We discovered his identity through our library card records, of all things. His mother is also in the system. She showed up on one of the security cameras we tapped into in a location south of here, called Colorado Springs."

Keldon stopped in his tracks and swung to face his underling. "And the boy? Did you get the boy as well?"

Marcus stiffened under the intensity of his commander's glare. "No, sir, the boy was not with her and has not appeared on any of the security camera footage. She is sure to know his whereabouts, so we will have him soon. And sir, she appears to be a Zarminan."

"What? A Zarminan? Are you absolutely certain?" Keldon stood nose to nose with Marcus, one hand grasping his throat, ready to squeeze if the answer displeased him.

"Yes sir, without a doubt. DNA analysis, taken to identify her as our subject, confirms her Zarminan origin. We should have an identity match by the time she is delivered."

Keldon stepped back, hands clasped behind his back as he stormed off toward his office. "Make sure she is restrained and heavily guarded once she arrives. I will handle this interrogation personally. Make sure nothing happens to her before I arrive, Marcus. I will hold you personally responsible if she is damaged." He slammed his door before hearing Marcus's response and paced his office at a frantic rate.

How is this possible? Could the Zarminans have traced us here? — No that would be inconceivable. Our security encryption protocols are perfect. Absolutely impenetrable. He stopped pacing in mid-stride and closed his eyes as if trying to recall a long-lost memory. *What was that memo from the emperor's council several years back? Something about a Zarminan spy suspected of penetrating our encryptions? Yes, I recall now, the spy was captured, but so severely injured in the battle he died before we could interrogate him. No threats to our systems since, though. Reports concluded he was unable to pass along what, if anything, he learned since no further breeches occurred. Yet, here is another Zarminan so close to our base of operations. It cannot be a coincidence. I need to drag the truth out of her. At least her presence explains how the boy came into possession of the puzzle box. Perhaps she is simply a refugee here and assumed guardianship of him as part of her cover to blend in.*

Two hours later, Keldon Ankara, supreme overlord of the Earth invasion forces, unlocked the door to a tax preparation storefront, currently unused since tax season was over. He turned on the lights and signaled for his driver to stand guard inside the front lobby. He passed two cubicles and entered the passcode to unlock the door which looked to be nothing more than a storeroom entry.

The room inside was much more. The Skutaran secondary communications center was heavily soundproofed and secured against electronic surveillance. Manned by three Skutaran technicians seated at terminals listening intently to their ear implants, they collected messages from bases across the planet, prioritized them, and relayed them on to the main base below the library, thus providing an extra layer of security to keep their operation secret. Beyond the next door guarded by two military officers, Keldon found a solitary woman sitting on the edge of a folding cot. A chain secured her ankle to a bolt in the wall, her hands cuffed to a heavy leather belt around her waist. Her light brown hair was disheveled, hanging down across one eye and a large bruise appeared on her left arm. She wore a green sweater and faded jeans, but was bare-footed. Keldon took a data pod from one of the guards and leaned in to ask him a question. "My orders were explicit. She was not to be harmed. Why is she injured?" He pointed toward her bruised arm.

The guard cleared his throat and responded in a low voice. "She tried to run when we approached her so we fired our stunners. She hit her arm against a car in the parking lot as she fell. The damage is only superficial and was unavoidable if we were to remain inconspicuous."

Keldon stepped into the room without further comment and shut the door behind him. He swiped through the information in the data pod, casually glancing at the woman from time to time. She remained unresponsive, as if not even aware of his entry. Keldon tapped the screen and the pod went dark. He placed it in a pocket in his vest, re-buttoned his suit coat, and tugged on the sleeves. "So, Mrs. Madrid, my name is Keldon Ankara. What brings a Zarminan to this wasteland of a planet?"

A few moments passed in silence between them before Emily raised her face to look her captor in the eyes. "I might ask the same of you, Skutaran. This is not your world. You have no business here. If you value your life, and the lives of your companions, you should release me and flee this world while you still can."

Keldon laughed and pulled up the lone chair to sit in. "I don't think you are in any position to threaten me, woman, but you can save yourself by delivering the boy to us. We have certain questions for him as well. Perhaps you are both merely innocents caught up in circumstances beyond your reckoning. If so, we will release you both without harm. So tell me, where is the boy?" He leaned back in the chair, crossing his legs and folding his arms across his chest.

Emily smiled at him. "What boy? I was out shopping and your thugs grabbed me off the street. I don't know anyone named Zarmilla, or whatever you called her. You've got the wrong person."

Keldon nodded and stood up, returning the chair to its place against the far wall. "Good. I hoped this would be an interesting battle between us. I will enjoy killing another Zarminan. I hope that you won't die as easily as the last. Regardless, you will give me what I want." He opened the door, gave strict instructions to the guards, and left Emily alone in her prison.

On the drive back to the library, he called Marcus on his private line. "Get me all the information you can about the Zarminan spy we killed about ten years ago. I need to make certain this appearance of another Zarminan so close to our final preparations is not a threat."

"That request will take some time, sir. Data from so long ago will be archived back on Skutara and will require your official passcodes to open. Do I have your permission to utilize them?"

"Yes, Marcus. And add a rush priority notice to the request."

"Yes, sir. Right away. Will there be anything else?"

Keldon thought for a moment, glaring out the window at nothing in particular. "Yes. Cancel my afternoon appointments and have someone take over the four o'clock study session for me. I'm going to get something to eat and go back out to interrogate the prisoner. Something is wrong and I mean to find out what is going on. Relay the data request to me as soon as it arrives." He disconnected the call without waiting for a response.

***

Justin sat with Kevin and Myah at their usual table in the mess hall. They arrived early to get ahead of the lunch rush, and to get their burgers before all the sweet potato fries were gone.

"So explain to me again how Superman and Batman can actually fight each other. If Superman is so powerful, he could kill Batman without even trying, and there is nothing Batman can do to even slow him down." Myah stuffed another fry in her mouth as she tried to understand her friends' obsession with pulp fiction superheroes.

The boys looked at each other, then back at Myah, responding in unison. "Kryptonite!"

"Right, the strange green rock that can kill an otherwise invincible person. That makes perfect sense." She rolled her eyes and took another bite of her burger.

"Kevin threw his arms in the air and slammed them on the table. "Of course, it makes sense. Kryptonite is a radioactive mineral from his home planet. Since they are both from the same world, the radiation is still deadly to him."

Myah lifted a stray strand of hair out of her eyes and shook her head. "You two do realize that the universe doesn't really operate like that... right? I mean really, the odds of even a tiny particle of rock from an exploding planet, which simply doesn't happen either, reaching the same planet a lone survivor landed on, would be beyond calculation. The distances are too great. And don't even get me started on chunks of matter traveling interstellar distances in only a few decades. Even if the pieces could find Earth, they would have taken millions of years to arrive."

Kevin fell back in his chair, eyes wide and slack-jawed. "Now you're the one being ridiculous. First of all…"

"Justin, Myah, Kevin, come with me right now. No questions, just come to my office." Jonah called out in a commanding boom of a voice from the entry to the mess hall. The three gaped at each other, jumped to their feet and headed after him.

They found Jonah sitting on the edge of his desk in front of three chairs. He waved them to sit down and signaled his adjutant to close the door.

"There's been a change in plans. Get hold of yourself, Justin. There's no way to ease into this so…your mother is missing."

Justin sat with a blank expression for several seconds. He blinked, refocused his attention on his uncle and tried to respond. "What did you say? Mom is…is missing? I don't understand."

Kevin leapt to his feet. "You promised she was safe. You promised. What happened? What about my mom? Is she okay?"

Myah took Justin's hand as Jonah knelt in front of him. "I only got word a few minutes ago. The team protecting her informed us she complained about feeling trapped in the safe house for so long. They kept a close eye on her until this morning. She apparently got up early, got away without their hearing a thing. She left a note telling them she was going shopping and would be back soon. They tracked her to the mall near downtown, but when they arrived, she was nowhere in sight."

He looked up at Kevin and attempted a smile. "We checked on your mother, Kevin. She is fine. There is no reason to believe the enemy knows anything about you or her."

"This is all my fault," gasped Justin. "I never should have taken that stupid box out of the house. We both have files there at the library. They must have recognized my photo and discovered her too. How could I have been so stupid?"

"No Justin, there's no way you could have known anything. At the time, you didn't know anything about any of this, or even your true heritage. If anyone is to blame, it's me. I should have warned you about showing the symbols to anyone. But don't worry. Your mom is an old soldier. She knows how to handle herself in an emergency. If they are looking for you, they won't hurt her, and she will never expose you."

"I know, Uncle Jonah. That's what scares me. I know she would sacrifice herself to keep me safe. What if she...what if she does something to herself..."

Myah took Justin's face in her hands and turned him to face her. "Don't go there, Justin. We will find her before it comes to that. Jonah is right; she is a fighter. You need to trust in her, and us. I promise."

Jonah stood up again and sat back on his desk. "We are doing everything we can to find her, Justin, but we need your help."

Justin looked up at Jonah through eyes brimming with tears he fought to hold back. "Me? What can I do?"

"You can look for any messages they transmit with any information relating to her and where they might be holding her. They'll need to check back with their records on Skutara just in case there's any information they can use on her. Look for those signals. They will lead us to her."

"Why not bust down the library doors and blast them all? We know that's where their headquarters is located." Kevin faced Jonah, his jaw set in anger.

"What if they're holding her someplace else? The library can't be their only base. We don't know everything we need to mount an operation yet. We still have time, but we do need to find her soon." He turned his gaze back to

Justin. "Can you hold it together long enough to help us find where they have her?"

Justin looked first at Myah, who squeezed his hands harder, and then at Kevin, who nodded his agreement. He took a deep, calming breath and shook himself. "What exactly am I looking for?"

Chapter Twelve

"I don't like this. You could get yourself killed." Justin tried once again to talk his friend out of risking his life in a plan to rescue his mother. He wished he could be there with Kevin and his uncle, but Jonah had forbidden Justin to leave the base. The success of the entire mission depended on him and his ability to decipher the Skutaran communications. All he could do now was stay in touch by highly secured video calls. "The Zarminans have others who can do this."

"Not on your life. It's my turn to contribute something to this war." Kevin sat watching out the car's window toward the series of storefronts they had identified as the source of the Skutaran signals, and potential hiding place for Justin's mother.

Two days earlier, Justin discovered a series of transmissions discussing a prisoner the Skutarans considered a spy. Specialists at the secret Air Force base in Nevada traced the signals to the location sitting across the street from them now. Efforts continued to trace the transmissions to those who were receiving them, but this proved to be much more complicated.

Jonah turned to his left and rested his arm on the back of the passenger seat he occupied. "Justin is right, Kevin. We have others who can do this. You don't have to risk yourself."

Kevin let out an exasperated groan. "We've been through this already. I know what the guy looks like, and most of the other librarians. If any of them show up, we have confirmation of their base of operation at the library. Nobody else knows what they look like. And they most likely will not know me. I'm not the one on their radar like all you aliens. No offense. And who here will look most inconspicuous hanging out in front of a 7-11 drinking a Big Gulp and reading graphic novels?"

Jonah nodded, his face stern. "Alright, but we will be right here. If you see anything, or if anything seems amiss, give the signal and get out of there. No heroics. Understand?"

Kevin smiled and saluted. "Yes, sir!" He jumped out of the car and strolled to the 7-11 two doors down from the apparently vacant tax preparation office.

"I have a bad feeling about this." Justin sulked as he slouched in the sofa in his uncle's office watching the drama unfold hundreds of miles away. Myah left her chair and sat next to Justin, patting his arm. "He'll be fine, Justin. You've seen how well he does in training. And he's right, the rest of us aren't as familiar with the suspects, and certainly would stand out like a sore thumb trying to stake out the place."

Justin shifted his position to get more comfortable. "I still don't have to like it."

Beads of sweat dripped down Kevin's forehead as he stood up to refill his Big Gulp, grab some Ding Dongs and a roller tube steak, for the second time. Three hours in the hot sun was starting to take its toll on him. He could only read so many graphic novels and definitely could eat only so many warmed-over hot dogs. *Wish I could play Grand Theft Auto on my phone. Not a chance of even looking at another computer app until this thing is over. No way do I want my brain scrambled.*

Just as he reached the door, he heard the crunch of tires pulling into a parking space nearby. Trying not to look obvious, or suspicious, he sidestepped the door and leaned against the window, opening up his book to the last page he'd read, keeping one eye on the car. Kevin's heart jumped nearly out of his throat. The door to the tax office opened and out stepped the head of the Mission Viejo library, and his assistant librarian. The head librarian pulled a set of keys out of his pocket and locked the door behind him. The two walked over to the metallic taupe sedan and climbed inside. Before the door shut, Kevin overheard the beginnings of their conversation.

"The woman has a powerful will, but she cannot hold out for long. Tomorrow we should discover who she is, and where the boy has gone. It is almost as if..."

The closing door cut off the rest. He peered over the top of his magazine as the car pulled into traffic and sped off in the direction of the library. As soon as they were out of sight, Kevin tossed his cup into the trashcan next to him, slammed the magazine closed and ran across the street, hopping into the back seat of Jonah's rented vehicle. "That was him! He came out of the tax office and just drove off."

"Woah, calm down, Kevin. Are you sure? Absolutely certain it was the librarian?"

"No doubt about it. I'd know that grouch anywhere. He always did give me the creeps. It's him alright. Mrs. Madrid must be in there too. I heard them talking about a woman they were trying to get information from. They said she couldn't hold out much longer. We need to get in there now."

Jonah pressed a few keys on his smartphone and pulled his gun from its shoulder holster under his jacket. "You stay here, Kevin. Now it's our turn. "

"But..."

"No buts!" Jonah's voice was harsh and commanding. "You will stay in this car until I return. You did great out there, but you are not trained for this sort of situation." He softened somewhat and put on a smile. "Besides, your mother will kill me if she ever finds out what I've gotten you into so far. I'd have to leave the galaxy if she discovered I let you join us today."

Kevin crossed his arms and slumped back into the back seat, scowling.

"Don't be a jerk, Kevin." The communication monitor crackled with Myah's voice. "If you get killed I'd never hear the end of it from Justin here. He's already whiney enough today. Don't make me have to endure more."

"Hey, I'm not whining," chimed in Justin. "But I'm on their side with this one, buddy. You helped us find my mom. Let the soldiers take it from here."

Kevin put his feet on the seat back in front of him as he slumped even further. "Alright. I'll stay put. But I don't have to like it."

Jonah stepped back and grabbed the car door before closing it. "Thanks, Kevin. We won't be long."

Kevin sat up and watched as Jonah, flanked by two others, with guns drawn, but held low, crossed the street. He noticed two more individuals, one man, one woman, taking up positions on either side of the tax office entry, Jonah signaled to the man on his left to take the lead. The man jogged ahead and knelt next to the office's door, hidden from inside by the closed blinds in the windows. After a quick look inside, he waved for the others to join him. As they lined up behind him, the point man made short work of bypassing the electronic lock on the door. He looked to Jonah for confirmation to proceed and then raised a hand with five fingers extended. Folding each finger in a countdown, at zero, the five charged the door and disappeared inside the office. Kevin saw the flashes of the laser pistols used by the group, then nothing. He waited for what seemed an eternity, bouncing his leg nervously.

"That's it, I'm going in there." Kevin threw open the car door and jumped out, barely registering the shouts of his friends over the monitor.

Charging across the street, Kevin took a position next to the open doorway as he had seen the others do, and quickly leaned over to look inside, pulling back just as fast. Not really seeing anything, he took a longer look and saw the two bodies of the Skutaran guards lying on the floor in the back of the office next to another open door. Stepping slowly across the threshold, Kevin looked around for something he could use as a weapon and grabbed the empty glass coffee carafe from the unplugged coffee maker on top of a file cabinet. He advanced toward the back door, carafe held high. At the door, he glanced at the two bodies and saw they had large burn holes in their chest and were not breathing. Satisfied that these two at least were not a threat, he stepped beyond the doorway. Boxes were piled up along both walls of a short hallway, ending at a stairway leading to lower levels. Kevin swallowed hard and tried to see down the staircase, but only heard muffled voices. Heading down the staircase, Kevin tried to be as quiet as he could manage, but the fourth step creaked so loudly, it brought two of the Zarminan soldiers running, pistols up. They lowered their guns as soon as they recognized Kevin, who continued down to the basement with hands raised.

"We have a visitor," one of the men told Jonah, signaling toward Kevin.

Kevin's heart stopped and he let out a gasp as he saw the woman strapped to a table, tubes running from her arms to plastic bottles hanging from hospital style IV stands. The woman soldier examined the bottles and turned back to the victim.

"Veritol solution, sir. Looks like they tried drugging her into talking. I'll give her a shot to counteract the effect." She pulled a vial and syringe out of her belt pouch, set them aside and started removing the needles from the woman's arms.

The victim's face was bruised, and one foot looked like it had been badly burned on the bottom. It took a moment for her identity to register.

"Mrs. Madrid!" Kevin cried as he ran toward his friend's mother.

Jonah caught Kevin in mid-step. "Careful, Kevin. Let the medic do her job. She's okay, just drugged. We need to make sure she's stable before we take her out of here."

"What happened to her? What did they do?" Tears welled up in Kevin's eyes.

Jonah took Kevin's shoulders and faced him. "Emily is a soldier, Kevin. She is well trained and was prepared to face this sort of thing. The medic will fix her up. Remember how quickly Justin recovered? He was much worse than this, so there's no need to worry. She'll be fine before you know it."

From the table, a groan escaped from Emily's chest. "Well, shit, this didn't turn out like I planned." She tried to laugh, but it turned into a violent cough. She grabbed her ribs in pain. "Aargh. That hurts." She turned her head and saw Kevin. A scowl darkened her face. "Jonah, are you out of your mind? What is Kevin doing here?" Then her eyes shot wide open. "If you brought Justin here, I'll skin you alive. Tell me you aren't that stupid." She coughed again, wrapping her arms around her chest and sucking in air through clenched teeth.

"Justin is safe, Emily. He's still back at our base. Kevin is the only one who could identify your captors so he had to come along. Right now, he is disobeying orders coming down here. He was ordered to stay back in the car and out of danger. We're going to escort him back there now." Jonah waved for one of the soldiers to approach and take charge of Kevin.

Emily exhaled carefully as the pain receded and held out one hand toward Kevin. "No, Jonah, it's alright. Come here, Kevin."

The teen looked up at Jonah for permission. Jonah nodded and extended a hand to let him know it was okay.

Jim Cronin • 124

Kevin approached Emily slowly, reaching out his hand toward hers. When they connected, she pulled him close.

"My brave Kevin. I'm so proud of you. Thank you. I'm so sorry you got mixed up in all of this, but it's obvious Justin chose his friend well. Thank you." A tear fell down her cheek and dropped to the table. The two held their careful embrace for a few moments before Jonah spoke up.

"Time to go, everyone. Let's go home." He pointed toward two of the soldiers. "You two take charge of cleaning up the mess upstairs. I don't want us to have to deal with any local law enforcement." He waved and led the way upstairs, followed by Kevin, and the two remaining soldiers supporting Emily Madrid between them. Back in the car, Kevin connected with Justin on the communications monitor and passed the device to Emily.

"Mom! Are you alright?" Justin's expression took on a look of grave concern as he saw the bruises on his mother's face."

"I'm fine, honey. Nothing the doctors can't remedy. I'll be much better by the time we arrive there."

Justin could barely contain his excitement. "You're coming here to the base? Really? That's great. I've missed you. I was so afraid something awful happened to you."

"Don't worry, sweetheart. I'm fine. We'll see you soon. And, by the way, you have one amazing friend here. I may have to steal Kevin away from his family and adopt him."

Kevin blushed and tried to slink into a corner of the back seat.

Justin smiled and nodded. "Yeah, I know, Mom. He's pretty cool."

***

Zach pressed the red disconnect button on his smartphone and gave a shout. "We found them! Get packed, Davidson, we need to get to Aurora, Colorado."

Davidson startled up from his semi-comatose state of watching Judge Judy. "Colorado? Why Colorado?"

"One of our contacts at the ARPC on Buckley Air Force Base took some photos of some suspicious activity there yesterday. Take a look." He tossed the phone to Davidson who caught it in one massive paw, then carefully tried to scroll through the images attached to the text with the smallest of his considerable fingers. He stopped at one of the photos and used his fingers to enlarge the image. "Him. A Captain at Groom Lake, but not ours. I think he's one of them."

"How about the others? Do you recognize any of them?"

Davidson flipped through the images, occasionally stopping to enlarge portions of them. "That woman looks to be in bad shape. You do that?" He gave Zach a scowl, threatening violence if he didn't like the answer.

"No, not me. No idea what happened to her. Is she one of them?"

Satisfied with Zach's response, Davidson grunted in reply. "Never seen her before, but the kid here looks familiar." He leaned in close to the image, expanding it as large as it could go. "Yeah, that's him. He's a friend of that Justin kid that survived the ATV wreck. He's got to be one of them. What are they doing in Aurora?"

"That's what we're going to find out. Get yourself cleaned up and packed. We hit the road in half an hour." Zach headed off to his room and began shoving clothes into an old backpack. Davidson stretched, yawned, and scratched his days' old beard before lifting himself up and heading off to his own room.

**

Keldon Ankara released his grip and Marcus Dakar collapsed to the ground, gasping for air. "No more of your pitiful excuses, Marcus. You have failed our rebellion for the last time." The leader of the Skutaran invasion forces stormed to the door of his office and threw it open. "Guards! Take this traitor away and keep him restrained until the next ship can infuse his brain with a new engram." Two very large guards entered the room and gathered up the former second in command, hauling him out of the ornately decorated underground office.

"You'll never get away with this, Ankara! The emperor will learn the truth of your schemes on this planet. It is your incompetence that allowed the Zarminans to locate our remote facility and for the woman to escape. My family is powerful and has the emperor's ear. You have not heard the end of this outrage. You will never overthrow the emperor." Marcus's voice faded as the guards dragged him down the passageway leading to the cells on the lowest levels of the facility.

Returning to his desk, Keldon Ankara lowered himself into the well-padded chair and popped a handful of grapes into his mouth. He picked up the single page report on the incident at the remote facility and slammed it onto his desk again. *Well, they may have recovered their operative, and discovered our operations there, but they are too late. Nothing can stop the operation now. In three weeks, we will release the codes throughout the Earth and bring these simpering fools to their knees. In three weeks, I will bring a new army with me to overthrow the blind, ignorant fools ruling our world and show them how true power is wielded in the hands of one who knows how.*

He tossed the papers into the incinerator next to his desk and punched the button on his phone connecting him to his personal secretary. "Prepare a list of the most qualified candidates to replace the traitor. Have it on my desk in the morning. And bring in the schedule for tomorrow's programs in the library."

Chapter Thirteen

A sudden buzzing noise, accompanied by a tightening on her left arm, startled Emily Madrid awake from her dreamless sleep. Squinting against the bright lights, she slowly turned her head to observe her surroundings. Banks of electronic devices next to her bed displayed rows of wavy lines and numbers. A pole suspending a bag containing a clear liquid fed the fluid into her left arm. A large vase of stargazer lilies and brightly colored daisies, her two favorite flowers, sat on a stand by one wall. She frowned at the realization that the only available light was from the glare of fluorescents in the ceiling outside her room. The curtains around her bed were pulled open so she could see what was going on. Military personnel passing back and forth let her know this was not a normal hospital.

Emily smiled as her gaze revealed Justin fast asleep on a small sofa and Jonah, lightly snoring in a chair, slightly too small for his large frame. He startled awake as the doctor, wearing his captain's uniform and carrying a clipboard with Emily's medical records opened the sliding door.

"How are you feeling today?" the doctor asked as he tucked the clipboard under his arm, squirted some disinfectant on his hands from the dispenser by the door and rubbed his hands together.

She examined her arms and saw the almost completely faded bruises. Taking mental stock of the rest of her body, she smiled with satisfaction.

"Much better, doctor. I'm guessing you have access to our Zarminan medicine since I can barely feel any effects from my captivity and interrogation… Unless I've been unconscious for several weeks."

The doctor, Captain Collins by his name tag, chuckled in reply. "No, not at all. We admitted you yesterday. We maintain a staff of your people here just in case and they treated you. I'm here to simply monitor your condition." He checked the panel of readings next to her bed and made note of the readings on his papers.

"Speaking of which… where exactly are we? And why doesn't my room have a window?"

Jonah spoke up from his chair as he stood and stretched himself to loosen stiff muscles, and signaled for the doctor to leave. "Our secondary base of operations at Denver International Airport. You were in such bad shape we couldn't risk going all the way back to Groom Lake. They have everything to care for us here, and some very skilled personnel, so we flew to Peterson and then an Air Force ambulance to the secure facility here."

"That explains the lack of a window. Not much of a view from the underground tunnels." She reached for the remote lying next to her pillow and raised her bed to a more comfortable sitting position. She looked at her son, still asleep on the sofa, her brows furrowing in concern. "How is Justin dealing with all of this?"

Jonah sat on the bed, smiling at his sister-in-law. "You should be very proud of him, Emily. He has a strength to him that reminds me of Karl. He is mastering his ability at an astonishing rate, possibly surpassing anything Karl was able to do. We are making tremendous strides against the Skutarans, all due to him."

"I am proud of him." She smiled, glancing at her son's curled up form beneath the blanket. "But I still worry about him, as any mother worries about her child. I know he must take on this burden, but it is difficult. To me, he will always be the little rascal who ran into my arms to tell me his latest adventures in the back yard, or come crying to me whenever he was scared or hurt."

"He is no longer that little boy, Emily, but he still needs us to guide him in this new life he must live. The war is upon us and —"

"Mom! You're awake!" Justin leaped from the sofa to his mother's bedside, nearly toppling the IV stand in the process. "Are you okay? I thought they would—"

She pulled Justin into a firm embrace, smothering the top of his head with kisses. "I'm fine, Justin. I'm just so happy to see you again. Jonah has been telling me how well you're doing. I'm so proud of you. Your father would be proud too."

Justin sat up, wiped the wetness from his face, and smiled. "Why didn't you tell me I wasn't from Earth? That we're not from Earth?"

She rustled his hair and gave him a wide-eyed questioning look. "And how would that have worked out for you? Could you have told anyone, even Kevin, without endangering us all? What little boy could safely keep such a secret?"

Justin looked abashed and lowered his face. "I'm not so little anymore."

Emily pulled him into another long hug. "I know, sweetheart. Time got away from me, and then everything happened so fast, there was no time. We were going to tell you that evening of your birthday, but…"

"Things went sort of whack, didn't they?"

"Yes, they did, indeed. Speaking of Kevin, where is he? I believe I owe him a huge thank you for everything he's done."

Jonah coughed and stood to retake his chair. "Now that the enemy knows about you and Justin, we have to believe it won't be long before they learn about Kevin and his mother as well. Myah has gone with Kevin to retrieve your silver box. It contains the next stage of your training, and you can't be risked. They should return here tomorrow morning."

***

Edward Davidson, ex-soldier, and member of the Red Angus Coalition (R.A.C.) leaned against the door of his leader's car studying his map of south Aurora and its vicinity as the growing storm clouds drifted across the sun's face. They would build into full blown thunderstorms come afternoon. Zach went over the plan one last time before they split up. "The Costco is here, on Cottonwood, just off Parker Rd. and the Southlands Mall is here." He zoomed out of the image on his phone to encompass both the sought-after locations they intended to search. "At E470 and Smoky Hill Rd. We meet at the fire pit there. Got it?"

"Got it," rumbled Davidson.

Zach Litson, leader of this mountain region cell, nodded, confirming the locations as he sat in the front seat of his car noting the locations on his own phone map. "Right. Our uniforms give us the perfect cover to pass around these 'person of interest' posters so, if our intel is correct, and these are two of the favorite hangouts for the local kids, somebody is bound to recognize him. Once we have his name and address, we can set up a surveillance team and snatch the kid at our first opportunity."

"We sure this kid is one of them? One of the aliens?" Davidson continued studying the map as he spoke.

Zach stiffened at the question. "Are you having doubts, Corporal?"

Davidson pulled back from the car window, giving Zach a glare. "No, no doubts."

"Even if he isn't one of the damn aliens, he's traveling with them. The boss left new instructions for us to learn what they are up to around here. If we can interrogate him, and if he is one of them, then there will be one less of them to worry about."

"Nothing less than they deserve." Davidson gave the coalition salute, his hand forming a sign language letter E pressed against his chest, and stepped toward his own vehicle parked across the lot.

As he entered the Costco, Davidson quickly located the food court with its red and white picnic table style tables. He pretended to search among the nearby aisle of metal shelves full of bulk packages of almost anything a person could want. All the while, he scouted the area for likely subjects for his inquiries. After only a few minutes, a likely group of teens bustled into the food court and claimed a table. Amid a great deal of laughter, they made their choices from the menu posted above the counter and gave their money to two of their companions who made their way to purchase the food for everyone. A few minutes more, and the group was happily gorging themselves on slices of pizza, hot dogs, ice cream cones, and an assortment of drinks.

Davidson assumed the demeanor of a soldier on a mission, approached the table of teens at a march, and held out his poster showing the enlarged photo of Kevin Samson, a bit out of focus, but still recognizable. "Any of you recognize this boy?"

The group grew silent as they stared up at the massive stranger. One of the louder girls of the group wiped her mouth, swallowed the last bit of pizza, and stared up at him. "Why ask us? We're just hanging out here. We didn't do anything."

"I never said you did. I just want to know if you can tell me who this boy is. Schools are closed so we are checking out all the possible locations he might spend time with his friends."

The girl kept staring at Davidson, refusing to look at the photo. "Why? What's he done?"

Davidson controlled his rising frustration with an effort and tried to look more relaxed to put the kids more at ease. He tried to add a friendlier, less menacing tone to his bear-like voice. "No, it's nothing like that. We simply need to find him to ask a few questions. He might be a witness in an investigation we are conducting. He is not a suspect or anything. We just need to ask him some questions. That's all. Do you know him?" He pushed the photo forward again.

The girl and her companions studied him a bit longer, then slowly began to examine the image of Kevin in the back seat of a car.

A dark-haired boy gulped down a sip of his soda as he looked at the image. "Isn't that that Samson kid? I think he was in my Language Arts class with Dr. Collins."

"Yeah," chimed in one of the girls. "That's him. Curtis? Kyle? What's his name?" She looked toward another member of the group.

"Ken? No, wait... Kevin. Yeah, Kevin Samson. That's him." The boy smacked the table with one hand and pointed at the photo.

Davidson smiled and pulled a pen from his pocket to write the name on the back of the poster. "Kevin Samson. You sure this is him? Do any of you know where he lives?"

The first girl scrunched up her face and leaned back on the bench. "Eww, no. He's just weird. We just know him from some classes at school. He hangs with that real weirdo, Justin. Now there's a loser." The rest of the group laughed as they grabbed more of their food and started chatting amongst themselves again.

Davidson folded the poster and put it into his shirt pocket along with the pen. "Thank you. You've been a big help." He turned and headed back to the parking lot.

Fifteen minutes later, Edward Davidson stepped out of his car in the Southlands shopping mall parking lot behind the Barnes & Noble store and headed toward the central street to locate the fire pit where he was to meet with his cell leader. He watched the crowd with a sense of foreboding. *How many of these people are not human? How many are aliens in disguise, just waiting to overthrow and enslave us? How long before everyone wakes up and realizes the danger we are facing?*

It wasn't long before he located the pit. There was no actual fire on this warm summer afternoon, and Zach Litson was sitting in conversation with two teens. Zach saw his approach and waved him in.

"Looks like my partner is here now, so I want to thank you again for your cooperation. Your information will help our investigation." He shook their hands and stood up to join Davidson.

"Did you learn anything?" he asked Davidson as they walked back down the sidewalk.

"Got a name, maybe a name for a friend of his as well."

"Great. We can compare notes back in the car."

Minutes later, seated together in the front seat of Zach's vehicle, the two men shared information.

"So we are looking for a kid named Kevin Samson, and his friend is Justin, maybe Jason with a last name of Matren, Madrid, or something along those lines. These two get off their school bus in the Seven Hills neighborhood, but nobody knows them well enough to provide an address. Anything else?" Zach looked up from his notes to face his co-conspirator.

Davidson scratched his head in thought. "Those two don't seem to have had many friends."

Zach nodded in reply. "At least we have a good start with their names."

"Maybe the local library will have more information on them. They seem to be a couple of smart kids, maybe they have library cards or something."

Zach pulled out his phone and tapped the Google maps app icon. "Good idea. Where would the nearest libraries be to Seven Hills?" He tapped in the required information and sorted through the results, zooming in and out of the view several times to narrow down the choices.

"Here it is. Mission Viejo library is the most likely choice, maybe Tallyn's Reach."

He set the phone, with the map still open, on his dashboard mount. "I'll take Mission Viejo, you go to Tallyn's reach. Same approach as with the kids. You good to go?"

Davidson tapped in the library's name into his phone and watched as the map function located his next stop. "Yeah, I'm good. Meet back at the motel?"

"Yeah, the motel in a couple of hours."

***

"So you're looking to find this boy, Kevin Samson, and you think we might have his address on file?" The large dark-skinned man who identified himself as Keldon Ankara, head librarian, stood behind the counter examining the ID card offered by the man in an ill-fitting lieutenant's uniform. He handed the ID back to the man, a fake ID Keldon thought, based on the man's lack of military crispness. "And why is this boy of interest to the Air Force?"

Zach grabbed onto the first thing he thought might be a valid excuse for an MP to be searching for a civilian youth. "Yes, a few weeks back there was an incident at the base involving a shooting and car chase. One of our officers was involved, and we think this boy was a witness to the event. We just need to ask him some questions."

Keldon Ankara rubbed his chin as he thought. "I see. Why don't you come back to my office and I'll see what I can find in our system." He waved Zach around the counter and led him to the small cubicle back behind the shelves of books and supplies. He signaled for Zach to sit in an old wooden chair with faded padding while he took the seat behind his small metal desk. He unlocked the computer screen and put on a smile. "Tell me the boy's name again."

Zach looked down at his notes again and looked up, mouth open to speak, but froze before uttering a sound. His eyes were fixed on the handgun, a type he did not recognize, aimed at his chest. The librarian's finger pulled on the weapon's trigger and Zach felt an agonizing pain shoot through every nerve in his body before passing out.

The blackness vanished into blinding white light as Zach awoke to find himself strapped down to what could only be described as a hospital examination table. Testing his strength against the restraints proved futile and only caused new pains to shoot from already abused muscles. He closed his eyes in an effort to protect himself from the painful glare of the intense light above his head.

A deep, resonant voice spoke from behind him. "Ahh, you are awake at last. Time for us to have a conversation." Zach opened his eyes to see the figure of the head librarian step out of the shadows to his side.

"What's going on here? Who are you?"

"The question we need to answer here is who are you? Don't insult me with any further attempts at claims to be military police. We both know that is only a fabrication. I will ask you once, politely. Who are you, and what is your interest in this boy and the car chase you spoke of?"

Zach tested the strength of his restraints again to no avail and tried to survey his surroundings, but only shadows filled the room outside the narrow perimeter of the light above his head. "Okay, I'm not an MP, you've got me there. I work for some people the boy's mother owes money to. A lot of money. They want me to send a message to her, through him, but she and the boy seem to have disappeared. The library seemed like a good place to start looking."

Keldon smiled, an evil joy gleaming in his eyes. "I was hoping you would continue to resist. I will have the truth from you, and I do so enjoy getting the truth this way so much more. Shall we begin?"

Chapter Fourteen

Davidson waited through the night for Zach to return, but sunrise still gave no sign of the cell leader. *Something's gone wrong. Zach would have at least called to check in by now.* He stumbled to the coffee maker on top of the small refrigerator, grabbed the water reservoir and carried it to the bathroom sink to fill. He replaced the reservoir, popped in a K-cup, placed a Styrofoam cup in position, and punched the on button. Stepping over to the window, he peeked out through the curtain. *What if they got him? Those damn aliens must have captured him and God knows what they're doing to him now. I've got to do something, but what?* A beep from the coffee maker alerted him to the finished brew. Grabbing the cup and taking a long draw of coffee, Davidson tried to think of a plan.

That kid! I got his address from the library. He must be part of it, maybe even one of them. If I can find him, maybe he'll lead me to Zach.

Swallowing the last of his coffee, Davidson finished getting dressed, buckled on his service revolver, something he hadn't worn since leaving Groom Lake, and headed out the door. He pulled his taser from the glove compartment and tucked it into its holder on his belt. He parked down the block, just in sight of the house with the address provided by the librarian. It looked empty, but Davidson decided to sit and watch for a while before taking any action. There was no place else to go anyway.

The sun passed its zenith when Davidson watched a black sedan pull up to the curb in front of his surveillance target. Two youngsters stepped out of the car. One was a blond girl dressed in black; the other was the boy from the photograph. Davidson slouched down until he could barely see them over the steering wheel. The two walked up the driveway and toward the front door. The boy—Kevin Samson, was it—opened the front door and they went inside.

Exiting his vehicle, Davidson shut the door quietly and strolled as casually down the street as he could manage. At the Samson house, he took care not to make any sound as he approached the still open front door. Voices came from inside.

"This is her day off, she must be out shopping or something."

"Did you check the garage? Is her car here?"

"You're right, I'll check... be right back."

Davidson entered the hallway and peeked around a corner to see the girl with her back to him. Withdrawing his taser, he took careful aim, and fired. The crackling of electricity sounded as the wires stretched out and impacted the girl's shoulder. She stiffened, and fell to the floor twitching, then going still as the charge ended.

"Myah, are you okay?" the boy called from another room.

Davidson switched the weapon to his left hand and pulled the revolver from its holster, pointing it in the direction of the voice.

"Myah, what..." Kevin froze at the sight of his friend lying motionless on the floor, then saw the man aiming a gun at him.

"Who are you? What did you do to her?" He ran to Myah, feeling for a pulse in her wrist and examining her eyes for trauma as he had been taught back at the base. He felt a tingle in his arms and hands and watched as she gave a quick gasp, but remained dazed.

The man waved the weapon at Kevin. "Step away from her, boy. It's just a taser, she'll be fine. We need to have a talk."

Kevin looked back down at Myah and noticed her eyes were now focused on him, and she gave a slight squeeze of his hand, then winked and closed her eyes again. Kevin realized he blocked the man's view of her, so he squeezed her hand back and stood. "What do you mean we need to have a talk? Who are you?"

Davidson smiled, but his eyes remained dead. "Who I am is not important. This may take a while. Have a seat over there." He signaled for Kevin to sit in a padded chair across the room and followed him, leaving Myah behind them.

Once Kevin sat down, Davidson pulled a sturdy wooden chair in front of him and sat, the taser still aimed at Kevin. "So are you one of them?"

Kevin, confused, stared at the man, trying to think of how to respond. "One of who? What are you talking about? This is my house, what are you doing here?"

Davidson lifted the taser, aiming it at arm's reach, and hit the test button so an arc of electric sparks crackled between the points. "I'll ask the questions today. You give me answers. Are you one of them? Or are you a traitor working with them?"

"Traitor? What? Are you whacked? I'm telling you, man, I have no idea what…"

Davidson leaped from his chair, His gigantic frame lunged at Kevin, and held the taser inches from his nose, growling in Kevin's ear. "The aliens! Are you one of them? I don't want to hurt you, kid, but we know you're involved. So I'm only going to ask one last time. Are you…" Davidson's world went black as something hard slammed into the back of his head. His limp body collapsed to the floor.

"Hello, boys… I'm baaack!" Myah stood over Davidson's inert form, holding a snow globe in her left hand. "You alright, Kevin?"

"Took you long enough."

Myah kicked the taser across the floor, knelt down next to Davidson, rolled him over and began to tie his hands behind his back with a zip tie from her belt pouch. "I needed to know what was going on, who he was. Once he started talking about aliens, I intervened. We need to get him back to the base to find out what he knows, and who he's working for."

Kevin walked over to pick up his assailant's weapon, but stopped in mid-crouch and looked back at Myah. "Did you quote *Independence Day* just then? I thought you didn't watch scifi."

Myah sighed, stood up and went over to Kevin. "You remember after Justin's accident, I told you about the pair-bond?"

Kevin searched his memory for a moment then suspicion filled his face. "Yeah, what about it? You said something about Zarminan soldiers working in pairs and you might have done something like that to save Justin."

"Maybe we should sit down for this. Anything to drink in the kitchen?"

Kevin grabbed a Monster energy drink for himself and the Coke Myah requested, and then joined her at the table. He popped the top and took a long swallow, wiped his mouth with his hand, and waited for Myah to spin her tale.

She took a sip of her Coke before beginning. "I never intended to pair-bond with Justin, but I had no choice. He was going to die, if you remember. You happened to be in contact with him as well, and you felt the effects too."

"Yeah, I remember, so what?"

"Well, I've never heard of it happening to anyone who wasn't a Zarminan, but you became a part of the bond as well, apparently. A triad-bond so to speak." She took another sip of her drink. "I talked it over with Jonah, to get his thoughts on it, and he had never heard of a triad forming before either, much less with another species. But we think that you and Justin must have already formed some sort of pre-bond connection. Somehow, unconsciously, after so many years of your close friendship together, some of his energy must have slowly leaked into you. Then, when the three of us were in contact at the moment I created the bond, all of us were connected."

Kevin jumped up and paced around the kitchen, his hands clasped on top of his head. "Well you just need to undo it, then. Like now! I'm not ready to be married. Not to anyone. Get rid of the damn thing."

"I'm sorry, Dave... I'm afraid I can't do that."

"You're kidding me. *Space Odyssey*? Really?

Myah gave a look of disgust. "Yeah, that's one of the more unfortunate side effects of this particular bond."

"Side effects?"

"Yes, you see, the bond goes deeper than anything you have here on earth. The pair-bond connects two individuals on a much more fundamental level. It builds a shared psycho-emotional state in which the two understand each other as well as they understand themselves. It's what allows our soldiers to work so effectively together, and why we have such low fatalities during battles. The pair-bond helps them work effectively as a team, even out of sight of each other. And if one is injured, the other can provide enough healing energy to keep him or her alive until more urgent medical care arrives. I bonded the three of us by accident, so now I am starting to respond to you and Justin using the same stupid movie quotes you two use as a communication short-cut."

Kevin thought for a moment, finishing off his drink. "So this is something between guys and girls on your planet? I thought you said Justin and I had already begun a type of bonding."

"Most frequently, yes, but not always. The bond can be made between two males, or two females just as effectively."

"This is sooo weird. So what is it doing to us?"

"I'm so connected to your minds that I'm taking on some of your quirks, like odd movie quotations. It's something you two do all the time. Now I'm starting to do it. I don't even like those movies. But before long, and with some training, we should be able to anticipate each others' moods and actions without thinking."

"Isn't there some way to undo it? Maybe one of your doctors knows a cure..."

"No, the only way to end the bond is through death." She gave Kevin a sideways glance with an evil grin. "I guess I could just kill you and be done with it, at least for your part."

Kevin startled at first with this revelation, but then felt her humor in his mind. He grinned back as he thought of a test. "Surely you're joking."

Myah gave a groan and replied. "Yes, I'm joking... and don't call me Shirley." She tossed her empty can of Coke at him. "Will you stop that!"

Kevin laughed. "So weird... but kinda cool too. Does Justin know about it yet?"

"No, not yet. I wanted to talk it over with Jonah and the doctors when I first realized all three of us might be bonded. Then everything went nuts, and here we are."

A groan from the other room brought Kevin and Myah back to the reality of their situation. Myah stood up and headed toward their prisoner. "I'll check on our guest, you go get what we came for."

A few minutes later, with Kevin supporting the still groggy intruder, and Myah keeping the taser trained on him, the three made their way to the car, secured the stranger in the trunk, and headed north toward DIA.

Kevin sat quietly, staring out the window for several minutes before bringing up the question which had plagued him since learning about the new base of operations. "So, along with aliens, are the Reptoids, New World Order, Illuminati and other conspiracy nut ideas about DIA true too?"

Myah laughed. "No, just us. Although the rest of those hair-brained conspiracy theories help conceal the truth about us, so we try to encourage them whenever possible." She gave Kevin a discerning look. "Really, you Earthers will believe anything. What's with you people?"

Kevin turned to look out the window again. "Hey, don't look at me. My whole world has been turned on its ear lately. Just checking to be sure what else might be going on."

"Fair enough," She replied, then grinned mischievously. "Come with me if you want to live."

Kevin groaned as he smiled. "Yeah, I guess that about sums it up."

***

Zach's mind went into overdrive trying to figure a way out of his predicament. The sight of several unfamiliar, but sharp and painful-looking implements his interrogator displayed for him sent chills up his spine, but his training helped him project an air of calm.

"Alright, you obviously are not a librarian, so tell me what you want and maybe we can come to an agreement. I have some very powerful and influential friends. Perhaps we can help each other."

Keldon picked up a long, waved-blade instrument with twin points. He brought the device close to Zach's face and pressed a button on the handle. A bright blue light stretched between the points, and even a foot away, Zach felt the heat.

Keldon smiled as he turned the instrument from side to side. "And why should I listen to any more of your lies, when this will give me the truth, and provide me with some much needed entertainment as well?"

Zach's mind raced for a way out, but decided he wasn't getting paid nearly enough to go through what this false librarian intended to do to him. "You're one of them, aren't you?"

Keldon hesitated, brought the implement a few inches closer, and looked his prisoner in the eye. "One of who? Be very careful how you answer this question."

"We know the boy is mixed up with a group of aliens here on earth. My boss hired me to learn who they are, and what they are doing here. My crew and I have been tracking them for months with nothing to show for it, and then this boy shows up and all hell breaks loose. He must be someone important so we've been trying to find him and take him in for questioning. From your reaction to my questions when we first met, and the look of that toy there, I figure you know exactly what I'm talking about. I don't know what your game is, but I think I might be able to help you."

Keldon kept his finger on the button, but pulled the blade back from Zach's face. "So you think I belong to a group of aliens invading your planet, and you offer me your assistance? Do you take me for a fool?"

"I'm not a fanatic, like some of those I recruited for this job. I never believed in UFO's or Bigfoot. But I've seen enough to know something big is going on, and for now, aliens here on Earth are as good an explanation as any. At least it fits some of what I've seen, especially recently. Whatever's going on, I'm not about to sacrifice my life for a bunch of crazies who just want to prove their insane conspiracy theories. If the pay is good, I don't really care what side I work for. And I do have some skills you might find useful."

Keldon's eyes narrowed and his forehead furrowed as he examined his prisoner for possible subterfuge. "Yes, we might have uses for one like you, a practical man with no convictions other than his own preservation." He turned to place the tool back on the tray. "You will stay here with us while I decide what to do with you…"

"Zach, Zach Litson."

"Mr. Litson."

"I prefer Zach."

"Very well, Zach. You will be our guest until we find a use for you. If you prove to be of no value, then I will have the pleasure of disposing of you after all, just like we did with your boss, Phillip Bork. You are one of his soldiers, aren't you?"

Zach stared at his captor. "You lie. I spoke with Bork two days ago."

Keldon typed a few commands into his wrist pad and began to speak in Phillip Bork's voice. "Are you referring to the conversation we had about you tracking down the two boys for interrogation?"

"How did you…"

"We have been the puppet master here for quite some time, Zach. Now I simply need to decide if you can be a useful puppet, or if I need to clip your strings."

He signaled for one of the others from the shadows to release Zach and escort him to another room in the bunker. "And, by the way, your friends were right. We do come from another planet, and have been here for some time now. We will discuss further details the next time we meet."

Several hours later, Zach found himself seated in front of Keldon Ankara in his ornately decorated office.

"We have decided you can indeed be of use to us, Zach. It will be your responsibility to run interference for us, and try to disrupt our enemy and prevent them from stopping us in what we have come here to do."

"And, if I may be so bold, who is your enemy, and what have you come here to do?"

"It's very simple. Our enemy is another group of aliens, from Zarmina. We have come to Earth to raise an army to take back to our world, Skutara, and reclaim it from those who humiliated me and forced us into exile."

Zach thought for a moment, rubbing his stubbly chin with one hand. "Fair enough, but I don't fancy becoming part of this army you're raising. I want nothing to do with going into space or risking my life on some other planet. You need to give me some assurances that once this is all over, and you and your new army leave Earth, that I stay here. Otherwise, the deal's off."

Keldon smiled in return. "Of course. We only need twenty million or so of your people to recruit. We can afford to leave you behind, if that is your wish. There are over seven billion of you to choose from, after all."

Zach nodded and leaned forward. "Now tell me exactly who I'm dealing with, and what you need me to do. I already have access to fifty of those nutcases who can't wait to rid the Earth of a bunch of aliens. All I have to know is where to point them."

An hour later, Zach was again led back to his quarters. Before Keldon could turn to other matters, Stephen Grozny, his new second in command, raised a concern. "I am not sure making that promise to him was wise, my leader. If he proves to be a skilled soldier, we could make good use of him as a host for one of the engrams."

A laugh escaped Keldon's lips. "And of what value is a promise made to a traitor? Let him think he is safe, then, if he proves able, we can implant him with whatever engram suits our needs."

Back in his room, Zach reviewed the plans he and the alien discussed. He also began to make plans for his escape when the time came. He had played this game before and had no intention of letting them break their flimsy promises. In the meantime, he would play their game.

Chapter Fifteen

Davidson woke in his cell. Well, if he was honest with himself, it was more of a dorm room set up than a prison cell. Just a locked door to keep him in, but otherwise, he had a television to watch, regular food, which was better than he had been eating since he left the base, even a private bathroom behind the curtain to his left. How long was it now, three... no four days since he found himself tied up in the trunk of that car and brought to wherever this facility was. Stretching, he rose up from the bed, a reasonably comfortable one, relieved himself in the bathroom, and began his hour-long routine of calisthenics. After the workout, he showered and readied himself for breakfast, always delivered at 7:30. Once he finished with the eggs over easy, toast with blueberry jam, sausage, orange juice, and coffee with one packet of Truvia as requested, he waited for his captors to lead him to the room where they questioned him. Time passed, but nothing happened. Seven-forty-five, according to the digital clock on the wall, and nobody came to collect him. Maybe they had given up, maybe they were changing tactics. No matter, he still wouldn't cooperate. The aliens were the enemy, and he would not give them any information. The sound of the door being unlocked brought him out of his thoughts.

A big man, a civilian, entered and closed the door behind him, then pulled out the desk chair and sat down. "Hello. I thought you and I might have a bit of a chat today."

Recognition clicked in Davidson's head. This was Captain Madrid, from the base. He wasn't wearing his uniform, but it was him. He was one of the aliens, according to the reports he had seen. "I'm not talking to you either."

Jonah sat back, crossing his arms. "Fair enough, and I promise not to knock your brains out for almost killing my nephew."

"Never meant to kill him, only strand him and his friends out there so we could capture him. I'm glad he didn't die in the accident."

"I thought that might be the case. Your motor pool chief and I had a long talk about you. He couldn't believe you were responsible. The chief is a good judge of character, and he believed in you. He's the reason you're not in a federal prison right now. I want you to come with me."

"Still not going to talk." Davidson looked Jonah straight in the eye, unafraid, challenging him to do his worst.

"That's fine. I won't be asking any questions. I want to show you something." He stood up and stepped toward the door, motioning for Davidson to follow.

Outside the door, a guard fell into step behind Davidson, but remained at a distance. After several twists and turns, Jonah stopped in front of a large double door. "When we go in, stay quiet. All I want you to do is watch and listen." He opened the doors and Davidson followed him into a large gymnasium, complete with basketball court, racquetball courts, free weights, treadmills, and a steam room.

He startled to recognize a trio of teens shooting hoops, what appeared to be a game of horse, only a short distance from him, and well within his hearing. The yellow haired girl was the one who'd surprised him back at the house, knocking him unconscious. The boy standing next to her was the kid, Kevin, he had tracked down to interrogate in his house. The other boy, taking a shot from the corner over his head, was the Madrid kid. The one who was supposed to have been nearly killed in the accident he had caused. There he stood, no sign of any injury, playing basketball with his friends. He should at least be sporting a couple of casts or be in a wheelchair. Nobody could have gotten away from that wreck without severe injuries at the least. Nobody, that is, unless he was one of the aliens. Maybe they had quick healing powers or something. Nothing else could explain what he saw. He decided to follow Captain Madrid's advice and listen as they took a seat in the small bleachers. The Madrid kid, Justin, he thought, waved at Jonah, who simply waved back and indicated he should stay put and keep playing with his friends.

"Oh! Just a bit outside! That's a big R for you." Kevin yelled out as Justin's shot missed the hoop by about six feet.

"Hey, you know I'm no good at basketball. At least I'm trying."

The girl laughed and joined in the good-natured heckling. "Do, or do not. There is no try."

Justin looked at her, raising his hands in dismay. "Seriously? You're doing it again. This bond thing is so creepy. Anyway, it's your shot now. I'd like to see you do any better."

Myah retrieved the ball and walked to the same corner of the court for her turn. "You think it's creepy for you, well try looking at it from my shoes. I'm stuck inside the head of you two weirdos. I don't even know half of what those references are about. They just pop into my head, like I'm stealing them from one of your brains before you can say it out loud. Not cool." She took one quick look over her head and, one handed, sank the shot.

Kevin picked up the ball as it bounced toward him and gave a few quick between the leg dribbles as he replied to Myah. "Same. Only for me, it's more like 'I know Kung-Fu!' I could never do this before, but now, I know how and only need a couple of tries before I get it. Being in your head is no picnic either." He took up a position at the top of the key and sank a left-handed skyhook shot. "See what I mean?"

Justin chased down the ball and headed back to the position Kevin had set for the next round of shots. "So what did I get out of this? Kevin becomes a super jock, and Myah gains a great sense of humor." That earned him a serious scowl from her. "But I'm still me. What gives?"

"I don't think so, Justin," replied Myah. "Think about it. Your skill at decoding the messages has improved since the bonding. You seem more focused. Also, when we've talked about Zarmina to help you with learning about your heritage, it's like you already seem to know things after we talk for only a minute or two. Your end seems to be more on the brainy side, while Kevin's is more the physical side. Which, if you think about it, is exactly what we need. That is how the bond is supposed to work. It gives each partner the strengths they lack from their partner."

"It's still pretty weird." Justin attempted the shot and winced as the ball bounced hard off the backboard.

Jonah stood up, signaling for Davidson to follow him. Out in the hall, the guard fell into step at a discreet distance as before. "So what did you see back there?" Jonah directed the question at Davidson, but kept his focus straight ahead.

"Kids shooting hoops."

"Exactly," replied Jonah. "Keep that thought in mind over the next few days. Three kids playing hoops. Nothing unusual about it at all. Something you could find in any neighborhood in the country. Except…those kids… one from Earth, one from another world, and one from both. Think about that before we talk tomorrow. You hungry?" Jonah led Davidson around a few more intersections to a cafeteria. After picking up their trays, ordering a burger, and filling their cups with soda, the pair sat at an empty table in the corner where they could observe the others in the room and began to eat. "Food's not great here, but definitely better than back on the base, wouldn't you say, Corporal?"

Davidson took another bite. "Not bad." He watched the room of about a dozen tables and various groups, mixed military and civilian, each in their own conversations. After a few minutes, he glanced over at Jonah. "Aliens here too?"

"Some. Some Earth civilians. All the military are yours, though. One hundred percent US of A army." Jonah shifted in his chair to face Davidson more directly, then leaned on his elbows. "We are not your enemy, Davidson. We are here to help. There are other forces here on Earth you do need to worry about. Yes, aliens, but not from my world. We are here, with the blessing of your government, and of most governments of earth, to help stop them from taking over your planet. I know you hate aliens, Corporal, but we need you to examine those beliefs and compare them to what you see here. Your chief back at the motor pool led me to believe you are much more than you seem. That you are capable of self-examination and willing to change your perceptions, given good enough evidence." Jonah waved his hand in front of them toward the people in the room. "Take a look around you. Does this look like we are invaders? Think about what you witnessed back in the gym. You can be of great help to us, Davidson. Alternatively, you can spend the rest of your days in confinement. It's up to you. We'll talk tomorrow." Jonah rose and signaled for the guard to take the prisoner back to his cell.

That evening, as Davidson sat in the dark on his bed, his mind struggled with what he had always believed, trying to justify those beliefs with what he witnessed today, and every day since his capture, and even back at Groom Lake. The more he thought about it, the less the Red Angus propaganda made sense. He was a proud and fierce defender of his country, and, ever since he was a kid, believed aliens from outer space were real, and posed a threat. This belief, and his staunch patriotism, often put him at odds with his classmates back in high school, so he often found himself on the outside. But did that threat really apply to all aliens? Not all foreign governments were a threat. Could it be possible not all beings from other worlds were a danger? These were the thoughts troubling his mind as he drifted off into a difficult and frequently interrupted sleep.

Davidson woke early the next morning. After an extended period of heavier than usual calisthenics, he took a long shower, all the while continuing to sort out his thoughts. The guard arrived on schedule at o-seven-thirty and escorted him to the cafeteria for breakfast. Again, the room's occupants were a mix of civilians and military, all chatting amiably about perfectly normal topics one might find in any office. Families, work, scores of last night's game, all so normal. He looked in vain for some sign of who among the civilians were the aliens. Downing the last gulp of coffee, black with one packet of Truvia. He took his tray to the return slot, and followed the guard to Captain Madrid's office.

"Two questions," Davidson rumbled in his deep voice as he sat across the desk from Jonah.

"Go ahead," answered Jonah. "I'll answer if I can."

"You really a Captain?"

"An honorary rank, given me by your president. I am my planet's liaison to your government, so the rank provides me with a familiar level of authority your people can work with."

Davidson frowned for a moment, then relaxed. "Fair enough. What about the kid? How did he recover so fast?"

Jonah tilted his head as he studied Davidson before answering. Nodding, and giving a brief smile, he responded, "We have advanced medical technology that mends wounds and many ailments much more rapidly than you have here on Earth. We are working with your medical authorities to synthesize versions of our treatments to treat human physiology. Your world is in for some amazing breakthroughs in the next few years, provided we win this battle with the others."

Davidson sat back, folded his huge arms across his chest, and stared at Jonah, as if trying to read the inside of a book through its cover. He grunted, and extended one large hand. "Alright, I'm in."

Jonah smiled, grasping Davidson's hand. "Glad to have you on our side, soldier. You understand there will be a period of debriefing, and the guard will remain at your side until we know we can fully trust you, but I think that won't be necessary for long."

Davidson nodded, but with a warning glare in return. "I'll be watching you too."

***

Deep underground beneath the library, Zach Litson, now an agent of the Skutarans, listened to the crackling of the radio receiver. "Alpha-One reporting in. We've secured the vehicle and the devices. We are go for operation mayhem at o-six-thirty. Over."

"Roger, Alpha-One. You are go for o-six-thirty. Repeat, go for operation mayhem at o-six-thirty. Beta-Two, what is your situation?"

"Beta-Two here. Everything is ready at our end."

"Roger that, Beta-Two. Operation Mayhem is a go at o-six-thirty. Do you copy?"

"Roger, base. "Go for o-six-thirty. Over and out."

Zach lowered the volume on his receiver and turned to face Keldon Ankara. "Everything is ready to go, sir. Our enemy won't be able to pay much attention to you when all hell breaks loose in in what they thought were their secure facilities. All we have to do is sit back and wait until the morning."

Keldon scowled at the human. "For your sake, I hope you are correct. We cannot afford to have the enemy disrupt our plans when we are so close to completion."

"Don't worry, sir. My men are committed to this operation. They won't fail."

"We'll see about that. Remember, your life depends on it," Keldon fumed as he left the room.

Zach swallowed hard as he watched Keldon leave, and returned to go over the plans they had worked on for several days. "You idiots better not screw this up," he muttered under his breath.

Chapter Sixteen

"So what's inside the box?" Justin sat across the desk from his uncle, turning his birthday present over in his hands, listening to the clank of whatever it contained moving inside.

"No idea. None of us have been able to open it. We didn't dare use a cutting tool for fear of damaging the contents. And, so far, we haven't been able to make any sense of the symbols on the outside. All I know is, before he died, your father made me swear to get it to you. He was convinced it was intended for you."

"For me? What are you talking about?" Justin stopped turning the box over and stared at the symbols carved on its surface.

"Again, not a clue. All I know is he found this during the raid on that Skutaran facility, and insisted I gave it to you when you were old enough. Why, or what he knew is a complete mystery. My guess is it has something to do with your ability to decode the Skutaran signals. Look carefully at the symbols. Do they mean anything to you?"

Justin continued to study the carvings, when his eyes shot open in surprise. "I think they've changed since I first saw them. Something seems different." He dug into his pocket and brought out the rubbing of the symbols he made for the library before everything went crazy. "I saved this, in case it was important or something, but look. See? They've changed." Justin compared the rubbing to the box and they were, without question, different.

Jonah leaned in close, shaking his head in confusion. "Those symbols are carved into the metal of the box. They can't change." He compared the rubbing to all sides of the box without success.

Taking the box back, Justin touched the carvings with the fingers of one hand, and felt warmth rising from the box. A faint whisper began to grow in his mind, until it became something like the jumble of voices mixing together in a large crowd. One phrase stood out from the jumble of noise. "Aeon rises once more."

"Oh, this is weird."

"What?"

"Feels like I just chugged a couple of Monster Gronks!"

"A what? What's a Monster Gronk?"

"An energy drink, Monster, named after Gronkowski, the Patriots tight end or something. Wow, this is a real rush!" The whisper grew in intensity, but his mind filled with rapid-fire images rather than words.

Jonah took the box away from Justin and set it on the desk. "I think that's about enough for now. Are you alright?"

The noise in Justin's head faded as soon as the container left his hands, but a slight tingling sensation continued. He looked up at his uncle, pupils dilated and slightly unfocused. "Yeah, I'm okay, I think. What was that?"

"You tell me I didn't see or hear anything. You sure you're alright? Maybe I should call in the medic to check you over." Jonah reached for the phone.

Justin's gaze followed his uncle's hand toward the phone, but stopped as he caught sight of the silver box. The symbols were glowing on its lid and reforming themselves into something he recognized. "Wait! Look at the box!"

Jonah froze, phone in hand ready to hit the speed dial for medical help, and turned to look at the box. "What?

Justin pointed emphatically. "Look! Right there! It's changing… glowing! I think I can read it now!"

"I don't see anything, Justin. What can you read?"

Justin laughed, his hand going over his mouth. "You aren't going to believe this."

Jonah, impatience starting to show on his face, leaned forward, both hands on the desk. "Tell me, Justin. What does it say?"

"'Speak friend, and enter'."

Jonah scowled in confusion, glaring back and forth between Justin and the box. "Say that again?"

Justin looked up and smiled. "'Speak friend and enter.' You know like in *The Fellowship of the Ring*."

Awareness slowly dawned in Jonah's eyes. "The movie? What does that have to do with anything?"

"To get through the Doors of Durin and into Moria, Gandalf had to say the word 'friend' in Elvish so their quest could continue. All I have to do is say 'friend', and it should open for us." Justin looked down at the box, cleared his voice, and spoke. "Friend."

"Nothing's happening." Jonah sheepishly realized he actually half expected it to work.

Justin concentrated for a bit, then jerked upright. "Of course! How do you say friend in Zarminan?"

Jonah watched his nephew, calculating the risk, and made his decision. "Shusa."

Justin again focused on the box and enunciated as slowly and clearly as he could. "Shusa!"

Immediately, a thin sliver of a crack formed around the top edge of the container, as if allowing the lid to appear and function. Justin reached out and lifted the lid off, revealing the contents for the first time in centuries: a small cube, roughly two centimeters square, nearly transparent, but with a red spark glowing inside. Before Jonah could react, Justin grabbed the cube and held it up in front of him. The spark grew brighter, then turned a brilliant green and began to melt, giving the appearance of a green, transparent liquid mercury amoeba crawling around Justin's palm. The tiny blob stretched out toward Justin's ring finger, wrapped itself around, and formed a beautiful silver ring with a band of emerald green in the center.

Justin felt a shock at first, watching the cube's transformation, but felt reassurance and calm emanating from his new ring, and began to smile. "There is no spoon!"

Jonah grabbed Justin's hand and tried to remove the ring. "There is no what? Justin, stop talking in riddles."

"Ouch! Don't do that!" Justin pulled his hand back, rubbing the ring finger. "I don't think it can come off. It feels like it attached itself to me and...wait, hold on a sec... let me see your phone."

"Why do you need my..."

Justin snatched the phone from Jonah's desk and called up his text messages. Choosing one at random, he opened the text and stared at the screen. "This is insane. I can see him. I can see the person who sent this, and I know what he's thinking, or at least what he was thinking when he sent this to you. Hold on! You have the guy who tried to kill me here?"

Jonah sat back, hands in his lap, eyes wide in amazement. "How do you know that?"

Justin gathered his thoughts and began to explain. "I followed the trail of this text, like an electronic path, back to its source, and then jumped into the mind of the lieutenant who sent it to you." He held up his hand and examined the new ring. "It's kind of like what I can do with the Skutaran signals, but more. I actually saw the guy who sent the text, and got into his head. So weird."

"Try another one," said Jonah.

"But what about..."

"In a minute. Try another text."

Justin selected a different message on the phone and concentrated on it. "This one is fuzzier, like static on a radio." He increased his focus, but soon gave up. "No good. There's something, but I was like trying to break through a wall to see it." He lost focus for a second, then grinned. "Oh. The ring says I need to practice more. And what about the guy who tried to kill me? Is he really here?"

Jonah stood up and stepped around the desk, taking Justin by the shoulder. "Come with me. I need to explain a few things before you meet him."

Fifteen minutes later, Jonah and Justin arrived in the detention area. Justin stopped short of the video screen monitoring the prisoner. "You sure it was an accident? He didn't want to kill me, but only strand us so his friends could kidnap us? Not sure how that's much better."

"He's got some pretty strange ideas about aliens and some other conspiracies out there, but I'm convinced he's not a bad sort. He was fed only the information his friends wanted him to have about us, but he is rethinking all of that now. He asked to talk with you. Maybe you can help him turn the corner. Can you do that?"

Justin approached the monitor and gaped at the monster of a man he saw sitting on his bunk reading. The ring sent out waves of comfort and peace. "Yeah, I can talk to him. What should I say?"

Jonah gave Justin's shoulder a good shake and chuckled. "Just be yourself, kid. Do what feels right."

Taking a deep breath, Justin stepped in front of the door to the cell and walked in when the lock clicked open. The man on the bunk took Justin's breath away. He never imagined a human could be so big. Yeah, in the movies, Dwayne Johnson or Arnold Schwarzenegger looked huge, but he always figured Hollywood magic played a big role in that. This guy looked like he could bench press a bus... fully loaded. "Hey! You wanted to talk to me?"

Davidson looked up from his reading at Justin, marked his place, shut the book and set it on the pillow as he sat up, swinging his massive legs to the floor. Sitting on the edge of the bed, he was almost at eye level with Justin. He nodded at Justin. "Hey, kid. You okay?"

The deep, rumbling voice fit the man, but still caused Justin to shuffle half a step back.

"Yeah. You the guy who tried to kill me? Why did you do that?"

Davidson hung his head. "Never meant to hurt you, kid. Glad you're okay."

Justin found the chair and sat down. "Same. Thanks to Zarminan medicine. Did they tell you about that?"

"Yeah. You really an alien?" Davidson looked up at Justin, studying him.

"Guess so, but I was born here on Earth. I've been to Zarmina, though. Pretty cool."

Davidson grunted as he thought. "Why are you here?"

"Like I said, I was born here. But I guess you want to know what our intentions are for the Earth. I thought they told you all that."

"I want you to tell me." The huge man's gaze was penetrating.

Justin began to realize the man was far more intelligent than his communication skills suggested. He swallowed hard before continuing.

"We're like the Avengers. All we want is to help Earth defend itself against another bunch of evil aliens, posing as librarians, from taking over and enslaving everyone."

"Evil alien librarians?" Davidson cocked his head as he thought about this information.

"Well, the ones we know of are pretending to be librarians anyway. My job is to try to find out where their main base is, then lead our soldiers to them so they can stop the invasion."

Davidson absorbed this before continuing. "Why you?"

"Me? I have some sort of ability to read the code behind their technology. The Skutarans, that's what they're called, are embedding a type of brain wave code in all of our technology to brainwash everyone or something. I haven't figured it out exactly yet, but I'm getting close. Something I inherited from my dad, from what my uncle tells me."

Davidson leaned forward on his huge arms. "What about after?"

"After?" Justin puzzled over this question for a moment before realizing what the man wanted to know. Everything depended on his answer to this one question. "Oh, you mean after we win? What will the Zarminans do?"

"Yeah."

Justin took a deep breath, exhaling slowly. "Then we leave. Well, not me, probably. Or maybe I will too. I don't know yet. The only interest we have here is to help Earth defend itself. If we are invited to stay, we can help with some new tech, but only if Earth wants us to stay, and even then, no soldiers. Only ambassadors and tech people."

"Just like that?"

"Just like that. Like I said, man. We're the Avengers."

Davidson sat back, relaxing for the first time. "Okay. Thanks kid."

"We good?"

"Gotta think more on it, but I think, yeah, we're good." Davidson picked up his book and laid back down on the cot.

Justin stood up and left the room, not sure how well he had done, but the ring felt warm and comfortable, easing his mind. An image of Captain America flashed in his mind, giving him a thumbs up.

Jonah made sure the cell was secure, gave a few instructions to the guard on duty, and walked back down the hall with Justin. "So now we need to focus on getting you some practice time with your new ring. Seems to me the enhancement to your ability will be the key to finally winning this war, but only if you can control it better. What do you need?"

Justin thought about it and images raced through his brain. "I need some time alone, just me and the ring. I think it has some things to tell me before I understand enough to use it."

"I think I know the perfect place. You like the mountains?"

***

The sun rose over the desert, already at a scorching 87 degrees. The two soldiers, dressed in tan camo fatigues, drove down the dusty road toward the main gate, a dozen mailbags in the back of their army issue truck. The sentry scanned their badges and admitted them when his pad gave a green light. The pair drove through the base, stopping at various buildings to drop off the heavy sacks, and picked up the postbags of outgoing mail. Their last delivery was the motor pool, where they were directed to a drop-off location by the chief's office. As the soldier set the bag down, he reached inside the bag and flicked a switch, then watched the red LED numbers begin their countdown. He shouldered the last of the outgoing mail sacks, deposited it in the back of the truck, got in the passenger side, and the two sped off. Five minutes after leaving the base, they pulled over to the side of the road and stepped out to watch. Seconds later, they saw bright flashes and, one after another, huge fireballs rising into the sky above the base at Groom Lake. The sound hit them less than thirty seconds later. Even five miles away, the explosions were impressive. The soldiers gave each other the sign language letter E salute to their chests and got back in their vehicle.

The man in the passenger seat pulled his phone out of a pocket in his shirt and dialed the familiar number.

"Alpha One here. Mission accomplished. Repeat, mission accomplished. Fifty-One is hot." He hit the cancel button and replaced the phone in his pocket.

Zach Litson sat in his car on a side road near Denver International Airport's Pike's Peak remote parking facility. He smiled as he listened to the report of a successful attack at his former assignment. He dialed a second number and a voice answered before the first ring ended.

"Bravo Two."

"Bravo Two, you are late. Report."

"Traffic tie-ups delayed us a few minutes, but we are approaching the gate now. Over."

"Get a move on, Bravo Two. You were supposed to coordinate attacks with Alpha One."

The two men, dressed in airport tarmac maintenance uniforms, sped toward the security gate at the far east end of the airport in their battered Silverado. The camper shell covered the truck bed, filled with a haphazard collection of toolboxes, spools of cables, orange hazard cones, and other equipment, but the false floor of the bed hid their deadly cargo, one hundred pounds of C-4, set with a remote detonator switch hidden in an app on the driver's phone.

As they approached the eastern security gate, the pair noticed several extra TSA vehicles parked next to the guardhouse, TSA agents and Federal agents with protective vests and high-powered rifles, as well as two bomb sniffing dogs.

The man in the passenger seat sat up straighter, one hand on the dashboard. "Something's wrong. Maybe we're too late."

"Yeah, traffic slowed us down longer than I thought. Should we abort?" The driver began to decelerate.

"They've already seen us. If we turn around now they'll only chase us down."

"So we're screwed either way."

The driver nodded, tugged at his body armor to make sure it was secure, and gripped the wheel harder. "Yep. We might as well take as many of them with us as we can. Damn aliens have got to know we won't surrender without a fight."

The passenger double checked his protective vest and helmet, tightened his seatbelt and braced his feet. "What the hell. Punch it."

The driver floored the gas pedal and about fifty yards before the gate, he engaged the four wheel drive, and turned off the narrow road. Gunfire erupted as the men at the gate opened fire, exploding a rear window and putting several holes in the side panels of the truck. Others ran to their own vehicles and started up the engines, preparing to give chase.

"Hold on!" The driver gritted his teeth and held the wheel in a death grip as they impacted the chain link fence surrounding the nearby runway. Metal posts flew into the air as sections of the fence broke loose. The front bumper of the truck broke away, but the Silverado continued its cross-country rampage,

"The passenger pointed ahead and to the right. "Runway ahead, looks like a plane is about to take off."

As the driver looked to his right, he saw a seven-twenty-seven begin to roar down the runway. "No choice now. Hang on."

Just as they hit the edge of the runway, the plane's nose rose in the air. A powerful burst of air hit the truck as they passed behind the aircraft, into its jet wash, nearly knocking the truck over. Regaining control, the driver aimed toward the taxiway that would take them to concourse B. To their left, the pursuit vehicles steadily gained on them.

Another active runway loomed ahead, a Delta 767 landed in front of them, with another on approach in the distance. They sped across the runway, dodged a United 737, and took aim at the gateways of Concourse B. A TSA car and two federal marshal vehicles, all with lights and sirens flashing, pulled in behind them.

Gate twenty-nine was the access point to the tunnel system underneath the airport. The same tunnel system every member of Red Angus knew hid the underground facilities housing the aliens working in concert with the New World Order, all conspiring against the US Constitution.

Most of the gates held aircraft from United Airlines awaiting their passengers. Even at this early hour, many flights would be full. As they approached their target, dodging and swerving around three airliners headed out to the runways, the conspirators saw two more police vehicles pull in front of the access point to the underground tunnels, blocking their way. The officers aimed their weapons at the truck and opened fire, now heedless of collateral damage.

Gunfire erupted around them, dozens of rounds making holes in their windows, tires, and side panels, wounding both men. The loss of control when two of their tires exploded caused the truck to veer drastically, right into the path of a transport cart hauling a train of passenger luggage to be loaded on one of the nearby planes. Jerking the wheel to try to maneuver around the cart caused the truck to flip onto its side, crash through the police vehicles, and skid to a metal-screeching halt just inside the entrance to the tunnels. The gunfire ceased, but the two heard the approach of heavy boots at a run, shouted commands, and barking dogs.

"You! In the truck! Hands out where we can see them. Now!"

The two saw officers in heavy riot gear cautiously take up positions in front of the windshield, aiming their AR-15s.

"Final warning! Hands out where we can see them. We will fire if you resist!"

The man in the passenger seat closed his eyes and pressed the app button.

From his position about three miles away, Zach watched as flames and debris flew into the air. The blast of the sound wave was powerful even at this distance, but it wasn't right. There shouldn't have been such massive flames from a blast deep underground. Something was wrong. Even as he considered what might have happened, several more explosions, again with balls of flame, erupted above the concourses. Getting back into his car, he flipped on the police band receiver and heard the chaos erupting. Calls for ambulances, more police, all available firetrucks both on and off the airport. Reports of planes exploding, extreme damage to the concourse, many casualties, possible terrorist attack, all overlapping each other in the frantic calls for help. Zach gunned his engine and drove away from the airport, swearing at the incompetent idiots he had to work with in this operation.

Chapter Seventeen

Dust and small pieces of the ceiling rained down on everyone in the underground facility as the lights flickered, went out briefly, then flickered back on. The rumble of a powerful explosion shook everything around them.

"Holy crap on a cracker! What was that?" Kevin grabbed the edge of the table where he sat eating lunch with Justin and Myah.

Myah's eyes went wide, and she jumped up, running toward the door. "Explosion! A big one, and close by! C'mon!"

Kevin and Justin stared at each other for a second before tossing their chairs aside and chasing after Myah. They caught up to her in the hallway just down from Jonah's office. Dozens of individuals, military and civilian, entered and left the office in a flurry of controlled chaos. Myah caught the arm of one civilian she knew as she passed by at a near trot.

"What happened?"

The woman looked at her—shock showed on her face. "There was an explosion up on Concourse B, Gate 29, Reports are sketchy, but it looks like hundreds of people are injured. Fires everywhere up there. I gotta run." She hurried down the hall, disappearing in the growing crowd.

Kevin gaped at Justin, his voice barely under control. "Houston, we have a problem."

Justin gaped back, fear growing on his face. "Inconceivable!"

"Yeah, I know... I do not think that word means what you think it means. Get a grip, you two." Myah rolled her eyes, grabbed Justin by the arm and pulled him forward, closely followed by Kevin.

The trio edged their way into Jonah's office and waited to one side until he had a chance to notice them.

Jonah handed a quickly scrawled note to one soldier, hung up his desk phone, and looked up, seeing them.

"Good, you're here." He waved them over. "Myah, take Kevin and get topside. You both have some first aid training, and Kevin has at least a start on emergency situations. See what you can do to help. Keep your eyes and ears open and see what you can learn."

The two headed out and Justin automatically followed, never noticing he was not included in the instructions.

"Not you, Justin."

Justin stopped in his tracks and spun to face his uncle. "What? Why not? I can help."

Jonah locked eyes with Justin, his voice calm, but stern. "Not this time. We can't risk you up there, it's too dangerous. Besides, you have something important you need to do." He quickly glanced down at Justin's ring.

"But…"

"No buts. We need you to learn to control whatever ability enhancements that thing is giving you. We know the Skutarans are getting close to completing their mission. We need you if we have any chance to stop them in time. We can handle the emergency topside. You need to do this. Now go. Do what you are here to do."

In his mind, an image of Captain America stood, arms crossed, impatiently tapping his foot flashed for a second. He knew Uncle Jonah was right, but that didn't mean he had to like it. "Yes, sir." He turned and saw his friends had stopped and overheard the instructions.

Kevin shrugged. As Myah pushed him down the hall, Justin yelled after them, "Go! You need to help the others!"

Kevin shouted back over his shoulder as he ran. "I'll be back!"

Since all airport operations were shut down, and the regular access to the surface was severely damaged, Kevin and Myah ran through the underground train tunnels to Concourse B. The noise of screaming people got louder as they neared the passenger doors for the trains. Security personnel were helping everyone down to the empty tracks, guiding them back toward the main terminal. Kevin and Myah used their high-level security clearance badges to gain access to an Employee's Only door in the tunnel and took the stairs up to the main level. As they opened the door, the stench of smoke from burning jet fuel filled their nostrils, causing them to shrink back for a second. A cacophony of alarms and people assaulted their ears. Dozens of injured fled past them toward the train access area. Sirens blared outside along with the roar of flames from at least four jets caught in the explosion, and the incredible tremor of tons of fire retardant foam spraying onto the flames. Kevin and Myah looked at each other, took a deep breath, and ran to give aid as best they could.

***

Justin sat down at the peak of the sand dune and pulled off his shoes. He dumped what felt like an entire sandbox out before replacing it on his foot. His mind still dwelled on the troubles back in Denver, his friends and family, as well as the hundreds of innocent people hurt in the tragedy at the airport. He couldn't rid his mind of the image of the towering plume of black smoke rising above DIA as he flew out of Buckley Air Force Base.

Yesterday, his uncle had sent him off to this remote area and another of their fronts in Hooper, Colorado, a small town only a few miles directly west of the Great Sand Dunes National Park. He learned from some of the locals about the UFO Watchtower just outside town and the prevalence of UFO sightings in the area. Though not as widely known as places like Roswell or Area 51, Hooper had its share of believers, but more the tourist type, not the hard-core theorists. The idea was to send him off somewhere quiet and remote so he could focus on discovering how to gain control of the ring and fully develop what it could do to increase his natural ability to read Skutaran messages.

Justin held his ring hand up in front of him, examining the green band in the ring's center, and spoke to it. "I don't know what I'm doing. What do you want from me? And no more Captain America. Tell me what I need to do. How do I see into the minds of the Skutarans who are sending the signals?" He sighed and lay back on the sand in frustration, staring up at the snow-capped mountains and deep blue sky. The view calmed his thoughts and he started to focus on the beauty of his surroundings and the sound of the wind shifting the sand around him.

"Finally. I was wondering when you would relax enough for me to get through to you, Aeon."

Justin jerked up to a sitting position and looked in the direction of the voice. His mouth dropped open. "Gandalf?"

"Well, you said no more Captain America, so yes, but I'm only taking these forms so you have a frame of reference to work with. I'm not actually here, still in your head, but close enough."

Justin continued to stare at the apparition, an old man with a long white beard, white cloak and pointy hat, and noticed the sand was now golden and shimmering as it moved, and the sky was a deep purple, with brilliant stars gleaming overhead. "But, you're Gandalf…"

The vision sighed and pulled off his pointy hat. "Yes, we've established that already. Before I can help you with your talent for seeing the messages, you need to know more about me. We need to establish a bond and this is how I've always done it."

Justin reached out and watched as his hand went through the vision. "You're not really there?"

"No, Aeon. I'm in your mind, but I thought this would help you learn to trust me. You have very powerful feelings toward this character."

"Yeah, you're great... I mean he's great... I mean... whatever." Justin turned to face the vision directly. "Why do you keep calling me Aeon? My name's Justin."

"Well, yes, and no." The figure of the aged wizard pulled out a long-stemmed pipe as he explained. "While you are the person of Justin Madrid, the Zarminan youth born on Earth, you were chosen by my brother, Aeon, to be the vessel for his eternal struggle to bring forces of the universe into balance. It is through Aeon's spirit, rising within you, that you can read the codes of your enemy."

Justin gaped in disbelief at the old man before him. "So... Aeon reads computer codes to balance the universe?"

Gandalf smiled and puffed an intricate pattern of five interlocking smoke rings in the air. "This time, yes. He provides whatever power is necessary to balance the evil creating the disturbances. Last time, in another sector of the galaxy, he gave a young woman the ability of persuasion. Through him, she learned to convince the leaders of vast armies to end a war that was leading both sides toward genocide."

Justin mulled over this news. "But why me? There has to be others better than me to handle this."

Gandalf shook his head. "Aeon has a mind of his own. I never see why a certain individual is chosen, but he almost always chooses the right individual. Once he makes the choice, he calls to me to provide the training. Come, I have much to tell you before we begin your lessons."

"You can really help me? What do I need to do?"

"For now, just listen." The scene around Gandalf blurred and morphed into a scene from an alien world. Not too dissimilar from Earth, but the sky was orange, the vast ocean beyond the cliff they sat on was too dark and thick to be water, and the terrain speared to be frozen, but not rock. "This is my home, or at least the first location I can remember. It is a world on the other side of the galaxy, but not unlike a moon in your star system. The one you know as Titan. My home was cold, with liquid methane taking the place of water. The beings there were far more advanced technologically than any in this entire sector, but had the curiosity to explore like most sentient creatures. They designed Aeon and me to go out among the stars and learn what we could of other civilizations. Unfortunately, during the three thousand years we traveled, our creators destroyed themselves when they tried to use the core of their world as an energy source. They set off a chain reaction of events which made the world uninhabitable within months, and we were left to wander the galaxy and learn."

"I'm sorry. It must have been terrible." Justin tried to touch Gandalf's knee in sympathy, but passed right through it.

"At the time, we had not yet become fully sentient, so no, we felt nothing other than the need to continue our primary function, explore the galaxy and learn as much as we could. As the millennia passed, we began to realize that we were spending more and more time in self-reflection and feeling connections with some of the species we were observing. The more we learned, and the more sentient beings we encountered, the more self-aware we became. Eventually, we became fully sentient and able to override our programming with our own sense of purpose."

The ancient wizard puffed another intricate design with his smoke as he continued his tale. "It was Aeon who first felt the balance of energy in the universe shifting. He went in search of the imbalance. However, he realized he could not fight the problem alone, so called me to aid him. We discovered our abilities complimented each other when confronted with such crisis. While Aeon could choose and empower another sentient being to correct the imbalance, one with some latent ability hidden in their genetic make-up, he could not communicate effectively with them. I, on the other hand, was able to follow his lead, and guide the chosen ones to fulfill their destiny and restore balance. This became our new purpose."

Justin watched in amazement as Gandalf blew another of his incredible smoke designs, this time, a spaceship flying among strange planets. "What, exactly, creates the imbalance you and Aeon need to fix?"

Gandalf slumped his shoulders as he replied. "Many species, as they gain in knowledge and power, seek to dominate rather than co-exist with the natural balance of the universe. When one species becomes so powerful that they threaten to end the lives of entire species, or harm them to the point of imminent extinction, this creates the sort of imbalance we are summoned to prevent. This is what the Skutarans are about to do on your world, and their own. Aeon found you, and I am here to train you in the abilities he has bestowed on you. This is why we travel the universe."

As Gandalf related this tale, images of vast reaches of space, filled with stars and nebula of incredible variety, and scenes from hundreds of alien worlds appeared around them. Justin struggled to take in the immensity of it all.

"Fortunately, incidents requiring our interjection are few, so we spend most of our time exploring and learning everything we can, as our original programming directed. We still find it comforting and enriching."

"So how old are you?"

The image of Gandalf rubbed his beard in thought and then smiled. "The last time I visited this planet, the only life forms were fish in the seas and a few insects and plants starting to colonize the land. By then, I had observed the birth and death of hundreds of stars."

Justin struggled to grasp the vast ages this intelligence had witnessed, but got lost in the attempt. "Okay, really old. Are there others out there like me?"

"More than you can imagine, but fewer than you might think. I have encountered countless systems with intelligent beings. Among those, some became travelers within their star systems, while some few even learned to travel between the stars but none survived for long. There have been many with unique abilities, some like yours, others of a completely different nature, and they are the ones I have searched for over the last few millions of years. They are the ones who have the potential to make real differences among their people, for good or ill. I have made it my task to find those individuals and guide them."

"But my uncle told me my father had the same ability to read the code. Why didn't you and Aeon choose him?"

"Beings with talents like the ones we search for send out unique disturbances through the cosmos. Aeon felt a disturbance, not you, but another similar to you, and made his way to this sector again. He followed the disturbance to some nearby systems, but had some difficulty isolating the source. Eventually, he located the Skutarans on an isolated moon, but they were the source of the imbalance, not the one he sought for. Something about the location caused him to stay. The origin of the call he felt appeared to be nearby, and getting closer. It took several years, spent sitting on a shelf in some back room of a laboratory, disguised inside that silver box, but eventually, Aeon felt the presence of what had drawn him to the area. Turns out it was your father. Aeon reached into his mind and found the rudiments of talent, but very undeveloped. By then, I had arrived to join Aeon in the box. I reached out to your father and convinced him to take me so I could learn more. At his touch, I sensed your presence, and the power of your talent. Somehow, your father's talent was masking the strength of yours so it made the search very confusing. Before I could learn much, your father was fatally injured. I only had time to give him a compulsion to send me to you."

The scene showing Justin's father and his discovery of the silver box played out around them, but went dark before he died. The original scene of the ring's home planet returned.

"Wait, you knew my father? Can you tell me more about him?"

"I thought that would have been obvious. You knew he sent us to you, so of course I knew him, but not like I am getting to know you. We were only together for a few minutes before he died. I am sorry about that, by the way. I can feel your pain over his loss."

Justin hung his head as a tear traced a path down his cheek. "Oh, I just thought that maybe…but no, you're right, there wasn't time. I'm sorry. Go on."

"Not much left to tell. After your uncle gave us to you, Aeon rejoiced and filled you with the ability to fully utilize your latent ability, and more. Then, I began studying you." He laughed, replacing the hat on his head. "The reason I took this form, and the images of Captain America, is that they were so strong in your mind. Those characters have made a powerful impact on you. The images were so strong, I became intrigued and decided to investigate them further. That was when I found the stacks of discs on a shelf near where you kept me, so I sort of watched all of them while you slept. I think you may have accidently caught me at it one night when you woke up unexpectedly and saw the energy streams between me and the discs."

Justin thought for a bit, and then smiled. "Yeah, I remember that night. I thought it was a dream."

"No, I planted that thought in you as you slept. I did enjoy those movies. Wonderful action, and intriguing stories. Your world has some amazingly creative minds. Maybe I'll hang around longer once we are done."

"What do you mean, 'when we're done'? Where are you going?"

Gandalf shook his head. "Pay attention Padawan, I told you my purpose is to roam the galaxy searching for others like you. There have been others before you, and there will be more after you. I must find them."

"Oh, yeah. And you just mixed *Star Wars* with *Lord of the Rings*. They don't go together."

"I know, but it made my point. Shall we begin? I think you're ready now." Gandalf stood up, the golden sands and violet star-filled sky returning.

Justin joined him in walking along the sands. "What do you mean I'm ready now?"

"While we were talking, I explored your mind, making a few minor adjustments here and there, to help you understand what you need to know, and open you to the possibilities. Nothing too big."

Justin jerked to a stop, raising his hands to his head, feeling for any changes. "You went in my head and changed stuff? That's just wrong!"

"Oh, stop being such a wimp. I only made a few tiny alterations. Nothing major. You are still you, only now you are better able to understand what you need to know to use your full potential. Do you trust me?"

Justin slowly lowered his hands and began walking again. "I guess so. Okay, what do I do first?"

"To begin, you need to understand the nature of brain waves and how to recognize them inside the signals you already know how to isolate. There is a subtle—"

"Hey, kid! Wake up!"

Justin felt someone shaking him as he fought his way back to alertness. "What? Where's Gandalf?" He looked around, seeing only the normal sand dunes he had been exploring earlier in the day. A park ranger knelt beside him, concern filling her face.

"Gandalf? That your dog or something?" She helped Justin to his feet, brushing sand off him. "It's getting late and the park is closing for the night. Let me give you a ride back to the campground." She pointed toward a dune buggy a few yards away.

Justin quickly gained his senses as he reoriented to the real world. "No, not a dog. I was having a very realistic dream. Sorry. What time is it?" He realized the sun had sunk lower in the sky than he remembered.

The ranger hopped into the driver seat and started the engine. "About four-thirty. We try to get folks off the dunes by six. Gets too dark for a good search party if anyone turns up missing after that." She hit the gas and the car sped off, spraying rooster tails of sand behind them.

As they bounced along, Justin realized the entire experience spanned only two hours. He felt the heat of a mild sunburn on his arms and face, but he would not have been surprised to learn he had been asleep for days. There was too much to absorb all at once. He needed to allow himself time to understand everything Gandalf—the ring—taught him. He needed to practice, but he knew what he needed to do now to learn control and to search for the creators of the Skutaran signals. Back at the campground, Justin started up his scooter, checked out to him by people at the safe house in Hooper, and headed back toward town.

***

"You sure you're okay now? How's Mom, and Myah, and Uncle Jonah?" Justin watched Kevin's face as they face-timed together. They had stayed in touch every night over the past two weeks since the attack at the airport.

"It was all *Twilight Zone* for a while, but it's good now." Kevin's face went slightly blank, as if recalling the horrors of those first few days. He suddenly perked up and changed the subject. "But enough about us, How are you and Gandalf doing? Man, that is so weird, don't think I'll ever get used to saying that."

Justin laughed. "Same. It's like the Doctor says, I just hold tight and pretend it's a plan." He leaned in closer to the screen and began to whisper. "He, it, whatever, told me not to reveal too much yet, but you gotta see this. Watch." Justin set his hands gently on the keyboard and closed his eyes to concentrate, then jerked back like he had received a shock. "Hey, you never told me you broke your arm in the concourse. What gives?"

Kevin stumbled for words briefly before answering. "It was only a flesh wound. Besides, we didn't want to worry you. The docs here got some of their Zarminan medicine modified for us humans so they fixed me up quick. See?" He waved his arm around to show it was completely healed, then stopped short, suddenly realizing what Justin had done. "Wait, how did you know? Did your mom or somebody tell you?"

"Nope. I followed your signal back into your mind. You told me."

Kevin's mouth dropped open. "Okay, don't panic. Where's my towel? You can read minds?"

"Sort of. But only with someone currently on line. Gandalf tells me I will eventually learn how to get into people's heads long after they have logged off. He says everyone leaves a trace of their brain wave patterns behind when they create, or use a program. I don't really understand it all yet, but if we want to eliminate the Skutaran's from ever attempting this on another planet, we need to make sure they don't remember even the possibility transferring one mind to another."

"So that's how you found out what they were up too? You read their minds?"

"Only partly. During one of our talks, Gandalf told me about how the Skutarans planned to implant their digitized criminals into the brains of humans to build an army. One of the first lessons he taught me was how to locate the details of the plans and how to find those most responsible. Have Uncle Jonah and the others been able to make anything of it all yet?"

Kevin shook his head. "Since the bombing, everyone's been too busy to focus on that one. Not enough left of the truck or the terrorists to make any positive ID. The security guard at the gate recognized the truck, but we don't know for sure who was driving it. Your uncle wanted me to ask if you can help with anything in that area. Maybe if we can find out who those guys really were. Think your new talent can do the trick? Help us Obi Wan, you're our only hope."

Justin smiled. "It's my destiny."

"Okay, man, gotta split."

The two friends signed off in unison: "May the force be with you." And Justin's monitor went dark.

Chapter Eighteen

"During our early talks you mentioned one of your partners in Red Angus named Zach Litson. What can you tell me about him?" Jonah sat behind his desk, arms crossed and legs stretched out under the desk. Across from him sat the hulking figure of Edward Davidson, former member of Red Angus, a group of UFO conspiracy theorists, currently a willing participant in the war against the Skutarans.

Davidson looked up at the ceiling as he thought. "Not much. Mercenary, smart, I don't think he ever really believed. The type who mostly only takes care of themselves. Why?"

"We got word from Justin last night that he traced some signals back and found him in some of the information related to the bombings here and back in New Mexico. Do you think he is capable of organizing that big of an operation?"

Davidson's gaze lowered to focus on Jonah. "Yeah, if he had the resources. Red Angus is full of folks who would be willing to pull it off for him. We had operatives in both areas."

"Where would he get the money and equipment?"

"Bork."

Pulling in his legs, Jonah sat up straighter. "Who the hell is Bork?"

"Zach's boss. Don't know much about him, but Zach always called him when we needed anything."

Jonah studied Davidson for a moment, and then leaned forward on his elbows. "Think you could track down Bork and Litson if we gave you clearance?" "I'm a mechanic, not some computer jockey."

"True, but Myah and Kevin are pretty good with computers. I think, with your help, they might have some luck locating them for us. You with us?"

Davidson's eyes narrowed, returning Jonah's studying gaze. "Yeah, I can do that."

"Good. I'll make the arrangements. You meet with Myah and Kevin tomorrow and get us a lead on both of those men so we can haul them in. They have a lot of innocent lives to pay for."

Both men stood and shook hands before Davidson left the room.

***

Deep underneath the Mission Viejo library, Zach Litson worked to control his fear. Bluster and bravado, along with the positive spin on events he concocted, were his only chance of survival.

Keldon Ankara snarled at the human whom he had trusted to end the Zarminan interference of his rebellion. "You have failed me. Your operatives made a lot of noise, but only managed to destroy human operations, killing only humans, and bringing attention to us. I should end your incompetent existence right now."

Zach held Keldon's glare without flinching, even if his insides were twisting in knots. "What do the humans matter? We caused enough disruption to tie up their operations for weeks. They will be so busy helping their human allies that you will be able to continue without delays. You said yourself that you only needed a few more weeks to start implanting the engrams. I've given you the time you needed, even if we didn't manage to kill the Zarminans."

Keldon thundered back, reaching out and grabbing the human by the throat, pinning him against a wall. "Do not try to play mind games with me, human. Your task was to kill our enemies, especially the boy who they seem to believe has some power to destroy us. Not only does the boy still live, but not one Zarminan died. And you have the gall to claim this as a victory?"

Zach gasped for air in the chokehold. He barely managed to squeak out a reply. "We can still be of service. I can direct my men to find the boy, and his friends. They can deal with him while you and your people complete your work."

The alien commander dropped the wheezing man, who landed on the floor in a heap. "You will handle the boy and his friends yourself. Use your network to locate them if you must, but I will expect you to end them personally. No more failures." He stormed out of the room.

Zach remained on the floor, rubbing his sore neck until he was sure Keldon was gone. Regaining his feet, he returned to his communication desk and began to coordinate a new series of actions to find the Madrid kid. According to his sources, he was not at the DIA facility with his friends any more. Only faint rumors of his whereabouts were beginning to surface. The other two had not left the safety of the more secure areas since the bombing, so he would have to wait and watch. They could not stay put forever. He had to hope they would expose themselves soon. His own life depended on it.

***

Myah spoke to Justin about his latest intelligence and plan to end the enemy threat. "Are you sure about this? You've only had a couple of weeks to get a handle on your new talent. I've got a bad feeling about…"

Justin laughed as he listened to her. "Relax. Gandalf has some pretty weird ways of speeding up my learning, so I'm good. You sound more and more like Kevin every day."

"Ugh, you don't have to tell me. And it's not just him. Talking to you, even over the phone, I get this overwhelming feeling to trust you. I keep seeing this image of three guys with a cartoon ghost on their overalls pointing some ridiculous weapon at something. What is up with you two and your stupid movies?"

"Oh, yeah, that's *Ghostbusters*, the three main guys had to learn to trust each other to beat a supernatural…"

"Whatever!" Myah threw up her hands, grabbing her head as if trying to keep it from exploding. "We can deal with this later. Are you sure it will work?"

"If you build it, he will come." Justin smiled, knowing the response this would cause in his new tri-bonded partner.

"Stop doing that! I get it! Alright, we'll go with your idea, but I still think it's risky."

"It will work, Myah. It has too. Time is running out. We need to put a stop to this new threat so I can get inside the Skutaran headquarters. I can only make it work if I have direct access to their isolated system. Without any way to access from the outside, I won't be able to put a permanent end to their plans. Hang in there." He ended the call and returned the phone to his pocket.

He turned and saw Gandalf sitting on a rock nearby. He had been on a walk when the call from Myah came in. "Am I right? Will this work?"

Gandalf pulled on his beard as he thought. "I don't know, for certain. But it is a good plan. Come now. We have more work to do. You are almost ready."

Back in the deepest tunnels under DIA, Myah switched off her phone and turned, rubbing her temples to see Kevin standing behind her. "So annoying."

Kevin grinned as he replied. "Just keep swimming."

She narrowed her eyes dangerously, pointing a threatening finger at him. "Don't even!" Images and phrases of possible replies from several of her bond-partner's favorite movies jumped into her mind, but she fought to ignore them. She gave Kevin a shoulder bump as she passed him. "I need to hit the heavy bag for a while, unless you want to go a few rounds with me."

He called after her as she headed off. "Not feeling suicidal today. Think I'll pass."

"Coward!" she yelled back over her shoulder, giving him the Zarminan equivalent of the middle finger before vanishing around a corner.

Chapter Nineteen

Time was closing in on Zach. The Skutarans estimated only a week or two remained before they would solve the remaining difficulties in transferring the brain engrams of their imprisoned compatriots into human brains. Recent attempts appeared, at first, to be successful, but within two or three days, the subjects went violently insane before dying. Two Skutaran specialists died because of vicious attacks from the most recent test subjects, but they were encouraged at how close they were to finally reaching a solution. Zarminan forces attempted to infiltrate the base beneath the library, but were repelled easily. The soft-hearted enemy did not want to risk the lives of civilians. Cyber attacks continued as well, but proved fruitless since the systems responsible for the transfer process were isolated from the outside world. Keldon, however, only grew more paranoid at the lack of success Zach's conspirators had in finding the Madrid kid...until today when he heard from Delta group.

"We found him, sir. Near Hooper, of all places. We positively identified him at a ranch just outside the town. Looks like he's alone, but we'll keep an eye on him."

Zach frowned as he tried to remember where he had heard about Hooper, and then it clicked. Of course, Hooper, Colorado, home of the UFO Watchtower. Another conspiracy site actually connected to actual alien activity. *What could they possibly be doing in such a backwater place like that?* He wondered. *Could this be a red herring, or a trap of some sort? We need to be careful.*

"Send me some photos so I can confirm the ID. Keep an eye out for any potential threats. And let me know if the others show up. We can be there tomorrow afternoon. Make arrangements for half a dozen."

"In Hooper, sir? Nothing here, unless you want to set up a tent. Closest place would be in Alamosa, about twenty miles away. It's also tourist season here, so not sure what will be available."

Zach barked into his phone. "Get it done, Delta. No excuses, just find someplace as close as you can manage and let me know." He disconnected and dropped the phone on the table in front of him. Seconds later, his phone signaled a new text. He opened the message and grinned as he recognized the face of Justin Madrid, the kid who was the source of his current situation. The photo showed him sitting alone at a picnic table outside a small house on some ranch drinking a Monster energy drink. *I have you now. One more day and I can rest easy.* He took a deep breath and blew it out hard. He rose from his chair and headed toward Keldon's office. He would need permission, vehicles, and supplies for the mission to Hooper. Things were more difficult since the Skutarans replaced Bork as his supplier, but Zach was adaptable, and a survivor.

The next morning, Zach made a last minute check on the supplies, and confirmed the strategy with the five others he collected for this mission. Shortly after eight o'clock, the two metallic grey Dodge Durango's merged into the highway traffic to start what should have been a four hour drive. *Damn traffic.* Even at this early hour, an accident on their route early on brought everything to a crawl. *At this rate it could take over an hour just to reach the mountains.* Zach leaned heavily on the horn as a woman talking on her cellphone cut in front of him, probably thinking this lane would be faster. She lifted a middle finger at him out of her window in reply. While contemplating the wisdom of ramming her tiny car, his phone buzzed to life.

"Yeah."

"Good news, boss. The kid's friends showed up a few minutes ago. All three are here, and the one we think is the Zarminan in charge of everything."

Zach slammed on the brakes, narrowly missing the back end of another car which had jumped lanes while he was distracted by this incredible news. "You sure it's them? Send me a photo so I can verify their identity."

"It's them alright. I recognize them from the base. I'll send a photo now. You want us to take them out?"

"No, just keep an eye on them. Traffic is slowing us up, but we should be there by early afternoon. Let me know if anyone else shows up. This might be just the opportunity we've been waiting for. Don't let them out of your sight."

"You got it. Can't wait to give these damn aliens a taste of their own medicine."

Zach grinned at the irony of the situation. *How would these idiots react if they knew they were being used to help the aliens who were really trying to wipe out millions of humans? Not my concern, though. As long as I get paid, sides don't matter.* And this was going to be a paycheck he could possibly retire on.

Even outside of town, Highway 285 was packed with slow-moving tourists taking in the scenery. This forced Zach to drive the speed limit only sporadically, often recklessly passing other vehicles out of sheer frustration. Once, taking a chance as they approached a blind curve, he barely missed a head-on collision with an eighteen-wheeler. He decided to check in with the surveillance team in Hooper. "Any changes?"

"We followed the kids over to the Sand Dunes Park. They're acting like typical kids, climbing the dunes and jumping back down again. Right now, they're cooling off in the stream at the base of the dunes and eating lunch. You about here?"

"Shitty tourist traffic. Another couple of hours at the most though. No sign of any more of them around?"

"No, sir. Just the kids and one leader. Should be a cakewalk operation to take them out once you get here."

"Don't do anything until we arrive. Surveillance only. Clear?"

"Clear. Surveillance only."

The line went dead and Zach accelerated hard to get around another slow-moving motorhome.

Shortly after two-thirty, under a blue sky with quickly growing clouds, threatening their typical afternoon thunderstorm, Zach and his companions pulled into a vacant lot on the edge of Hooper. He turned off the engine and stepped out to talk with the man leaning against his faded red pickup truck, drinking a Coke. "Situation report."

The man, dressed in white t-shirt and old jeans with a pair of dirty work boots, reached inside the truck and took a pair of binoculars from his partner, handing them to Zach. He pointed off to the west toward a lonely ranch house. "They're back at the house now. Must be cooling off inside after their trip to the dunes. It's getting pretty hot out now, maybe the storm will cool things off."

Zach glared at the man. "Just stick to the targets. I don't need a weather report."

"Right. Still just them, nobody else has shown up. One road in," he pointed to his right, "entrance is about a mile or so back up the highway. Not an easy approach if you want stealth. Only other building is the barn. A couple of guys, probably the owner and a ranch hand, been in there for an hour."

Zach surveyed the layout of the ranch for a few minutes and handed the binoculars back to their owner. He glanced up at the sky and saw dark clouds over the mountains, showing sure signs of a big storm. Lightening danced over the taller peaks, and was headed their way fast.

"The storm should provide us some good cover during our approach. Thunder and heavy rain will mask our trucks, and likely nobody will be outside to see us. We can take them then."

Zach laid out a plan for his men to attack the ranch, made sure everyone understood their job, and returned to his Durango to grab a bite and wait for the tempest to arrive. He watched as the rain shadow approached the ranch, gave the signal and gunned the SUV, spraying grit behind him as he sped down the highway, light raindrops beginning to spot his windshield.

As the vehicles reached the entrance to the dirt road leading to the ranch, a flash of lightening nearly blinded the drivers, followed almost immediately by an earsplitting boom of thunder, and the heavens let loose in a torrent. The drumming of small hailstones bouncing off the roof made it nearly impossible to hear anything else.

Perfect, thought Zach. *Nobody inside will hear us coming in all this racket, If we're lucky, they may not even hear us enter the house. Surprise will be on our side.* He struggled to see the road through the downpour, but soon saw the house and barn looming at the end of the road.

Fifty yards out, Zach slowed to a stop and turned off the car's engine. He turned to the three with him, pointed to them and then to the barn. He watched as the cars behind him emptied and the occupants headed toward the house, two to the front and two in back. He looked at his watch. One minute to go. Zach pulled the neck of his jacket closed, opened the door and stepped out into a deep and muddy puddle, soaking his feet. Swearing at the rain, he strode to the front door, fortunately protected by a wide porch with a roof. Examining his watch again, he held up five fingers and started the countdown. At zero, he stepped back and let the largest man slam into the door, shattering it open. His crew stormed inside, guns raised and shouting threats at those inside. Simultaneously, the rear door burst in and two more armed intruders appeared. Zach turned to watch the three at the barn entering their assigned target just as thunder exploded overhead. He thought he saw a flash coming from the barn, but dismissed it as lightning.

Kevin and Myah jumped to their feet at the intrusion, the pieces of their game scattering on the floor around the table. Justin and Jonah, filling a bowl of popcorn and getting cold sodas for everyone, startled at the noise of the front door slamming open and took a step back toward the living room just as the back door splintered and guns were pointed at their heads.

"Hands up! Don't move!" Shouts from the intruders filled the house.

Jonah surveyed the situation and raised his hands in surrender, signaling for Justin to do the same. "Don't resist, guys. Myah, Kevin, you hear me? They'll shoot you before you can do anything." He nudged Justin to head toward the living room as the gunmen followed.

Kevin watched Myah's face grow determined, her eyes darting from one intruder to the next. Her fists began to clench. He reached over, taking her wrist, and shook his head. "Yo, Adrian, there's too many of them. Do what Jonah says."

She turned to snarl at him, fire in her eyes. "Seriously? Now?" But she gave in and unclenched her fists, a look of resignation replaced the anger, almost.

"Alright, everyone, take a seat, and don't try anything." The man waved his rifle toward the chairs around the table.

"Do as he says, guys. Stay calm." Jonah took a chair, and placed his hands of top in plain view. The others followed his lead. The gunmen took up positions around the room, weapons still aimed at the four prisoners.

Chapter Twenty

"Well now, isn't this nice. The whole gang is here."
Zach strode victoriously into the room, his rifle held at a
jaunty angle over his shoulder. He circled the table,
enjoying the obvious fear he and his men instilled in his
captives. At least three of them.

Jonah stared up at Zach as if challenging him.
"What do you want? We don't have much money, but you
can have it, and our car. Just don't hurt the kids."

Zach smiled at Jonah. "Now isn't that touching?"
He gave Jonah a blow to the back of his head with the butt
of his rifle. "We know who you are so you can cut the crap.
We want to know what you're doing here. I'm here to find
some answers." He studied the faces of his captives and
settled on Justin. "I think I'll start with this one." He
grabbed Justin by the collar and pulled him to his feet.

"No!" Myah and Kevin started to leap up, but the
sound of four rifles being raised and aimed at them brought
them to an immediate halt.

"Sit back down, you two. Your turn will come soon
enough." Zach growled at the two, his eyes lingering longer
on Myah, causing a sneer to creep onto his lips.

"It's okay, guys, These are not the droids you're
looking for." Justin, although shaking slightly, kept his face
stoic as he went with Zach into the kitchen, followed
closely by one of the large guards.

Kevin and Myah regained their chairs, Myah
shaking her head and pinching the bridge of her nose.
Jonah kept an eye on the guards along the walls, one of
them following Zach and Justin into the kitchen. The
remaining three lowered their weapons, but stayed alert.

Shutting the door behind him, Zach slung his rifle over his shoulder and waved for Justin to sit at the table. "So, what shall we talk about?" He took a seat opposite Justin, his back to the door smashed open in the break in. Rain spattered through the undamaged screen door and pooled near the entry.

Justin focused on the calendar hanging on the wall to his left, maintaining his unemotional affect. "I've got nothing to talk about to you, except to give you fair warning. If you surrender now you won't be hurt."

Zach laughed out loud. "In case you haven't noticed, kid, we're the ones with the guns. Oh, and if you think your friends in the barn are going to help you, my men took care of them already." He reached into a pocket of his jacket and pulled out a large pair of lineman pliers and placed them on the table with a bang.

"We can do this either way, kid. Doesn't matter to me, but you might think about how many fingers you want to leave here with." Lightning flashed outside the window and door, followed by a massive explosion of thunder, shaking the house.

Justin thought he caught the image of a huge shadow approaching the back door out of the corner of his eye, but kept his focus on the calendar. He shrugged and turned to face his captor, smiling as he noticed the shadow out back getting very close. "Hello, my name is Indigo Montoya. You killed my father. Prepare to die."

Zach opened his mouth to respond just as another burst of lightening filled the room, along with almost simultaneous thunder. The guard suddenly grabbed at his neck; a small dart had embedded itself just below his left ear. He swayed and collapsed unconscious to the floor in a heap. Zach, distracted by the commotion, only halfway managed to unsling his rifle as a monstrous hulk of a man filled the doorway, charged at Zach and flung him across the room. Edward Davidson took two steps to cross the floor and gave his former partner a massive kick to the gut. Air exploded out of Zach's lungs as he crumpled even further on the ground. He then took the opportunity to check on Justin. "You okay, kid?"

"I'm good." Justin turned away so he didn't have to watch.

"Edward, what are you doing? We're friends." Zach barely gasped out the words as he tried to breathe.

Davidson picked him up by the shoulder, tossing the rifle to the other side of the room. "You lied to me, Zach." He landed a vicious fist on Zach's nose, breaking it, and probably several other facial bones as well, from the sound of it.

Zach landed with a thud, but managed to stay conscious, raising one feeble hand in defense. "No, let me explain…"

"You killed innocents." Davidson's size fourteen boot landed with a crunch, cracking several of his ribs through his Kevlar vest. He picked up Zach's limp body, slammed his head against the wall, knocking him senseless. Satisfied, Davidson walked across the room, picked up the discarded rifle, it looked like a toy in his hands, and checked again with Justin.

"Sure you're okay, kid?"

"Yeah, but was that necessary?" Justin looked up at his rescuer, craning his neck, sadness in his voice.

Davidson looked from Justin to Zach, unconscious on the floor, and back again. "Yeah, it was."

"He's right, Justin. The fool will survive so we can question him, but he had to pay a price for his actions." Emily entered the room and replaced her pistol in the holster on her hip. She stepped over to Justin, pulled him into her arms, and held him tight. "You sure you're alright? I was so scared for you."

Justin returned his mother's embrace. "Yeah, Mom. I'm fine." His voice shook as the tensions released from him.

Meanwhile, in the living room, the noise from the kitchen distracted the three guard's attention just enough for Kevin, Myah, and Jonah to react. Reaching under the table, they each grabbed their pistols, which they'd hid there that morning, and opened fire.

Tiny darts struck home in each of the guards, one in the neck and two in the arm. The guards started to aim their weapons at the prisoners, but appeared to find the effort to be too much, and dropped to the floor. Their arms began to spasm, their eyes fluttered back in their heads, and the guards fell unconscious to the floor. The effect of the paralyzing drug required less than five seconds to incapacitate the men. Jonah, Myah and Kevin leaped to their feet and yanked the rifles from the drugged men, tossing them aside.

"Well done, you two. They'll be out for hours. Let's get them prepped for transport back to DIA."

Kevin and Myah looked at each other, then the kitchen door, ignored Jonah, and headed toward the kitchen, tranquilizer guns at the ready. After only three steps, the door opened and Davidson strode through, ducking and turning his shoulders slightly to fit through the small doorway. At least it looked small next to him. Emily and Justin, each with one arm around the other, followed him through the doorway. Justin broke away from his mother and practically ran to Kevin and Myah. The three friends froze for a second before enfolding each other, wordlessly, into a group hug. After a moment, all three showed a flush of red on their faces and awkwardly broke the embrace.

The three stood in embarrassed silence until Myah blurted the first thing that came to her mind. "Why didn't I take the blue pill?"

The boys focused on Myah as her face changed from the light flush of awkwardness, to the crimson of annoyance. They smiled in unison, opening their mouths to respond, but Myah pointed at each of them in warning. "Just don't. Not a word. Either of you." She stormed off to another room calling back over her shoulder. "Glad you didn't kill yourself, or us, Justin."

After the brief reunion, they busied themselves restraining three attackers, including those Davidson dragged in from the barn. The sound of a car engine roaring to life, and tires squealing in mud, caused everyone to snap to attention. Racing to the front window, Emily and Jonah watched as Zach sped off down the gravel road in his car.

Jonah slammed his fist into the wall alongside the window. "Damn, I thought he'd be out for hours."

Justin turned to Myah, his voice hushed. "How could he even move? Davidson messed him up pretty bad. I thought we would have to carry him out of here on a stretcher."

Myah shook her head. "Trained mercenaries are used to pain. He had no choice but to try an escape, even if he had to drag himself away. Better than becoming a prisoner."

Emily cursed under her breath; her fingernails carved small half-moons into her palms as her fists tightened. "I'll call it in. Maybe we can still pick him up on the road before he gets too far."

Davidson's face turned to stone as he strode toward the front door. "I'll handle Zach."

Jonah grabbed Davidson's wrist, the only part of his arm small enough to grab. "Hold on, big guy. We can't have you running off after him like this."

Davidson turned to face Jonah and Emily, who had joined her brother-in-law in confronting him. "You still don't trust me?"

Jonah and Emily shared glances, Emily nodded and went to help the others.

Jonah released Davidson's wrist and smiled. "Go ahead, but stay in touch. Don't try to do anything on your own."

Davidson grunted and stepped out onto the porch. His long strides took him across the dirt yard to the barn where he swung the large doors open and went inside. Moments later, one of the three vehicles they had hidden there upon their arrival two days ago came to life and sped off down the road toward the highway. Jonah watched as the car vanished in the distance.

Myah appeared behind him, arms crossed over her chest. "You sure about him?"

Jonah let out a heavy breath and turned away from the window. "Yeah. I trust him. Don't ask me why, but I do."

Justin searched his mind for the place Gandalf resided and found him sitting under a massive oak tree eating a granola bar. "Where did you get...? Never mind. Did you have something to do with helping Uncle Jonah trust him?

Gandalf swallowed and held up the granola bar, admiring it. "These are wonderful. Much better tasting than lembas bread." His eyes twinkled as he glanced up at Justin. Maybe just a bit. He is your uncle, so I can feel his mind faintly. You need that giant in this quest. You can rest easy about him."

As they finished loading the last of the attackers, still heavily drugged, into the back of the remaining two vans, Justin stood in front of the others, struggling to hold back his emotions. "Thanks guys. I don't know how to..."

Kevin simply grinned back as he interrupted his friend. "The needs of the many outweigh—"

Myah cut him off mid-sentence. "—the needs of the few—"

Justin finished the quote as he rushed in to embrace his friends. "Or the one."

Emily looked up into Jonah's face, worry filling her expression. "Is he up to this, Jonah? Are all of them really ready?"

Jonah smiled back as he placed his arm around his sister-in-law's shoulder. "Yes, I believe they are. Justin did uncover their communications alerting us to this attack. He seems to have gained control over this ability of his."

She sighed, looking over Jonah's shoulder at her son and his friends. "I know. But I'm still his mother, and I'm worried about him."

"I am too, Emily, but he knows what this is about, and we don't really have any options left. Let's take this war to the real enemy for a change."

***

Four days later, Zach Litson jerked awake, finding himself tightly restrained in a chair facing a large computer monitor, and three Skutarans, including Keldon, were busy with the images and readouts on their monitors. He felt an intense desire to blink and bring relief to a powerful dryness in his eyes, but two clamps held them open, and head restraints forced him to look at the blank monitor. His memory of recent events slowly returned as he regained consciousness. After the disaster back in Hooper, he evaded any pursuit and made his way back to the library. There was one close call as he awoke in one of Red Angus' safe houses outside of Pueblo. Somehow, the traitor Davidson tracked him to the location and was approaching the entrance. Not wanting another confrontation with the giant of a man, and finding himself without a weapon, Zach sneaked quickly out the back door and narrowly escaped. His return to the library did not go as he had expected. Keldon had erupted into a fit of rage at the failure and beat

Zach to within an inch of his life. He had to find a way to regain the alien's confidence.

"Keldon, listen to me. I found the kid once, I can do it again. I can still be of value to you. I still have the Red Angus…"

"Be silent!" A blow to the back of his head sent stars shooting through Zach's vision. He had not noticed the guard behind him.

Keldon gave one of his sinister grins as he looked up from his console. "Well, Mr. Litson, you have decided to join us after all. I was afraid you might miss the final test of our engram revitalization process. It would be a shame for the guest of honor to miss his own party."

Zach struggled against his restraints. "You don't want to do this, Keldon. I know things that can be of use to you. I have connections. You still need me."

Keldon approached Zach and reached out, placing one hand on the chair as he leaned in close. "And I will have all of that information, without you. You should be honored. I have decided to use you as the host for my most trusted ally. Montok was one of our greatest generals. His ability to strategize and run a battle was unequaled. I will need him to run my revolution, and I will be rid of you. Your memories will be incorporated into his engrams, but you will cease to exist. Montok will have access to your Red Angus personnel if we need them for anything, as unlikely as that seems. The best part is, since only your mind will be replaced, they will believe he is you and follow his orders without question. You see? You are of no value to me whatsoever, except as a host. I was prepared to use another, one without your knowledge, but since you came back to us, we can proceed as planned."

"No! You can't do this! I'll do anything you want."

Keldon returned to the consoles and stood tall, facing the struggling man in the chair. "You are. This is precisely what I want you to do. Farewell, Mr. Litson." He reached down with one finger and pressed the Enter button on the keypad.

The monitor came to life, a seemingly random series of images, but Zach felt a jolt of electric energy shoot through his body. In his mind, he felt a growing presence. Despite his efforts to resist, he felt himself grow thin, almost like a he was becoming a shadow of himself cast by a light in a dark room. The other presence grew stronger by the second and he heard a voice, weak at first, but soon overpowering in its strength. Strange memories also invaded his mind. Thoughts of battles in space, of wars on far off planets, and plans of troop dispersals and supply lines crossing interstellar distances replaced memories of family and earthly places he knew. More and more, he felt himself vanish, replaced by a new entity, an alien being taking over his consciousness. Resistance indeed became futile. As the last of Zach Litson faded away, his final awareness was of a voice coming to life.

"Alive! At long last, alive again!"

"Welcome back, my old friend." Keldon touched the Enter button again, allowing the monitor to grow dark. He stepped up to the chair, holding what still appeared to be Zach Litson. He removed the restraints and eye clamps, briefly steadying the former earthling as he slumped.

Montok, now the new owner of Zach's body, took a couple of deep breaths and examined his hands, turning them over in front of him before looking up to see Keldon to his left. "Keldon? Is that you? How is this possible?"

"In time, General. In time. We have much to discuss, but you need to adjust to your new body. Our scientists assure me the process is permanent, but they will need to monitor your recovery during this adjustment period, a few days at most. We can begin our revolution once you regain your strength."

The general made an awkward smile. His control over this body would take some time to fully incorporate into his consciousness. "Yes, of course. I am weak. But tell me, how long has it been?"

"Fifty years, General. I managed to keep my part in the conspiracy secret for many years, but the emperor discovered me less than twenty years ago. I was able to escape with some of our allies and bring most of the engrams with us to this pitiful planet. It took a long time to learn how to reinstate you into a living body, but we have succeeded. Soon our army will be stronger than ever."

"That is good news, Keldon. I will rest now. We can make plans when I am in full control of this body. Thank you."

With the help of a guard, Montok made his unsteady way down the hallway to the residence area. Keldon returned to join the others at the monitors as they surveyed the data of the process. Once they were satisfied everything had gone as they expected, they turned off the computers, congratulated each other, and left to arrange for the final phase of their plans. Millions of engrams silently awaited revitalizing in the databanks, the only sign of their current status a blinking red light in the darkness as the Skutarans exited the room.

Chapter Twenty-One

Justin sat in his station, focusing on the monitor. His face fell blank as he appeared to stare into nothingness. Only minutes had passed since he began his search in the alien computer system for any new information about their plans. Emily and Jonah sat next to him, exchanging concerned glances at this unnerving state of emptiness in him. Without warning, Justin stirred, blinking his eyes and hands clenching and unclenching as he returned to normal.

"We're out of time. They just completed their first successful test and implanted an engram onto a human. It's only a matter of a day or two before they let loose for real."

Emily rolled her chair in close, placing her arms around Justin's shoulders, attempting to comfort him. "Can't you break into their system and shut it down from here?"

"No, Mom, I can't. They've got the engrams, and the system responsible for implanting them on everyone, offline. No connection to the outside world, at least until they are ready. And then it will be too late. I won't have time to do what I need to do to shut it down."

"But can't you…"

"No, Emily, he can't." Jonah cut her off as gently as he could, but still asserted his authority. "We've talked about this. He has to go inside to personally reach into the network and wipe out the entire database, and the minds responsible for creating it, once and for all,"

Emily opened her mouth to reply, but Justin interrupted her before she could raise any more objections. "Mom, I can do this… Trust me."

She let out a heavy sigh of resignation and gave Jonah one last look. He nodded in response. "Alright, Justin. I do trust you." She stood up and leaned in to give him a long hug. "But promise me you won't do anything stupid. Let Myah and Kevin do their jobs protecting you."

Justin smiled up at his mom as she released him. "I promise. But it is really weird how Kevin can do all that Kung Fu stuff all of a sudden. How did he learn it all so fast?"

"That's the nature of the bond, dear. It connects individuals in very complex ways. Myah has been training for years, so Kevin absorbed her muscle memories and mental aspects of the techniques from her as he trained. It's not so unusual if you think about it. You only took a few days to learn how to use your ability, and, back when you were training with them, didn't you pick up some skills pretty quickly too?" Emily ran her hands through Justin's hair as she gave him a motherly smile.

"I guess so." Justin hesitated, not sure if he should ask, but decided now was as good a time as any. "Is that how it was with you and Dad? With the bond and all?"

Emily's smile took a slow downward turn, and she turned away from her son, unable to look him in the eye as if she would lose all control. "Yes," she replied quietly. "And that's another reason I am worried about the three of you in this war." Without another word, she walked out of the room.

Justin turned to face his uncle. "Did I say something wrong?"

Jonah shook his head. "No, Justin. But you need to understand just how strong the bond grows over time. Your parents were together for many years, and faced many dangers together. Their bond was a powerful one. It nearly killed your mother to lose him. We don't know how the bond works between the three of you—nothing like this has happened before, that we know of. Some, though, believe the effects will be multiplied since there are three minds involved, with all of their thoughts and emotions feeding on each other. She is worried for all three of you if anything were to go wrong and we lost one of you. It could be devastating to the remaining two."

Justin sat silently, considering the possibilities. He searched in his mind and found Gandalf wandering along a tall mountain pass, feeding a mountain goat with some grain from a metal bucket. Before he could ask, Gandalf straightened up, the bucket and goat vanishing in a puff of sparkling dust. "Yes, what they say is true. I have searched through Zarminan history and found several examples of a triad bond, similar to yours. They were long ago, and the memory of them lost over time, but those were particularly powerful and tragic circumstances. You do need to prepare yourself for the possibility one of you will be lost during this endeavor."

Justin closed his eyes, returning to consciousness after only seconds. "I understand, Uncle Jonah." He stared off into the distance again, and then stood up from his chair. "I need to go find Kevin and Myah."

Jonah gave Justin a pat on the back, smiling at him. "Your father would be very proud of you, Justin. They're in the gym again, training."

Fifteen minutes later, after changing into his workout gear, Justin joined Kevin and Myah in the gym. A loud thump greeted him as Kevin, once again, landed on his back after an arm-drag throw from Myah. Kevin rolled with the fall and quickly regained his feet, taking a defensive stance as the two continued the match.

"Very good, Kevin," said Myah, slightly out of breath and glistening with sweat. "You nearly had me that time. Don't overreach next time. Balance is everything."

"Wax on…wax off. I get it. Let's go again." Kevin circled to his right, his eyes fixed on Myah's hips as she taught him to see an opponent's true intentions about where he or she will move next.

With an almost snake-like speed in striking, Myah advanced on Kevin, reaching to take hold of his exposed left wrist. In a nearly as quick twist, Kevin changed the angle of his arm and took hold of Myah's wrist, spinning her into a double-arm bar hold he remembered from the time he tried wrestling in middle school. He lifted her feet off the ground, turned his shoulder, and brought her to the mat. While still maintaining control with one hand, he gave a rapid series of blows, not actually landing as was performed during training, to her throat and solar plexus. Jumping to his feet, Kevin gave his impression of Muhammad Ali bouncing around the ring with arms raised in victory. "I'm the greatest!"

With a chagrinned look on her face, Myah got to her feet. "Alright killer, you got me that time. You're definitely improving. Care for two out of three?"

"How about giving me a shot?" Justin called out from the edge of the mat.

"Justin! You finally get tired of all that computer wizard stuff?" Kevin continued his bouncing around, giving a few quick shadow boxing jabs at Justin's stomach.

Myah stepped up to them, giving Justin an appraising look. "You stretched out properly?"

Justin grinned, excited at the chance to do something purely physical for a change. He had tried to keep up with his physical training, but kept falling behind with the demands of his true responsibility. "Give me a minute."

He carefully went through his warm-up routine to loosen every muscle as Myah and Kevin continued to spar. When he was ready, he stepped onto the mat. Kevin stepped off, ran over to the heavy bag and began dancing around the bag, landing jabs and kicks.

Myah took another swig of water as she waited for him. "You remember where we left off?"

"Yeah, me flying through the air and landing on my butt."

She laughed at the memory of the look on his face after that encounter. "Try not to do that again. Let's start off with a little review."

Justin took his defensive stance as Myah began to circle him. From the door to the gym, Jonah stood silently watching the three friends. He closed his eyes and, despite his normally agnostic feelings on the matter, began a supplication to Jutar, the Zarminan diety. *Please don't let this be their last time together. Watch over them, protect them. Help me protect them and keep them safe.*

In his mind, the voice of Gandalf echoed. "Trust in Aeon. He is fully risen in you now. Trust in yourself."

Chapter Twenty-Two

"Does anyone have any questions?" Jonah stood in front of the conference room, a holographic image of the five levels, one main level and four underground, of the Mission Viejo library projected to his left. The twenty soldiers in the room continued to study the image, committing it to memory.

"How firm is our intel on this layout, sir?" a squad leader in the front row called out.

"Solid. We have a secret informant who has provided these blueprints. You can rely on them." Jonah omitted the fact that Justin, through his ability to see into the minds of the Skutarans utilizing the accessible sections of their network gleaned these plans from their memories. This was not something he was ready for anyone other than those already in the know to learn. Justin's ability to read the codes was well known, but still considered somewhat mystical. No need to muddy the waters any further. This mission was too dangerous to risk.

He allowed another minute for any further questions, but the room remained quiet. "Very well, you all know your assignments. We rendezvous at the library in one hour. Dismissed."

The room erupted in an excited jostling of chairs and gear, the soldiers sharing good-natured jabs at each other as they exited. Once everyone was gone, only Jonah, Kevin, Myah, Justin, and Emily remained. Jonah stepped in front of them, examining each with the practiced eye of a leader.

"You are ready for this. You've trained well for it. The rest of us are here to support you. Kevin and Myah, stick close to Justin. Justin, follow their lead, and listen to Myah's instructions. It is their responsibility to get you inside and watch your back. Emily and I will try to be there as well, but we have other responsibilities that may force us to be elsewhere. Let's head out."

The small family—all of them felt this way about each other now—got to their feet, embraced each other, and headed out the door.

The drive south from their headquarters at DIA was silent, each person in the vehicle absorbed in their own thoughts. Kevin and Myah focused on a transfer of ideas and emotions through the bond. Though not in words, or anything tangible, the bond created a link between these two which simply allowed each of them to know what was going on with the other. Justin would have been included since their bonding was a triad, but he focused instead on a final meeting with his intergalactic mentor. In all previous times, he had manifested as Gandalf the Grey, but now, at the moment of the final confrontation with the enemy, he became Gandalf the White.

"You may be overdoing this a bit," said Justin as he squinted and shaded his eyes with one upraised hand against the brilliance of the light shining off his guide.

"Sorry. Sometimes I get caught up in the role. Your mind's images are incredibly clear about the characters of this story, particularly this one." The light dimmed to a soft glow of shimmering, almost iridescent halo around the figure.

"Thanks." Justin looked around, not recognizing any of the scenery. Then he noticed the three moons of various sizes hanging in the sky. "Where are we?"

"In your mind. Where else?"

"You know what I mean."

Gandalf chuckled and used a small tool to scrape the bowl of his long-stemmed pipe. "I do. I am simply trying to train you to be more precise in your thoughts. That will be critical in the hours to come. But to your question, this is what your scientists refer to as Kepler 62f. I visited some friends here once, long ago. They, of course, have a completely different name for their planet, but I don't think there is any way to translate it into anything you would recognize as language. Beautiful, isn't it?"

"There are people here?" Justin's head spun around as if on a swivel looking for signs of the beings who lived here.

"No, not people. More like coherent photonic beings. They existed at the quantum level, so you wouldn't be able to see them, even if they were still here... But enough about my reminisces. What do you require, Aeon?"

Justin sat on a rock and plucked what appeared to be a translucent, iridescent flower, twirling it in his fingers. "Stop calling me that. I don't feel like some super powerful being. Are you sure I'm ready for this?"

Gandalf leaned on his staff; the gem at the top glowed with a bluish-white energy. "It is only natural to have doubts before such a great undertaking, but yes, you are ready. You know everything you need to know to defeat the Skutarans." Gandalf's face grew stern. "You must stop them. This plan of theirs is an atrocity. The Skutarans, as a race, are not the most pleasant life forms to deal with, but these renegades cannot be permitted to succeed. It will lead inexorably to a shattering of the balance of universal forces we cannot allow. You know what you must do. We have searched throughout time and space to find you. I have trained you well in the abilities Aeon has seen fit to bestow upon you. Have no more doubts. You must do this."

Justin stared at the flower a while longer, then dropped it and rose to his feet. "*Klaatu barada nikto*. Let's do this thing."

Gandalf screwed up his face in response to Justin's statement. "That's really not what those words mean, you know."

Justin smiled and winked. "I know. It just seemed appropriate, somehow."

The alien world faded away, replaced by the sounds and sights of south Aurora, just as Jonah guided the car into the Burger King parking lot in the corner shopping center north of their destination. A line of shops hid them from any inhabitants of the library. It was not due to open for another two hours, so no civilians were inside, only enemy targets.

Jonah pressed a patch on his black vest to activate his communicator. "Alpha one is in position. Report."

In his earpiece—each of them had been fitted with one before starting out—Justin heard the other team members checking in.

"Beta two, in position, awaiting go signal."

"Delta three, in position." Davidson's baritone voice rumbled his team's readiness.

"Gamma four, ready. No sign of hostile activity."

Jonah pressed the contact again, "All teams go, repeat, go. Secure the target." He looked toward Emily, and then over his shoulder at the three teens in the back seat. "Final weapons check everyone. Stay together, No hesitations. Let's go."

The five black clad individuals stepped out of their car and headed toward the back entrance road to the parking lot. Fortunately, nobody was around to see the small assault teams converge on the neighborhood library. Rounding the corner of the buildings, Jonah signaled a halt and watched as the other teams closed into position. With a quick touch of the communication patch, Jonah signaled the others to move in. Each of the teams closed in on different access points to the building. One team broke open the front entrance, while another took the door to the community room, and the last entered through the rear door. Justin heard three muffled pops, and then a voice in his ear.

"All clear, Alpha team. Three hostiles down."

Myah turned to Justin, noticing his pained expression. "Don't worry, we're only using non-lethal paralysis rounds. If these Skutarans are really the criminals and traitors you say they are, we'll want to ship them off to their home world to face justice for their actions."

Justin smiled behind still worried eyes in response.

Jonah raised his hand and led them all forward with Emily bringing up the rear. In less than a minute Justin found himself in the center of the team, ushered through the main entrance and around the front desk, into the back room. Shelves of books and a variety of odds and ends cluttered the area, A pair of feet stuck out from behind one of the offices along one wall. He averted his eyes as they passed, not wanting to see the body.

Kevin called out from the back of the last cubicle. "Here's the elevator, just like you said." He held open what looked to be a normal closet door, meant to disguise the presence of the elevator. The others joined him as he pressed the button to open the sliding doors of the elevator proper.

A shadow darkened the small room as Davidson stepped through the doorway. "Zach's not up here. I'm going down with you."

Jonah shook his head. "Negative, Davidson. We need your team up here to keep any others off our back."

Davidson remained stoic. "Plenty of others for that. Zach is mine."

Emily reached out and held Jonah's arm. She gave a brief nod, and Jonah exhaled noisily. "Alright, let's get a move on."

The six crowded into the elevator, Justin safely tucked into a back corner. As the door closed behind them,

Jonah signaled each team to set up for the final stage of the operation. "Delta team, secure the main floor. Beta and Gamma, sweep and secure the top two basement levels, then reinforce Delta. We have the lowest level. Stay alert."

Justin watched the lights above the elevator door flash through B1, B2, and hold steady on B3. The doors slid open with a slight rattle and the team stepped out into the corridor, weapons raised. Jonah raised his fist, calling for a halt as they took up a defensive position. "Which way, Justin?"

Closing his eyes to see the floorplan of the facility in his mind's eye, Justin oriented himself in the plan and then opened his eyes. "To the left, then right, down the second corridor to the fourth door. That's the main access terminal room." He was relieved the construction plans for this underground addition to the library was maintained in the accessible network of the system. Somebody got careless with that decision. He tracked down the plans a couple of days ago, allowing Jonah to plan this infiltration.

"Kevin, Myah, take the lead. Justin, stay close. We'll take up the rear."

"I'll take care of Zach," said Davidson as he headed off to the right. "Somebody has to clear out the rest of this floor anyway."

Jonah opened his mouth to object, but one glance from Emily changed his mind. He watched as Davidson vanished around the corner, heard the crash of a door being kicked in and two quick shots fired before rejoining his team, already almost to the intersecting corridor. So far, each room they encountered proved empty.

Then Myah kicked open the third door. Six Skutarans sat around a table studying the readout on a monitor in front of them. As one, they raised their heads to stare at the intruders. Shocked looks and panic exploded in the room along with the pops of paralysis rounds being fired by the assault team. Three of the group fell to the floor immediately and the others sought shelter behind chairs and desks in the room. Emily stood guard in the hallway, with Justin behind her, as the others charged into the room. Within seconds, all the enemy scientists lay on the floor, conscious, but unable to move or speak. A quick survey of the room verified these were the only inhabitants, so the team exited, resuming their positions to continue down the hall. Just as they reached the access terminal room, two more doors further down the corridor flew opened and seven Skutarans stormed out of the rooms, their own weapons firing. As one, Myah, Kevin, Emily, and Jonah dropped into defensive position around Justin and retuned fire, dropping four of the attackers. The three behind got tangled up among the paralyzed bodies of their comrades and stumbled over them trying to reform. Myah and Kevin each downed one more, while Jonah took care of the third.

Kevin, kneeling next to Myah, gave her a sideways glance, and smiled. She rolled her eyes in response, but gave a half-smile, and the two recited the phrase in unison. "*Hasta la vista*, baby!"

Emily stood protectively over Justin, a small trail of blood running down her right leg.

"Mom! You're hurt!" cried Justin.

"I'm alright, honey." She replied, reaching into her med pack belt pouch. "This will take care of it for now." She gave herself a quick injection and the bleeding stopped instantly. "It just grazed me, so I'll be fine. Are you injured?" She gave him a rapid once over to make sure her son had not been injured in the exchange of fire.

"Myah, Kevin, get Justin inside. Emily and I will keep watch here in case more of their friends show up."

The pair nodded and took up protective positions in front of Justin as they opened the door and charged inside the dark room.

"You're too late, Zarminan. The process is underway. There's nothing you can do to stop it now." Keldon Ankara smiled as he rose up from his chair behind the controls. General Montok, in the body of Zach Litson, looked up from his study of the data coming across the screens in front of him. His hand, hidden from view by the computer, slid to his sidearm.

"Go ahead, punk, make my day." Kevin raised his weapon at the General's head, waving him to stand and step around the table.

Montok lifted his hands in surrender and did as Kevin told him. "The commander is right. Soon millions of your fellow earthlings will be ours. You are too late."

"Leave your gun on the table and step over there, hands behind your head. You too, Commander." Myah watched as the general unholstered his pistol and set it down, then aimed her rifle at the pair as they followed her instructions.

Kevin handcuffed them both and guided them, roughly, to a place to sit across the room. "Are they right, Justin? Are we too late?"

"Pay no attention to the man behind the curtain," said Justin as he sat down in front of the controls, placing his hands on the keyboard. His eyes closed.

Justin concentrated on the pathways and circuits as their images grew in his mind, gradually transforming to a series of diverging paths in a dark forest. He looked around for Gandalf, but the old wizard, the alien entity in his mind, never appeared. "Guess I'm on my own now," he said to himself, shrugging and starting down the main path. As he came to each new branch in the path, he sought ahead with his thoughts and followed the traces of energy leading to the main program of the Skutaran efforts to plant their engram into human brains. Soon, he came to the entrance to a cave in a hillside. In front of the cave sat a gnarled old figure of a humanoid creature Justin did not recognize. The figure, dressed in a tattered and faded red robe, peeked up at him from under the robe's hood, with his orange tinted eyes, each holding vertical black irises, reminiscent of a tiger's eyes. It spoke in a raspy voice in a language Justin did not know, but understood. This was the programming language of the Skutaran signals. He had reached the core. This was what he trained for. Time to reprogram the system. Justin began to speak in the programming language.

The Skutaran figure resisted his attempts to give instructions, but Justin remained persistent, fighting to wear down the figure's strength and bend it to his own will. As he focused, a large green and orange spider crawled to Justin and tried to crawl up his leg. Justin recognized it as an anti-virus type of protective program, sent to infect him and remove him from the system. "Oh no you don't," he said before the spider could bite him, and swatted it away, stepping on it as it landed on the pathway. He glared back toward the gnarled figure. "You'll have to do better than that."

Continuing to speak the codes that would alter the program, rendering it useless, Justin began to sweat with the effort as his enemy fought back. A loud growl startled him. Without losing his focus, he turned and found himself staring at a large blue hairy beast, its huge fangs dripping with a green fluid, most likely poisonous. The creature ran at him on two trunk like legs, four inch long claws on each of its six toes. Six more long talons glistened from each of the beast's raised hands. Justin lifted one hand and summoned a long, curved blade sword, which appeared from a mist that formed in his hand. He held the blade high and it began to glow with an intense golden light. The beast slowed its attack as the light grew in intensity. Speaking a few more words in the code language, Justin pointed his sword, and the creature came to a dead stop, writhing in agony. Seconds later, it howled as it burst in a cloud of atoms and blew off in the breeze. Justin let his sword vanish and returned his gaze to the robed figure. "Nice try, but your protections are useless against me." He continued to speak the code language, noticing small cracks starting to appear in the figure's face and robe. A black smoke leaked from those cracks. He was winning.

The computer core being shed his robe, roaring as he stood to his full height. Amazingly, it towered over Justin, seeming to grow more of itself as it stood. What was once a pitiful creature sitting on the path in front of the cave now appeared as a fearsome monster with thick muscles and long curved horns sprouting from its head. It called out in a deafening voice which echoed off the nearby hills. Justin stood firm, but fear began to grow in his heart. He now shouted the programming commands, summoning his sword again, projecting the blade's golden light onto the bellowing creature. The wind began to howl, dark clouds billowed and lightening flashed. The ground shook and the resulting fissures belched a sulphurous smoke, stinging his throat and eyes. Justin nearly lost his balance in the raging tumult, but regained his footing, and redoubled his focus. The cracks in the core creature he faced started to grow, the once small leaks of black smoke now streamed from its body. As he continued shouting code, the howling of the wind changed, sounding more like voices than a storm, as if millions of furious individuals crashed down on him. In the distance, Justin saw what appeared to be a vast army of Skutarans charging over the hills, headed toward him in a full out assault. The imprisoned engrams were about to be released.

Chapter Twenty-Three

An energy beam split the air between Jonah and Emily as they stood guard outside the main control room. A dozen Skutaran warriors, in full battle armor, charged down the narrow hall. Diving to the other side of the hall, Jonah squeezed himself into the limited protection of the doorway, pulled his own beam rifle from his back, and returned fire. Emily also abandoned her paralyzer pistol in favor of her rifle. The two fired a heavy barrage into the enemy, slowing their advance. Changing tactics, the Skutaran warriors brought forward a row of shields to protect those behind, who continued to fire through slim openings in the shield wall. Jonah and Emily watched as the enemy advanced on them in a precise, coordinated pattern. Their own weapons' fire was now useless against the shields, Jonah lowered his rifle and pulled a disrupter grenade from his belt. He pressed the activation contact and leaned out to throw the explosive. As his arm started forward, the impact of an enemy energy beam sheared through him. The grenade bounced limply down the corridor, far short of the target, exploding harmlessly between the forces, only scorching the walls. Jonah fell to the ground, clutching at the wound in his chest.

"No!" Emily looked on in horror as her brother-in-law fell. Unable to come to his aid amid the enemy barrage, she shouted in defiance, reaching for her own grenade. Knowledge of her imminent death gave a new fury to her determination to protect her son. As the explosive came free, a new sound, the shouts of a confused enemy reached her. She watched in amazement as the force in front of her became disrupted, many of them struggling to take up new positions to protect their rear. Loud bursts of what sounded like the energy signature of a tank blaster filled the corridor. Their shield wall fell apart, and Emily tossed her grenade into their midst. The explosion shattered the remaining Skutarans, killing all that remained. As Emily saw the enemy force defeated, she dove to Jonah's side, lifting his head into her lap, tears streaming down her cheeks. She looked in horror at the obviously fatal wound. Even immediate evacuation to a Zarminan emergency care facility would be of no help, but logic gave way to desperate hope.

"Jonah, hang in there. We'll get you to the medicals. They'll fix you up. Just hang in there." She tried to staunch the blood flow with one hand while holding his head in the other.

Jonah coughed, spitting up blood, grimacing with the pain. "Is Justin safe? Did we stop them?"

Emily, torn with grief, softened her voice. Years of training took over, giving her strength. "Yes, Jonah. We did it. Justin is safe, and the Skutarans are defeated. We saved the humans."

Jonah smiled, gave one last cough, and exhaled his last.

Out of the corner of her eye, Emily saw a shadow approach from the carnage of Skutaran bodies down the hall, but her tears blurred the image. The need to protect Justin reared itself insider her mind and she reached for the rifle she had discarded on the floor next to her.

"No need to do that, ma'am. They're all dead on this level now." Davidson's booming voice penetrated her grief and she dropped the weapon.

Davidson loomed over her as Emily sobbed, cradling Jonah's body. He gave her a few minutes before interrupting her mourning. "How's the kid, ma'am? Shouldn't we check on him?"

At the sound of her son's name, Emily jolted out of her grief and looked up at the giant of a man. "Yes, yes, of course. We still have a job to do." She gently set Jonah's head on the floor and rose, unsteadily, to her feet, rejecting Davidson's offered hand. Squaring her shoulders, she opened the door to the control room.

"Stop right there before we... Oh, hi, Mrs. Madrid. Sorry about that." Kevin stood up from his position behind a desk, returning his paralyzer pistol to its holster.

Myah rose up from her location across the room. "Is everything secure out there? Justin is still doing his thing with the computer." Her eyes settled on the prone figure of her commanding officer on the floor of the corridor outside the door. "Oh, no." Her hand went to her mouth, eyes wide with shock at the sight.

Kevin felt the shock through the bond and jerked his head toward the hallway. "Jonah... is he..." One look at the two women provided the answer to his unfinished question. A wave of sorrow washed over him, partly his own, partly Myah's through the bond.

As Kevin and Myah stared in shock, they unconsciously came together, embracing each other for support. Emily, too full of her own grief, only managed to give them each a gentle squeeze on the shoulders as she passed by to stand at her son's side.

***

The roar of the approaching army of Skutarans was deafening. Justin fought hard to shut down a rising tide of fear. Ignoring the charging enemy, he returned his full attention to the smoking beast in front of the cave.

"Time to end this." Justin gathered all of his energy and concentrated with everything he had as he raised his hands and shouted another string of command codes. The beast began to shrink, flinching back from the onslaught of new programming. Justin strode forward, forcing the now frail-looking beast back toward the cave entrance. It screamed in agony as new, larger fissures appeared, smoke now billowing from them, shrinking the beast back to its original form, now only clothed in a filthy breechcloth. Gaining courage and strength, his programming language grew more powerful by the second. The creature gave one last piercing scream and dissolved into a cloud of blackness. Justin completed his programming with a final command and staggered from the effort. He watched as the last vestiges of the code creature vanished in the breeze. The charge of the Skutaran army, the engrams awaiting implantation into new host bodies, continued unabated. They were nearly upon him now. Justin prepared himself for one last programming command. He faced the army, raised his hand one last time, focused all of his concentration, and shouted.

"You shall not pass!"

A wall of crystal-clear energy formed across the path between him and the enemy. The engrams crashed into the wall, clawing and scraping at the nearly invisible barrier. They were blocked. The wall continued to grow and surround the entire force until they were completely contained within its borders. Their howls of desperation grew almost pitiful, until he remembered what they had almost accomplished. With a final series of commands, he sealed off the crystal prison, permanently trapping the engrams.

"One last thing to do." Justin took a deep breath as he turned and strode into the cave. He had to remove the memory of this program from all those who were connected to it. He had to locate the engrams of those programmers who helped develop this atrocity. As Justin walked through the cave, his own energy illuminating the path, he became aware of a light growing in the distance. In six small alcoves dug into the sides of a large cavern at the end of the trail, Justin found six glowing crystal balls, each a different color. He touched one of them and felt the presence of one of the minds of a scientist connected to this program. Each of these orbs represented the minds of those who had helped build it. Justin concentrated, and his sword materialized in his hand again. With a powerful two-handed swing, Justin severed the first orb from its base, causing the light to go out. Repeating this action with the remaining five globes, his actions symbolically acted out the removal of this part of the six minds. Justin reset his shoulders and walked out of the cave, back into the light of day, or at least the daylight of this manifestation of the computer system he had infiltrated.

"Well done, Padawan." A smiling Gandalf appeared as if from nowhere at Justin's side. He let out a yelp of surprise and jumped back, reflexively taking a defensive stance.

"Don't do that!" Justin gasped as he regained his self-control.

Gandalf laughed and sat down on a rock which had not been there a moment before and pulled out his long-stemmed pipe. "Yes, very well indeed. I am sorry it came with such a price, though."

"Price? What price? What do you mean?"

"You will learn soon enough. For now, I wanted to congratulate you on a great victory and say my farewells."

Confused, Justin ran his hand through his hair and gaped at his mentor. "Farewells? You're leaving? Where are you going?"

"Wherever the cosmic winds take me, for now at least. I think I deserve a vacation... such a wonderful concept you people have. I have been on this particular quest for quite some time, so some time to just wander about the universe for a while is in order." He stood and took the reins of a large white horse, which also appeared out of thin air right before Justin's eyes. Mounting the horse, Gandalf trotted off down the path, vanishing in a blinding flash of blue-white light.

Justin stood staring at the empty air before jolting back to reality, remembering Gandalf's words about a cost. *Is everyone alright? Mom? Uncle Jonah? Kevin and Myah? I have to get back.* His thoughts focused on returning to his body at the console.

Justin's eyes fluttered as he returned to consciousness, aware of his mom calling to him.

"Justin, come on, honey, come on back. I'm here."

He felt the warmth of her touch on his forehead, bringing back memories of times he was in bed sick and she tested for a fever.

Justin gave a weak smile and managed a feeble greeting. "Hi, Mom. You alright?"

Emily gasped as the sound of his voice and enveloped him in a bear hug, her tears dripping on Justin's brow. Unable to respond verbally, she increased the strength of her embrace.

"Mom, I can't breathe. You're choking me," Justin gasped as his airways were nearly choked off.

Emily released her grip and sat back but kept touching her son's face and arms as she gazed at him with a pained expression. "Sorry, Justin. Yes, I'm fine. Are you okay? Did you do it?"

Justin blinked as the world came back into focus again, and the sounds of the others nearby caught his attention. "Yeah, it's over now. The program is dead, the engrams contained, and the programmers' memories are erased. It's done." He shook his head to clear it. "Is everyone else alright?" Trying to stand, a heavy wave of vertigo hit him. He dropped back down into his chair, closed his eyes, and waited for everything to stop spinning. His mind soon cleared enough to feel the bond with Kevin and Myah again, so he knew they were still alive, but something was wrong. A profound sadness filled the bond.

And he noticed his mother had not replied to his question. The world suddenly rushed back into him with a jolt. Beyond the doorway to the computer room, he saw Davidson covering a body with a blanket. Kevin and Myah stood next to the huge soldier, holding hands, wet streaks coursing down their faces. *Where did he find a blanket down here? What happened? Who is that?* His thoughts raced as he tried to form the words.

"Mom, what happened? Who is that?" He began to panic. "Where is Uncle Jonah?"

Emily choked on her reply. "I'm sorry, Justin. He… he didn't make it." She began to sob again, burying Justin's head in her shoulder in another strong embrace. "There was an attack. He died protecting you."

Justin's world crashed in on him as he recalled the words of the Gandalf entity. "I am sorry it came with such a price." This was the price it had spoken of. The man whom he had begun to regard as his surrogate father was gone, just like his actual father. Only this hurt so much more. He had no memories of his real father, but many of his uncle. Justin returned his mother's grasp, holding on to something that still remained of the life he knew.

After several minutes, Justin felt the pull of the bond and released his grip on his mother. He stood up and staggered to where his friends stood mourning the loss of the man who led them and taught them. Kevin and Myah opened up to let Justin join them, wordlessly holding each other, arms around each other's shoulders, gathering comfort from the bond between them.

Chapter Twenty-Four

A week later, the family, now including Myah, sat in silence as Tumarut, the spiritual leader of all Zarmina, concluded the funeral rites for Jonah Madrid. Dignitaries from all levels of the government, and several allied planets Jonah had helped over the years were present, all dressed in their finest to show their respect for the fallen hero. Even an ambassador from Skutara came to give his thanks for the capture and return of the traitors before they could create an interstellar incident. As tradition dictated, the Imperator rose from his designated place of honor on the dais as Tumarut sat in the chair next to his.

"Justin Madrid," he called out in his well-practiced orator's voice. "Come forward."

Emily and Myah had prepared Justin in advance for this portion of the ceremony, but he still retained enough of his Earther identity to be skeptical of his rightful place among these people. With a small nudge from Myah, he stood up and climbed the steps to take his place in front of the Imperator.

"Kevin Samson, of Earth, and Myah Helsinki, take your rightful place by the side of your companion and complete your triad." As Justin's companions took their places, murmurs arose in the assembly at the affirmation that a true triad bond actually existed. This part of the ceremony, for as long as anyone knew, had only formally sealed a pair bond. Everyone craned their necks to ensure they had a clear view of history in the making.

Tumarut again rose up, took hold of a transparent green crystal rod, intricately carved with a golden flame at its head, and stepped to the Imperator's side. He extended the rod to Justin, who took hold of the rod, his hand holding it just above that of the other man.

"Do you, Justin Madrid, son of Karl and Emily, nephew of Jonah, the sole heir of the Madrid family, take now the responsibility of leadership of your family? To protect those remaining members from harm, and bring prosperity and honor to your name, and the name of your ancestors?"

"I... I do." Justin's voice cracked at his first attempt at a response, but upon clearing his throat, he managed a clear reply.

The Imperator reached out and took hold of the rod above Justin's hand. "And do you, Justin Madrid, accept your role as equal partner in the triad bond with these two beside you? To protect and honor them as you would yourself and your family?"

"He smiled and glanced sideways at his friends as he replied. "Yes, I do."

"Then Kevin Samson, and Myah Helsinki, take hold of the rod alongside your partner."

The two placed their hands on the ends of the crystal rod.

"Do you, Kevin and Myah, pledge yourselves to honor and protect this triad bond above all else?"

Together, they responded, smiling broadly. "We do."

The flame at the end of the staff began to glow with an orange light, but remained cool to the touch. The light expanded and enveloped the three friends, almost obscuring them from view.

As one, the Imperator and Tumarat gave the official proclamation. "Before the eyes of all who are present, and the ancestors, we declare the bond fulfilled and established. May it never be broken."

The glow faded away as the two leaders released their grip. Together, as one, the new bonded trio bowed, first toward the leaders, then toward the gathered audience, and finally to the only other surviving members of Justin's immediate family. Emily, her parents, and several relatives nodded, returning the respect. They then turned and approached the cairn on which Jonah's final remains rested beneath the ceremonial flag of the Madrid family. Justin extended his free hand, still holding the bar with his companions, and pressed a panel on the support. As they stepped back, an electric hum rose in intensity, and an energy field surrounded Jonah's body. The field grew opaque with a blue-white energy and pulsed for several seconds. As it vanished, only the empty surface of the cairn remained. The triad then returned to the leaders and handed back the crystal staff and left the dais, officially concluding the ceremony.

At the reception afterwards, the triad was the center of attention, besieged with well-wishers and the curious, but it was Justin who received the bulk of the attention. Even Kevin's status as a visiting alien from another world could not compare to the son and nephew of two of Zarmina's heroes. The highlight of the encounters was when the Skutaran ambassador approached them with news of the complete round-up of all the traitors who had fled to earth. The ambassador especially wanted to express his gratitude for the help provided by Edward Davidson as their liaison with the officials of earth during the process.

"The young man seemed especially pleased when we loaded Keldon Ankara on board. He asked if it might be possible to accompany us to witness the traitor's engram imprisonment, but we had to respectfully decline. Skutarans are not as accepting of off-worlders as you Zarminans are."

During the next several hours of unending questions and offers of all sorts, thankfully Myah provided guidance as to how to respond appropriately to each and not give offense with his ignorance of Zarminan ways. The triad finally escaped the crowds and found their way to their assigned quarters. Plopping down on the long, well-padded cushion, they activated the foot supports to rise up from the floor and collapsed.

Kevin was the first to speak. "Yep. Strange things are definitely afoot at the Circle-K." Justin laughed and Myah groaned, giving one of her patented eye rolls.

"I hate to say this, but if I am ever going to really understand you two idiots, you are going to have to show me these movies you keep referencing. I have some notion of what you mean, but until I get some better context, I won't be as effective as I need to be in this triad."

The boys laughed and agreed to set up a marathon series of films to bring her up to speed. They then began to argue over what order to present them in, based on appropriateness, timeline, and interconnectedness of the various franchises. Myah groaned at the realization of what she was now committed to, but only out of habit. Her heart soared to feel the absolute joy of her companions' friendship, knowing that she too was included fully. The future of their unprecedented relationship remained a mystery, but nothing they would not work out over time. Zarminans were not consumed by the taboos of many Earther partnerships, but Justin was raised as one of them, and Kevin was not Zarminan. There would undoubtedly be complications, but they could deal with them later.

"So what now?" asked Kevin.

Justin turned his head to face his friend. "What do you mean?"

"I mean, are you staying here, or going back to Earth? We still have three more years of high school left you know."

Justin's face screwed up. He looked up at the ceiling in puzzlement. "I haven't even thought about that. I mean, everything's happened so fast, I never stopped to think about what would happen after."

"Same," Kevin replied. "It just popped into my head. I have to go back, at least for a while, to explain everything to my mom."

"Can I watch? That sounds like fun to see you try to explain about us and the humans on Earth nearly being taken over." Myah laughed at the thought of seeing Kevin try to tell his mom about all of it.

"Ha, ha, ha," said Kevin sarcastically. "You wouldn't by any chance have a second heart or anything to prove you're an alien, would you? That might at least help."

"Not a chance. Do you know many aliens with two hearts?"

***

Six months later, back in Aurora, Kevin, Myah, Justin, and Emily found themselves in the audience of a large crowd celebrating the grand reopening of the Mission Viejo Library. Its sudden closing was officially explained as due to a lack of money in the city budget, but neighborhood outcry was intense so the city managers gladly announced their capitulation and now the big day had arrived. Of course, at the highest levels of city, state, and federal government channels, intense efforts had been taken to repair and erase all traces of the aliens who had taken over the library.

Kevin's mother, surprisingly, took the news of Kevin's summer and Justin's identity fairly well. She was happy her son finally had a girlfriend, even if she didn't completely understand what they meant by a triad bond. Sometimes, it was better to let some questions go unasked.

The triad companions had decided they would take over Uncle Jonah's position as Zarmina's representative on Earth and continue the work of bringing new technologies and knowledge to the planet. All four of them would spend summers on Zarmina while Justin and Kevin learned the culture and customs of Justin's home world, at least until the two earned their college degrees. After that, only time would tell.

Now, as the various dignitaries concluded their speeches, and the audience applauded, the only ones who knew the truth simply smiled as they joined everyone and passed under the large banner above the entry welcoming the new staff to run the library. For now, they were glad life resumed its peaceful routine. The best part was how his classmates now accepted Justin as one of them. Whether it was his newfound confidence, or merely the fact he now participated with them and their video games and watched the same TV shows they watched, he didn't care. Life was good, so long as no more aliens threatened the earth.

About Jim Cronin

I am a retired middle school science teacher, working part-time as an educator at the Denver Museum of Nature and Science. I have been married for forty years to the love of my life. We raised two incredible sons, and now have four amazing grandchildren to spoil rotten.

I was born in Kansas City, Missouri and lived in Arlington, Virginia before moving to Denver where I attended High School and eventually college at Colorado State University, graduating with a degree in Zoology and a teacher certification. My wife and I currently live near Denver in the small town of Parker.

After writing The Brin Archives trilogy, I wanted to try my hand at reaching a new audience. The idea of a nerdy teenager with few friends suddenly learning the fate of all earth depends on him struck me as a fun scifi adventure.

Social Media

Website: http://jimcroninscienceedutainer.weebly.com/

Facebook: https://www.facebook.com/JimCroninScienceEdutainer/

Twitter: https://twitter.com/authorjimcronin

Goodreads: https://www.goodreads.com/author/dashboard

Acknowledgements

My thanks go out to many people who have helped during the writing of this story. First and foremost, as always, my loving wife who has put up with long hours of isolation while I sit and dream away at my computer, talking with the characters in my head instead of with her. I also need to extend a special thank you to Dr. Collins' second period 8th grade class at Sky Vista Middle School. They were instrumental in helping me learn the language of today's teens so Justin and Kevin could sound authentic. Guys, your help was invaluable, and I was incredibly impressed with your willingness to do this with such enthusiasm and insight. And thank you also to Dr. Collins, my former teaching partner, for letting me disrupt her class for this purpose.

If you enjoyed this story, check out these other Solstice Publishing books by Jim Cronin:

Hegira

His home world is dead; the victim of a supernova, but this does not stop Karm from attempting to save the Brin, his extinct species. Rescued by an alien race from a derelict spacecraft as a vial of DNA, then cloned, Karm must travel back in time, convince a small team of co-conspirators to join him in his quest, and outmaneuver a power hungry monarch and his fanatic brother, leader of The Faith, both absolutely committed to opposing him.

All of Karm's plans rest on the untested and controversial cloning theories of the young geneticist Dr. Jontar Rocker, and the abilities of his bodyguard, personal assistant, and surrogate niece, Maripa. Will their combined efforts be enough to overcome the power of the monarchy and the planet's most influential religion? Will Karm's secrets destroy the trust of his companions and ruin his campaign to save the Brin?

https://bookgoodies.com/a/B010E3EKC6

Recusant

In this sequel to Hegira, the Brin are thriving on their new world, but, in the 300 years since their arrival, some of the more powerful guilds, and members of the government have cooperated to violate a sacred trust. Maliche Rocker, descendant of The Saviors, uncovers a terrible secret and must fight those in power, including members of his own family, to save thousands of innocents from the cruelty of his own people. Will greed, prejudices and old rivalries tear apart their grand civilization? Or will another Rocker find the strength to once again save his people?

https://bookgoodies.com/a/B01KTVTMNK

Empyrean

Interstellar war has raged for centuries between the Skae and Gorvin Empires. The Skae claim their efforts to capture and harness the power of a black hole will eliminate all future energy shortages and allow all the planets to thrive and prosper as never before. The Gorvin believe they have evidence proving the existence of a fatal flaw in the Skae's plans. A flaw which would result in the destruction of half the galaxy.

Maliche and Jontar Rocker, along with a small band of Brin and Kolandi companions, must learn which side to believe in order to bring an end to the war. Only travel to the distant past will uncover the truth and reveal the fate of the galaxy. Will what they learn allow them to join with the Skae, the beings who saved the Brin civilization? Or must they betray their ally and fight with the Gorvin to bring peace and a new empyrean to all the planets? Time is running out.

https://bookgoodies.com/a/B077ZBQWDT

Project 9 Vol 2

A reality pill… Canoples Investigations returns… Are we computers? plus many other stories in this science fiction anthology from Solstice Universe.

Ten authors with eleven tales to tell: Ray Chilensky, K.C. Sprayberry, Rob McLachlan, Debbie De Louise, Jim Cronin, Rick Ellrod, Natalie Silk, Arthur Butt, E.B. Sullivan, and S@yr bring you stories to delight and entertain.

https://www.amazon.com/Project-9-2-Arthur-Butt/dp/1625264372/ref=asap_bc?ie=UTF8

Reviews for The Brin Archives

Hegira

"This is a great book! Just when I thought I had predicted what was going to happen next, the author threw a twist that hadn't even crossed my mind!! It has controversy, emotion, action and suspense! I definitely recommend reading this book! I can't wait to read the next book!!" - 5 stars by Larson

"Hegira by Jim Cronin is a very interesting and in-depth science fiction and time travel story that takes you deep into a new realm of danger. Hegira is a very well-written story that combines so many complex layers that I was thinking about it for days after I finished reading it." – 5 stars by Renee Taylor

Recusant

"Recusant (The Brin Archives Book 2) is an entertaining and gripping read. The story itself takes place a long time after Karm, Jontar, and Maripa guided their people from the brink of extinction. Whilst no knowledge is needed of the previous book, Hegira, I thoroughly enjoyed learning of the events which shaped the Brin's future on this planet. The manner in which the past was relayed was a stroke of genius; believable, interesting, and fitting in with the characters and plot development. Once again, Jim Cronin creates a cast of diverse and vivid characters, equipped with engaging dialogue and fully developed personalities. There are so many threads to this one tale, with hidden connections, plots and schemes, that it is impossible not to get ensnared." – 5 stars by K.J. Simmill

"Brilliant. Last year, surprisingly as it's not my favourite genre, this author's debut novel Heigra was one of my most enjoyed reads and if anything he has upped the game in this, his second book. It can be read as a stand alone but it is part of a planned series.

I like his books because I find them so easy to read. The world created is fantastic yet very grounded and believable. Intelligent commentary is made about the strengths and weaknesses of humanity in a totally natural way. And finally I find the author makes the genre easily accessible and I don't feel like I need a phd in applied science to understand the story.

Whether you enjoy sci-fi/fantasy or not this is a great read about prejudice, fear of the unknown and greed versus compassion and respect for different races wrapped up in an intriguing and exciting story. Can't wait for the next one." – 5 stars by Maria

Empyrean

"Empyrean is the final chapter in the trilogy, The Brin Archives, brought to us by Jim Cronin. This is as good as the previous two novels that trace the history of the Brin and their relationship with their saviours, the Skae. This is great science-fiction, easily readable, easy to understand (even the complicated technological bits) and easy to get involved with the characters. I loved that Cronin was able to neatly wrap up millennium of history in this final chapter. This an excellent author and a wonderful series. Highly recommend all three books in The Brin Archive series." – 5 stars by Rhea

"Empyrean is book three in The Brin Archives series by Jim Cronin, and is an action packed, delightful read. For fans of sci-fi, this will be a great treat. The reader is transported to an interstellar world with two powerful empires set against each other in the struggle to capture and control the power of a black hole in the galaxy. The Skae Empire believes that this could ensure a constant supply of energy to the planets, but the Gorvin Empire thinks the scheme could cause greater damage, destroying half of the planet. It is in this context that powerful heroes must dig for the truth to find a permanent solution to the interstellar wars that have gone on for centuries. Follow Maliche and Jontar Rocker and their companions as they embark on an epic journey in search of the truth. The outcome is far from anything the reader could imagine. This is an interesting story that is well-plotted and well-written, a story with an exciting setting. Jim Cronin has the gift of uprooting readers from their immediate reality and plunging them into worlds that are strange and yet make them feel as though they were a part of that world. The writing flows beautifully and it is enriched by vivid descriptions and exciting dialogues. Beginning a story in the midst of a crisis is an intelligent way to grab the attention of the reader and I couldn't resist reading on. In fact, the conflict is one of the strongest elements of Empyrean and it is developed with great skill. I loved the strong characters, the quick pace, and the compelling plot points. It's a great read." – 5 stars by Christian Sia